THE BODYSNATCHERS

MARK MORRIS

BBC BOOKS

Other BBC DOCTOR WHO books include:

THE EIGHT DOCTORS *by Terrance Dicks*	0 563 40563 5
VAMPIRE SCIENCE *by Jonathan Blum and Kate Orman*	0 563 40566 X
GENOCIDE *by Paul Leonard*	0 563 40572 4
THE DEVIL GOBLINS FROM NEPTUNE	
by Keith Topping and Martin Day	0 563 40564 3
THE MURDER GAME *by Steve Lyons*	0 563 40565 1
THE ULTIMATE TREASURE *by Christopher Bulis*	0 563 40571 6
BUSINESS UNUSUAL *by Gary Russell*	0 563 40575 9

DOCTOR WHO titles on BBC Video include:

THE WAR MACHINES *starring William Hartnell*	BBCV 6183
THE AWAKENING/FRONTIOS *starring Peter Davison*	BBCV 6120
THE HAPPINESS PATROL *starring Sylvester McCoy*	BBCV 5803

Other DOCTOR WHO titles available from BBC Worldwide Publishing:

POSTCARD BOOK	0 563 40561 9
THE NOVEL OF THE FILM *on audio tape*	0 563 38148 5/Z1998

Published by BBC Books,
an imprint of BBC Worldwide Publishing
BBC Worldwide Ltd, Woodlands, 80 Wood Lane,
London W12 0TT

First published 1997
Reprinted 1997, 1998
Copyright © Mark Morris 1997.
The moral right of the author has been asserted.

Original series broadcast on the BBC
Format © BBC 1963
Doctor Who and TARDIS are trademarks of the BBC

ISBN 0 563 40568 6
Imaging by Black Sheep, copyright © BBC

Printed and bound in Great Britain by Mackays of Chatham
Cover printed by Belmont Press Ltd, Northampton

This is for David Howe, for getting me the gig in the first place.

Thanks, as always, to my wife, Nel, for her love and support, and to my children, David and Polly, for being there.

Thanks also to the Sam squad - Jon Blum, Kate Orman, and Paul Leonard - for their generosity, enthusiasm - and input.

CHAPTER 1
FIRE AND BRIMSTONE

By rights the man in the corner of the room should not have been there at all. Yet as Jack Howe entered the tavern, accompanied by his colleague, Albert Rudge, he saw him sitting in what of late had become his accustomed place. Bold as brass he was as always, done up to the nines in his expensive overcoat, top hat, and thick muffler. His lily-white hands rested on the solid-silver lion's head that topped the cane he always carried. He sat there, quite still and calm in the stink and the squalor, amid the thieves and the cutthroats, the horribly diseased, and the hopelessly drunk.

Oh yes, he was a proper gentleman, no doubting that. In the filthy Whitechapel tavern populated by Jack and his cronies, he stuck out like a diamond on a plate of kippers. Jack thought it a miracle that the man had not been found garrotted in an alleyway before now, his pale, scented, well-fed body stripped of its clothes and valuables. He was asking for trouble coming here night after night as he did. And yet... there was something about him that made even big Jack Howe uneasy, something he couldn't quite put his finger on – not that he would ever have admitted that to Albert, who was nervous enough at the best of times.

Perhaps it was simply that the man was so... watchful. So still. When he moved it was in slick little movements, like a snake. Or perhaps it was something about his eyes, which were the only part of his face the man ever revealed, keeping his hat on at all times and his muffler pulled up over his mouth and nose. Yes, that might have been it. There was a queer cast about his eyes. Sometimes they seemed silver, and once or twice Jack could have sworn that he had seen them flash orange, as if the man had a fire inside him.

Harry Fish, the landlord, was polishing glasses with spit and a grubby rag. Jack ordered gin for himself and Albert, then the two men made their way through the ragged, smelly, drunken crowd to join the silent man in the corner.

He did not look up, or even move, until Jack and Albert were seated at his table. Then he raised his cold grey eyes and regarded them for a moment. Jack took a gulp of gin in an effort to repress a shudder. Six years ago Jolly Jack had been carving up the working girls of this parish, and the local word then had been that it was a toff doing the killings. Jack had never believed the rumour, had never thought a gentleman would have the mettle for such business. Now, however, looking into this man's stone-cold eyes, he wasn't so sure.

The man spoke, and his voice was a soft murmur. 'Good evening, gentlemen. I trust you have the merchandise?'

Jack nodded, and tried to make his voice as brusque as possible. 'We do, mister.'

The man blinked slowly. 'Splendid. I'd like to view it if I may.'

It was always the same – no pleasantries, no preamble, straight down to business. Not that Jack minded. He didn't want to spend any more time with this man than was necessary, however well he paid. He tilted his head back and finished his gin, savouring the acrid burn in his throat and gut. Then he gave a swift nod and stood up, followed immediately by Albert, who jumped to his feet as if he was afraid Jack would leave him alone with the man.

The man rose smoothly, and allowed Jack and Albert to lead him to the door. Jack couldn't help noticing that most people, hard-bitten East Enders though they were, glanced at the man with fearful eyes and gave him a wide berth. Yes, there was something mighty queer about him, all right.

He, Albert, and the man who had never given them his name stepped out on to a cobbled street, caked with the bodily waste of dogs, horses and humans alike. The streets were only ever cleaned around here by the rain, but after a while you hardly noticed; you got used to the stench of filth and sickness and death.

The fog was yellow as always, and so thick that the tall, dark slum buildings that surrounded them, the rookeries, where people lived ten or twenty to a room, could barely be seen. Their feet crackled on the cobbles as they turned left away from the tavern and plunged into the fog. Within seconds the fog had swallowed not only the tavern itself, but the welcoming glow from its windows.

For the next ten minutes the men wandered through a maze of alleyways and backstreets, most so narrow that they had to travel in single file. They passed clusters of children huddled together in doorways like sacks of rubbish, disturbed packs of rats, which scampered before them like living clumps of darkness.

Eventually they slipped down an alleyway and emerged into a cobbled courtyard of sorts, surrounded on three sides by the soot-blackened walls of more of the East End's ubiquitous slum dwellings. The fog was so thick here, and the buildings so tall, that the sky could not be seen. Grey rags of washing hung limply on lines that stretched from one side of the courtyard to the other, high above the men's heads, like the pathetic flags of an impoverished nation. In the far corner of the courtyard, smothered by the fog until you got close enough to reach out and touch its nose, stood a mangy horse, tethered to a ramshackle cart covered by a tarpaulin.

The man gave a hiss of satisfaction and hurried to the rear of the cart, slipping past Jack and Albert like a shadow. The two East Enders hung back, Albert pulling a thick rag over his mouth and nose and tying it at the back of his head as though parodying their employer's muffler-obscured features. Jack would have done the same, but was reluctant to show any sign of weakness to the man. Instead he took shallow breaths through his mouth, tasting the sulphur that yellowed the air, feeling it catch in his throat. Both Jack and Albert were used to bad smells, but this was far worse than the normal day-to-day odours: this was the high, sickening stench of bodily corruption. Their habit when they worked was to rub horse manure into the rags they covered their faces with. Though that in itself was a fetor that could make a man's head swim and his eyes water, it was preferable to the noisome stink issuing from the bodies of the recently dead.

Their top-hatted companion, however, seemed singularly unaffected by the smell that filled the courtyard. Lithe as a monkey, he clambered over the tailgate of the cart and yanked the heavy tarpaulin aside. Though the fog reduced him to little more than a blurred silhouette, Jack sensed the man's eagerness and was glad of it, thinking of the gin he would buy later. He knew all too well what sight the man was presently feasting his eyes upon – the heaped cadavers of men, women and infants, some still so fresh that the maggots had only just begun their busy work.

'How many?' the man asked, crouched like a ghoul above the grave pickings. 'How many tonight?'

Albert, who did not know his numbers, looked to Jack.

'Seventeen,' Jack said.

'And you were not seen? You left no trace of your work?'

'None,' confirmed Jack.

'Excellent,' the man murmured. He took one last greedy look at his booty, then dragged the heavy tarpaulin across, leapt down from the back of the cart and climbed up on to the seat behind the horse.

Jack stepped forward expectantly as the man reached into the pocket of his dark overcoat. Sure enough, the man's pale hand emerged clutching a fistful of coins, which he tossed on to the cobbled ground as casually as if he were tossing food scraps for hungry dogs. Jack held himself back as the coins chinked and rolled; he wouldn't be seen grovelling in front of anyone. Albert was not so proud, but he was scared – of both the man and Jack, and so he held himself back too.

'I will see you tomorrow, gentlemen,' the man said. 'The arrangements will be as always.'

'Very good,' said Jack drily.

Albert tugged at the brim of his cap. 'Thank you, sir,' he muttered.

The man faced front and flicked the reins to get the horse moving. Jack remained standing until the horse and cart and its hunched, top-hatted rider had been swallowed by the fog. Only then did he drop to his knees, his big hands groping through the slimy filth between the cobbles, greedily gathering up every last coin that the man had scattered on the ground.

Tom Donahue had no proper plan to speak of. His present circumstances, combined with the dreadful, gnawing pain in his hand, had pushed him to his wits' end these past several weeks. A month ago he had had a job and lodgings, and money enough to put bread and potatoes and sometimes even a little meat on the table. Now he had nothing. He was confused, exhausted, starving, angry and scared.

What perplexed him the most was the fact that, until recently, his ex-employer, Nathaniel Seers, owner of Seers's Superior Bottles, had been a kind and generous man, a true philanthropist, who cared about the welfare of his workers. Not long before Christmas, however, he had changed. He had become cruel and mean-spirited, unconcerned about those who toiled in his factory on the bank of the Thames.

Tom was unfortunate enough to have been one of the first to fall foul of his employer's new-found, unpleasing disposition. One morning he had been cleaning the machinery when he had caught his hand in one of its whirling cogs and injured it badly. Rather than showing compassion, as was his normal reaction to such a misfortune, Mr Seers had instead lambasted him for his carelessness, and even as Tom had lain there bleeding on to the floor, almost fainting with the pain of his injury, had dismissed him, claiming that an employee who couldn't work was of no use whatsoever.

As a result of his dismissal, Tom had been unable to pay his rent or buy food. He had spent Christmas, which was almost three weeks past now, sleeping on the streets, living on scraps and hand-outs. If his circumstances didn't improve soon, he supposed he would have to take himself off to the workhouse, though he wanted to put off that dreadful day for as long as possible. The workhouse was a harsh place with a strict regime, though at least there he would have a roof over his head and a little food to eat, and he might even be able to get some medical treatment for his hand.

Since injuring it, the pain had been growing steadily worse. Indeed, it had now begun to travel up his arm, attacking, it seemed, his very bones, to the extent that he often woke in the night, crying out in agony. Furthermore, the fingers had turned black and he could no longer use or move them. Additionally, the flesh had begun to swell and split and to exude a stench like rotten meat.

Tonight, for the first time since his dismissal, Tom had decided to return to the factory. He had little idea what he was going to do when he got there. It was already well after midnight, and despite the cripplingly long hours that the employees worked, the place would now be dark, the machines silent. Tom was so embittered by what had happened to him that part of him wanted to burn the factory to the ground, or at the very least cause as much damage to the machinery as he could. There was another part of him, however, that hoped Mr Seers would still be there (it was rumoured that recently he had taken to staying at the factory until the small hours, and sometimes not going home at all). Tom half believed that, distanced from the troublesome bustle of a normal working day, his ex-employer might be more convivial and accommodating, more prepared to listen to Tom's grievances.

Yes, Tom decided suddenly, this was why he had come; indeed, it had been his intention all along, had he but known it. If he could only convince Mr Seers that he was his final desperate hope, then surely the factory owner would rediscover the humanity, the benevolence, that he had sorely lacked these past weeks.

Despite his conviction, Tom's belly began to quiver with nerves as the factory came into view, a huge black edifice rising out of the fog, caged within a fence of spiked iron railings eight feet high. At first glance, unless a fellow was equipped for a rather treacherous climb, which Tom was not, the place seemed impregnable. Tom, however, knew that the factory was accessible at the back. It had been built on a bank twenty feet above the Thames, and a set of stone steps led first on to the towpath below and thence down to the river, this to provide access to the boats that transported far and wide the bottles that were made in the factory.

Tom made his way there now, shivering with the cold wind

blowing off the water. Although he could hear the gentle lap of water against the flood wall below, he could not see it, for the thick fog muffled what little light there was from the intermittent gas lamps along the riverbank.

He climbed the steps. There were only a dozen or so, but by the time he reached the top his head was swimming with hunger, fatigue and the as yet only slight delirium of his pain. He paused, panting, holding his injured and aching hand, wrapped in the soiled rag that served as a bandage, to the hollow of his chest for a moment, curling himself around it like a mother protecting her young.

Eventually, able to dredge a scrap more energy from deep within his rapidly failing reserves, he straightened up. Back here, behind the factory, was a jumble of outhouses – storage facilities, equipment sheds, stables for the factory's half-dozen horses. Tom was tempted to make his way straight to one of the stables now, lie down in the sweet, warm hay and go to sleep. He told himself that if Mr Seers was not here, then that was exactly what he would do.

He began to shuffle across the cobbled yard between the outhouses towards the factory. It was even darker here than it had been on the riverbank, damp colourless fog coiling around him, blending shadows and solids into a single shifting black stew. He walked with his good hand outstretched and questing from side to side. After a half-dozen steps his hand thumped against the wooden wall of a stable that had appeared to loom out of the fog as if it had crept up on him. He realised he had been veering to his left and realigned himself accordingly. A few steps further, and his feet became entangled in a discarded coil of sodden rope which almost brought him to his knees. Staggering, he managed to remain upright, though couldn't prevent himself from uttering a muffled cry that sounded in his own ears disconcertingly close to despair.

Regaining his balance, he moved forward again, and suddenly saw the faint, diffuse glimmer of a light ahead. He judged it to be a lamp affixed to the back of the factory, and moved towards it eagerly. He had taken no more than five steps, however, when he became conscious of a sound permeating the silence, a dull, irregular *thunk... thunk*.

He halted a moment, listening. Where was the sound coming from? It was hard to tell, for the fog seemed to distort his perceptions, to carry the sound hither and thither. He tilted his head to one side, then pushed his nose into the air like a hunting dog and turned a complete circle until he was facing the blurred light once again. He was not entirely sure, but the source of the sound seemed to be the light itself. A little more cautiously now, he crept forward.

Eventually the light grew larger, more distinct, and though it did not dispel the fog, it at least thinned it a little. Tom realised to his surprise that the source of the light, and indeed the sound – which was louder now – was not the factory, after all, but another outbuilding, this one a long, low shed where, Tom knew, various items of equipment used to repair and maintain the factory's machinery were stored. He realised that after colliding with the stable and realigning himself he must have over-compensated, veered too far to his right – or perhaps it had been after tripping over the rope that he had done this. In truth, the whys and wherefores of his misdirection were unimportant. What was important was the fact that the factory, or rather its grounds, was not deserted. Someone at least was here, which in his present state of disorientation Tom found of no little comfort.

He moved towards the window at which the light flickered and pressed his face to the glass. At first he saw nothing; his rasping breath produced a cloud of vapour which befogged the window. He rubbed at the glass with his good hand and looked again. In the light of several candles he saw the silhouette of a man with his arm raised behind his head. A second later the man brought his arm sweeping down, and Tom saw that he was holding an axe, which he thudded into an object on the long workbench.

Chopping wood, Tom thought, and then a number of details presented themselves, one after another, to his hunger-pain-exhaustion-befuddled mind, coiling slowly and lazily into his consciousness like pebbles sinking to the bed of a murky pond.

The first detail was this: the man chopping wood was his ex-employer, Nathaniel Seers. The second detail was Mr Seers's dishevelled state; he was in his shirtsleeves, sweating profusely, his dark hair hanging over his forehead in greasy strands. The third detail was more shocking: Mr Seers was wearing what Tom assumed was a butcher's or a mortician's apron, for it was spattered with blood and clots of tissue. The fourth and final detail was more than shocking, however; it was appalling, unbelievable…

On the workbench before Mr Seers was not a length of timber, but a partly dismembered human cadaver.

Tom couldn't help it. He let forth a thin, whooping scream. Instantly Nathaniel Seers's head snapped up, and now Tom saw something that was possibly even more unbelievable and horrifying than the axe and the blood-spattered apron and the riven corpse. What he saw, what he knew he saw even though his mind tried to deny it, was that Mr Seers's eyes were not even remotely human. They were pools of hideously glowing orange light, in the centre of which the pupils were no more than thin black slits.

They were the eyes of the very devil.

Too shocked to scream a second time, Tom stumbled back from

the window, feeling the mark of those eyes on him, their burning poisonous glare. Though he felt what little strength he had ebbing away, almost as if his life force was being sucked from his body, he somehow managed to turn and stagger into the fog. Now it seemed that the fog itself had become a live thing: Tom imagined yellow vaporous hands reaching out to grasp him, bloated, leering, malodorous faces forming from the darkness ahead.

He flailed at the fog as he ran, with his bad arm as well as his good, barely noticing the pain. More by luck than judgement, he negotiated the route through the outbuildings without mishap, and within moments was plunging down the steps that led to the towpath. However, even as he careered along the towpath itself, he knew that his headlong flight was hopeless, that the instant he had looked through that window his life had become forfeit. No mortal man could expect to gaze into the eyes of the devil and live to see another dawn.

In the equipment shed, dripping axe held limply in its right hand, the devil in the guise of Nathaniel Seers made no attempt to give chase. Instead it cocked its head to one side and adopted a look of quizzical concentration. After a few moments its glowing eyes suddenly flared brighter. The axe dropped from its hand and hit the floor with a clunk. Beneath the dark mutton-chop whiskers that the factory owner favoured, the creature's lips began to move. It appeared to be communing with something.

'Oh no!' exclaimed the Doctor as several pages of the magazine he was holding came loose and zigzagged lazily to the floor. His melancholy blue eyes widened in alarm as one of the pages alighted on a candelabrum containing five lit candles. Dry and crisp as an autumn leaf, the page immediately and spectacularly whooshed into flame. The Doctor closed the ailing periodical with a rustle of dry paper and a puff of dust, and slid gymnastically down the ladder he had been standing at the top of in order to reach the upper shelves of his library.

He tossed the magazine on to a reading table already covered with a scattering of scrolls and charts and sprinted to a dark recess between two tall sets of bookshelves. Wrenching a fire extinguisher fitted with a hose attachment from the wall, he turned and directed a jet of foam at the merrily crackling flames.

The instant the fire was out, the Doctor let the extinguisher drop to the plushly carpeted floor and ruefully assessed the damage. The candelabrum now resembled a melting wedding cake, and all that was left of the page was a sticky pile of mush and a few scraps of drifting black ash. The Doctor sighed deeply and ran a hand through the curls of his wild, shoulder-length hair. 'Good grief,' he murmured. 'Now I can't even repair you, can I?'

He moved around the TARDIS library, picking up the other spilled pages. When he had them all, he dropped them on to the reading table beside the magazine and placed a chunk of polished blue Nusalian rock, which served as a paperweight, on top of them. He dropped heavily into a high-backed, ornately carved armchair beside the table, leaned forward and picked up the now much-reduced magazine, a Christmas 1893 edition of *The Strand*. It was a vital issue, containing the original printing of 'The Final Problem', one of the pivotal Sherlock Holmes stories – and indeed, initially intended by Conan Doyle to be the last before a public outcry encouraged him to resurrect the famous detective. The Doctor had been planning to take the opportunity, while his latest companion, Sam, caught up on some much-needed sleep, to settle down with a nice pot of Darjeeling and a plate of dry-roasted gumblejack fritters and read it for the 437th time.

'The best-laid schemes…' he murmured wistfully, placing the magazine in his lap. Now in his eighth incarnation, he was a far more settled character than the majority of his previous incarnations had been. Nevertheless, his last violent regeneration, during which he had come closer to death than ever before, had shaken up his molecules so comprehensively that certain aspects of his character had come to the fore that had previously been buried so deeply within him they had seemed virtually nonexistent.

His romantic nature, for one. And his tendency to babble about his origins, for another. During his post-regenerative trauma, he had given of himself so freely, so uninhibitedly, that his scrupulously guarded secrets might just as well have been baubles, trinkets, of little or no value.

His plan, after his bittersweet parting from Grace – the woman at whom his perhaps misplaced attentions had been directed – had been to travel alone for a while, to contemplate, take stock, rediscover the silent, still point within himself. However, as usual, events had contrived to overtake him, and now he had Sam aboard. Seventeen years old, socially aware, brave, outspoken, full of enthusiasm and a sense of wonder that she tried to conceal beneath a patina of streetwise indifference ('cool' she'd probably call it), she was both a tonic and a burden – inspirational and maddening in equal measure.

The Doctor turned his thoughts from his companion and back to himself, which was something he had little enough time for these days. He looked around at his library – the tall bookshelves, the darkly ornate fixtures and fittings, the flickering candles in their holders, the Tiffany lamps, the plush, intricately patterned carpet – and he nodded in approval. Yes, this suited him very well. This, for now, reflected his inner mood and character:

sombre, thoughtful, tasteful, but with a hint of the impressive and the unusual too.

'And so modest, Doctor,' he murmured, gently mocking himself. It had started in his last incarnation, this sense of self-awareness, of his own very definite place in the complex machinations of the universe. One might almost call it a sense of grandeur, if such a phrase didn't stray too close, dangerously close in fact, to the way in which many of his foes viewed themselves.

Like and yet unlike. The incorruptibly good and the indescribably evil. Flip-sides of the same coin. Dark thoughts, Doctor. Dark thoughts.

'This won't do at all!' he exclaimed suddenly, snatching up what remained of the magazine and flinging it back on to the reading table. He jumped up, a tall, lithe, youthful figure, dashing in his frock coat, wing-collared shirt and grey cravat, patterned waistcoat and narrow-legged trousers. In a sudden flurry of energy, he dashed from the library, passing innumerable shelves stacked with all manner of books and periodicals, before reaching an innocuous-looking door propped open with a dog-eared copy of *The Ripple Effect* by Anton Bocca. He catapulted through the door, passed yet more shelves, and finally leapt down on to the parquet floor of the console room.

This was a vast Gothic cathedral of a place, dominated by a six-sided console that managed to look both quaintly archaic and awesomely advanced. The Doctor jumped up on to the raised dais surrounding the console and began to flick switches, push buttons and pull levers, his hands a blur of movement.

Co-ordinates set, he glanced up at the monitor screen, which he had reconfigured to resemble an early TV set from his beloved Earth. The screen flickered and then stabilised:

DESTINATION – LONDON, EARTH
LOCAL DATELINE – 11.01.1894
Victorian era

* * *

'Just time for a quick cup of tea before we arrive,' the Doctor announced, clapping his hands together.

'Wha–?' said Sam blearily, contorting her face in an effort to open one sleep-gummed eye. When she finally managed it, the Doctor was gone, leaving behind a steaming cup of tea on her bedside table, and an outfit carefully laid out on the high-backed wicker chair in the corner of the room. The outfit consisted of a coral-coloured jacket with puffed sleeves, blue bloomers, black Victorian boots and a straw boater-type hat with a coral-coloured band.

Sam considered ignoring the intrusion, turning over and going back to sleep, but hadn't the Doctor said something about arriving somewhere, and wouldn't it be just like him to go off and explore without her if she didn't get a move on? She sat up in her sumptuous four-poster bed, stretched, yawned, and ran a hand through her short blonde hair, making it stand up in spikes. She reached for the china cup and took a gulp of hot tea, immediately closing her eyes in satisfaction. The Doctor made the best cup of tea she'd ever tasted. Knowing him, he probably grew his own leaves or something.

She allowed herself a couple of minutes to come to, looking idly around her room. With its wood-panelled walls, impressive furniture and rich fabrics, it looked like something off the telly, like a set from one of those BBC historical things – *Pride and Prejudice* or something. The Doctor had told her the room had once belonged to Nyssa, whoever she was, but that it had been 'restructured' a bit since then.

Finishing her tea, she put the cup aside, then flung back her covers and crossed to the wicker chair, enjoying the feel of the plush carpet beneath her bare feet. On top of the pile of clothes was a small white business card with a weird symbol on it, and written beneath the symbol, in beautiful copperplate script, were the words: Wear Me.

Sam bridled. No 'please', no 'would you mind?', no 'I know this stuff isn't really your style, but'. God, it was just like being at home again. No, actually, it wasn't, because at least Mum and Dad encouraged her to express herself, speak her own mind, assert her individuality.

She knew she was being unfair, that the Doctor never asked – told – her to do anything without a reason, but it was the way he went about things that got her back up sometimes. She eyed the clothes she had peeled off and dumped on the floor before crawling into bed – ratty jeans, Chumbawamba T-shirt, loose-knit purple and grey striped jumper, green plastic lace-up boots with an orange sun symbol painted on them that she had found in the TARDIS boot cupboard – and thought: I'll wear them if I want, and if he doesn't like it, tough.

However, at that moment she heard the trumpeting of the TARDIS's ancient, powerful engines drifting from the console room, and, realising that they would be arriving at wherever they were going any minute, grabbed some clean underwear from a shelf in her vast, ornately carved wardrobe and picked up the pile of clothes that the Doctor had left for her. With a gesture of what she convinced herself was rebelliousness, she put on a Levellers T-shirt under the coral-coloured jacket, though buttoned the jacket up to the neck.

Fully dressed, she appraised herself in her dressing-table mirror, and though she pulled a face she had to admit that she looked kind of cool. The jacket was slim at the hips and made her

16

wiry body look more shapely than it was, the bloomers were comfortable; and the boots she could have quite happily worn in the company of her mates without fear of ridicule.

The only thing she wasn't sure about was the hat, though maybe she could just carry that around with her. She put on her Walkman (though allowed the headphones to dangle loose around her neck), bunged in a Mory Kante tape, then hurried through to the console room.

The Doctor was busy at the console, making minute adjustments to ease the TARDIS's passage from the Space/Time vortex. The rods of light in the transparent cylinder of the time rotor were meshing and then separating above the console like champing teeth. He was muttering to himself, flicking hair absently out of his eyes.

'Hi!' Sam shouted.

The Doctor raised a hand without looking at her, though whether in greeting or to urge her to be quiet she wasn't sure.

Undaunted, she stomped across the room and leaned on one of the four massive girders which curved up into the cobwebbed darkness above the console and supported the time-rotor mechanism. She watched the Doctor for a moment as he skittered around the console like a squirrel, and then she called, 'I gather from the gear that we're off back to Earth again. So what period are we going to grace with our presence this time?'

The Doctor grunted and gestured at the monitor screen. Sam read what it said there, and despite herself felt a tingle of excitement.

The Victorian era! Even now, despite all she had seen and experienced, which was enough to blow anyone's mind wide open, she couldn't get over the awe-inspiring fact that soon she would be walking about in the past of her own planet. It was an era she'd learned about at school, and had perhaps learned more about from watching films and TV serials based on Charles Dickens's novels, and the old musicals that they always put on at Christmas – *My Fair Lady* and all that.

Yet although her stomach was juddering with anticipation, she couldn't possibly let the Doctor know how excited she was. In what she hoped was a taking-this-kind-of-thing-for-granted sort of voice, she said, 'So what we gonna do this time? Catch Jack the Ripper or something?'

'We're several years too late for that,' murmured the Doctor, evidently preoccupied.

'Oh yeah, right,' she said, as if the Doctor had pointed out something she already knew, but which had briefly slipped her mind. Then a thought struck her and, her eyes shining, she said, 'Doctor?'

'Hmm?'

'Do you know who Jack the Ripper was?'

This time the Doctor looked at her directly. He appeared to consider her question for a moment, then said quietly, 'I know many things. Too many, I think, sometimes.'

'So you *do* know!' Sam exclaimed.

The Doctor pointed at her and frowned. 'You can't take that with you,' he said.

'You what?' said Sam guiltily. For a moment she thought he was referring to the Levellers T-shirt beneath her jacket, that maybe as a Time Lord he had X-ray vision, but just hadn't happened to mention it to her before. She felt herself beginning to blush at the implications of this, then realised he was referring to her Walkman. 'Why not?' she challenged.

'You know why,' the Doctor said, and then added more gently, 'Sam, you're far from stupid.'

She tried not to appear flattered by the compliment. 'It's a dangerous anachronism, right?'

'Right,' replied the Doctor.

'I knew that. I was just wearing it to annoy you.'

'I know,' the Doctor said, smiling.

The engines of the TARDIS reached a crescendo, and then began to quieten.

'So what do you think of the clothes?' she asked, half raising her arms self-consciously.

The Doctor blinked, and then his smile expanded into a grin as though he was only now seeing her for the first time. 'You look delightful,' he said.

Sam pulled a face. 'Oh, cheers,' she said, nonplussed. 'I don't think I want to look delightful.'

'How *do* you want to look?' asked the Doctor.

'I dunno. Cool. Confident.'

'You definitely look cool,' said the Doctor. 'In fact, you'll be one of the coolest people around. The 1890s equivalent of a... a Spice Girl.'

'I think I'd better take that as a compliment,' said Sam carefully. 'Otherwise I might end up giving you a slap.'

The TARDIS engines ground to a halt. The time rotor ceased its gnashing. The Doctor turned his attention back to the console, checked the instruments, then smiled. 'Splendid,' he said. 'We're where we're supposed to be. I'm getting the hang of this.'

He operated the lever that opened the doors and jumped down from the control dais. Sam hastily took off her Walkman, tossed it on to a nearby chair which the Doctor had told her had once been the throne of a pretender to the title of Earth Empress, and followed him outside.

In fact, she all but cannoned into the back of him, because he was standing very still on what appeared to be a towpath, surrounded by drifting fog, looking around suspiciously.

'Oof,' she said. 'What's up, Doctor?'

He frowned. 'This isn't right,' he murmured. 'This isn't right at all.'

Sam felt her spirits sinking. 'What's not right?' she asked dangerously.

'Well, look around you. It's dark.'

'So? It tends to do that at night-time. You've probably been too busy saving planets and stuff to notice before.'

'No, no, you don't understand. The TARDIS instruments distinctly stated that we had arrived in London at two p.m. on January the eleventh, 1894. As I see it, this could mean one of two things. Either some great catastrophe has befallen the Earth which has plunged the planet into darkness. Or…'

'Or?' prompted Sam.

'Or it's not two p.m.'

She sighed. 'What you mean is, you've got it wrong again. I bet we're not on Earth at all!'

'No no no no no,' said the Doctor quickly, holding up his hands as though to stem her anger. 'The TARDIS has probably just got her a.m.s and her p.m.s mixed up. She gets a bit forgetful sometimes. Dear old thing.' He turned and patted the TARDIS's chipped and battered exterior, then pulled the door shut. 'No, this is Earth all right. Smell that air.'

Sam did so, almost choking on the sulphurous fog.

'Only London smells like this,' said the Doctor cheerfully. 'It has a certain… ethos. A certain bouquet.' He paused, looking puzzled.

'What's the matter?'

'*Déjà vu*,' said the Doctor, then shrugged. 'Occupational hazard. Come on.'

He strode off along the towpath. There was a high, rough-hewn flood wall on his left, and on his right a drop into foggy blackness from which could be heard the gentle lap of water.

'Where are we going?' Sam asked, having almost to jog to keep up with his long-legged strides.

'We're going to a little bookshop I know to buy a copy of last month's *Strand* magazine. It should still be on sale.'

'Right. Er… why?'

'Because my issue met with a little accident.'

'God, are we living dangerously or what?' said Sam a little ruefully. Then she frowned. 'Doctor?'

'Hmm?'

'I think I might have spotted a minor flaw in your plan.'

'Really?' said the Doctor, surprised. 'And what might that be?'

'Where are we going to find a bookshop that's open at two o'clock in the morning?'

The Doctor stopped dead, and again Sam almost walked into the back of him. 'Ah,' he said. 'I wondered when you were going to notice that.'

'Oh yeah, sure,' she said. 'So what are we going to do? Go back to the TARDIS and wait for daylight?'

'Certainly not! Now we're here we might as well find out where we are.'

'Then what?'

The Doctor shrugged. 'We'll think of something.' He began walking again.

Sam fell into step beside him, wafting a hand in front of her face. 'Why's this fog yellow?' she asked. 'And what's that farty smell?'

'Sulphur,' explained the Doctor. 'Smoke pollution caused by thousands of coal fires. There's no central heating in this age, remember. The fog's permanent and always yellow – hence the phrase "pea-souper".'

'Maybe I ought to start a campaign against it,' said Sam, 'get in

21

there before the problem gets as bad as it is in my day. Don't people realise that they're poisoning the planet?'

'Keeping themselves warm is a greater priority,' said the Doctor.

'Well, it shouldn't be. Someone ought to make them see what a terrible legacy they're leaving behind for future generations. Besides, there's alternative methods of –'

She broke off, turning her face to peer into the fog ahead. Aside from the water she could hear lapping in the darkness to her right, there was now a different sound – the approaching clatter of rapid footsteps.

'Doc–' she began, but had not even had time to complete the word before a large, flapping dark shape hurtled at them out of the fog.

Before Sam could even blink, the Doctor had grabbed what she quickly realised was a man wearing a ragged coat and had swung him round by the lapels, dragging him off balance. As the man stumbled and fell to his knees, the Doctor wrapped an arm around his neck in an unbreakable headlock.

'Please,' the man cried, his voice shrill with panic and exhaustion. 'I beg of you, don't hurt me!'

'I have no intention of hurting anyone,' said the Doctor mildly.

'I beg of you,' the man said again, almost sobbing with terror, 'please let me go, else he'll catch me.'

'I don't reckon he's a mugger, Doctor,' Sam said. 'Look at him, he's scared stiff.'

The Doctor released the man and stepped back from him, showing his open palms. 'Perhaps we can be of some help,' he said gently. 'Is someone chasing you?'

The man seemed not to hear the Doctor's words. He was a wretched sight, his clothes tattered and dirty, his face pallid and thin with exhaustion and malnutrition. There was an awful, rotten stench about him that seemed to be due to more than simply a lack of personal hygiene.

'Is he a crackhead?' Sam whispered, sidling up to the Doctor.

The Doctor shook his head. 'No, he's just very poor and very frightened.'

'Nah, he's definitely out of it,' Sam said. 'You can tell by his eyes. There's this kid at school – Tony Blanchard. He's a total dopehead. He's got eyes like that.'

'He's ill,' murmured the Doctor. 'Partly delirious.'

'What's wrong with him?'

'Look at his right hand.'

Sam looked, and saw that the man wore a filthy rag around his hand, from which his fingers poked, horrendously black and swollen.

'Gross,' she breathed. 'What is it?'

'Gangrene,' said the Doctor grimly. 'I'm afraid our friend is not long for this world.'

'That's horrible. Can't you take him back to the TARDIS and operate on him to stop it spreading? Chop his arm off or something?'

The Doctor shook his head. 'The techniques required would be too far in advance of this time.'

'So?'

'So if I let him loose on the streets again and the wrong people noticed him, it could set up a temporal vibration, leading to a glitch in technological advancement.'

'That's crap!' said Sam. 'We're talking about a man's life here.'

'We're talking about millions of lives. The life of every person on this planet. Such a glitch may well lead to catastrophe. You, Sam, may never be born.'

'But that's mental. I was born. I'm here, aren't I?'

'That's open to debate,' murmured the Doctor, and then

quickly, before she could react, 'Listen. Our friend is trying to tell us something.'

The man climbed slowly and painfully to his feet, his eyes rolling in terror and delirium. He appeared to be muttering not so much to them as to himself.

'What's he saying?' asked Sam.

'Shh,' said the Doctor, and then raising his voice, 'Look, we really do want to help you.'

The man looked up at the Doctor and began to shake his head. 'No one can help me, no one can help me now,' he muttered.

'We can try,' said Sam. 'Come on, mate, just tell us what's wrong.'

She took a step forward. The man flinched back, his body going rigid. He pointed at her with his good hand. He looked like a cornered animal.

'Keep back!' he ordered, his voice raw and shrill. 'For your own sakes, keep away from me.'

'Why won't you let us help you?' asked the Doctor gently. 'You're obviously in some trouble.'

'Yes, sir, you might say that,' said the man, casting a fearful glance back over his shoulder. 'The devil himself is at my heels.'

The Doctor raised his eyebrows. 'The devil?'

'He's completely gone,' whispered Sam.

Though the man's eyes were still wild, the Doctor's soothing tone seemed to be anchoring him back into a semblance of reality.

'I've seen him, sir,' he hissed. 'Back there at the factory. He fixed his eyes upon me. Horrible they were, horrible! Glowing like lanterns.'

Sam saw the Doctor glancing curiously along the towpath behind the man, though she herself could see nothing but swirling fog. She wondered if the Doctor was thinking what she was thinking, which was that the bloke's gangrene was turning his brain to mush, causing him to hallucinate.

'Which factory's this then, mate?' she asked, trying to make her voice as soothing as the Doctor's.

It didn't work. In fact, it appeared only to have the effect of enraging the man. Without warning he lunged at her, barging her into the Doctor, and as the two of them went down in a tangle of arms and legs, the man leapt clumsily over them and continued his desperate, shambling flight along the towpath.

Sam's fall was cushioned by the Doctor's body, but under her weight he stumbled backwards, cracking his head on the wall at the side of the path.

'You all right, Doctor?' she asked, picking herself up to find him sitting on the slimy cobbles, rubbing the back of his skull and blinking sleepily up at her.

'What pretty fireworks,' he remarked. 'Are they yours?'

'Doctor!' Sam urged, shaking his shoulder.

He recovered in an instant, springing to his feet. 'Where's he gone?'

Sam pointed along the towpath. 'That way. Towards the TARDIS.'

'Come on.' The Doctor hared off, Sam running as fast as she could to keep up with him, wishing she had a pair of Nikes instead of these bloody boots. The Doctor's tall frame, his coat flapping behind him, became insubstantial as the fog shrouded it, and then was swallowed up altogether as he forged ahead. Sam heard him shout, 'Don't run. We want to help you.' His voice sounded flat, compressed, as if the fog was thick as cotton wool. Sam gritted her teeth, willing her legs to pump faster.

She had just sprinted past the TARDIS when an awful, gut-wrenching scream tore out of the darkness ahead. The shock of it made her jump, causing her to slip on the cobbles. She struggled to keep her balance, her arms pinwheeling, her boots skidding on the slippery stones. Another warbling scream, so saturated with terror that Sam felt cold, hard fear lodge inside her belly, seemed to shred the fog before it was abruptly cut off.

Part of Sam didn't want to see what was ahead of her, didn't want to see what had made the man scream like that. The greater part, however – her reckless bravery, her desire to help, and yes, even her curiosity – drove her onward. She licked her blotting-paper lips as she ran, trying without success to generate some saliva in her mouth. Suddenly she saw a figure ahead of her, a dark silhouette wreathed in fog.

'Sam,' the figure hissed, half turning towards her and extending an arm as a barrier, 'don't move. Don't make a sound.'

Such was the authority in the Doctor's voice that for once Sam obeyed it without question. She clattered to a halt, her lips clamped shut, trying to breathe fast and hard through her nose. She saw something move in the darkness beyond the Doctor, something that towered above him. She screwed up her eyes, trying to focus on it, but the fog made it indistinct. She couldn't even tell how far away the creature – if it was a creature – was. It could have been ten yards, or twenty, or more.

The Doctor held up a hand, urging her not to follow, then turned and began to edge slowly forward. It was obvious he wanted to help the man if at all possible. Willing her legs to move, Sam crept after him.

All at once the dark bulk ahead shifted, and Sam heard a sound, like a crocodile's slithering, magnified a hundredfold. She saw something waving vaguely from side to side twenty feet above her and looked up.

Her eyes widened in horrified awe. Could that be a head up there, on the end of a long neck?

It's a dinosaur, she thought. I'm looking at a bloody dinosaur!

Then she was clapping her hands over her ears as the creature let out a bellowing roar that seemed to rattle the stones in the wall lining the towpath, and reverberated out across the river, no doubt terrifying every boatman for miles around.

Even before the echoes of the roar had died away, the creature was moving in the darkness. At first Sam thought it had spotted them, then she realised it was actually turning to slide off the towpath. There was a huge splash and a great wave surged over the embankment. Water covered her boots, then, frighteningly, pulled her towards the river as it withdrew. The Doctor yanked her back, almost bruising her arm. As soon as the wave was spent, the Doctor rushed forward, splatting through pools of water that even now were draining back into the river. He stood right on the edge of the towpath, hands on knees, leaning forward as far as his balance would allow, peering down into the black water. Sam hesitated, then, deciding she was already as wet as she was likely to get, splashed forward and joined him, though as usual she could see nothing but fog and darkness. She could hear little waves lapping against the flood wall some way below her, however. She imagined the huge ripples of the creature's passage extending ever outward, a series of concentric circles like a widening shiver of fear on the dark skin of the Thames.

CHAPTER 2
POST-MORTEM

Twenty minutes later the Doctor and Sam were sitting on hard wooden chairs, watching impatiently as the stout, bewhiskered desk sergeant across from them recorded the details of their experience in a large, cloth-bound ledger. Why was it, the Doctor thought as he watched the man dip his pen into a small pot of ink for at least the five hundredth time, that all Victorian policemen seemed cast from the same mould? Not only did they all look the same, but they all operated with the same ponderous, flat-footed precision. Mind you, the same was true of law-enforcers and authority figures everywhere. No imagination, no intuition, no sense of urgency. No wonder the universe was forever in such a mess.

The Doctor had told Sam to let him do the talking – an order that she had greeted with a look of contemptuous defiance, but had nevertheless obeyed so far – and then had proceeded to tell the desk sergeant, whose name was Tompkins, a series of half-truths. He had decided to leave out the bit about the gigantic monster disappearing into the Thames. Instead he had said that while giving chase to the evidently desperate man they had encountered on the towpath, the two of them had heard a number of cries and the sounds of a scuffle in the darkness ahead. By the time they arrived on the scene, however, the man had been nowhere to be found. The Doctor offered the opinion that the man had been attacked, perhaps even killed, and then pushed or thrown into the river.

The sergeant had listened attentively, and was now engaged in the painfully slow process of writing down what the

Doctor had told him. His patience at an end, the Doctor leaned back in his chair, swung his legs up, and placed his still-damp feet on the sergeant's desk.

Tompkins glanced disapprovingly at the puddles of water forming around the Doctor's heels. 'Do you mind, sir?'

'As you were taking so long I thought I'd have a little nap,' said the Doctor acidly. 'I mean, let's face it, Sergeant, even if the poor unfortunate I encountered was still alive when he entered the water, he'll have drowned by now.'

Tompkins's frown deepened. 'What are you suggesting, sir?'

'He's suggesting that you pull your finger out, mate,' Sam said, unable to contain herself, earning herself a startled look from Tompkins and a warning scowl from the Doctor.

Diplomatically the Doctor said, 'I'm simply asking you to send some of your men down to the river to scour the area. We need to act quickly if there's any hope of rescuing this poor fellow.'

The sergeant regarded the Doctor with a deadpan expression. 'I'll be sending someone down there in due course, sir, don't you worry.'

'In due course?' the Doctor snapped. 'It may have escaped your notice, Sergeant, but a man's life is in danger.'

Now Tompkins's expression became a little pitying. 'You're not from round these parts are you, sir?'

In one swift movement, the Doctor swung his legs from the desk and leaned forward. 'That's very intuitive of you, Sergeant,' he murmured.

Tompkins sighed. 'What I mean, sir, is Whitechapel's not the sort of place you would normally expect to find a refined gentleman like yourself at this time of night, particularly not in the company of an equally refined young lady. And, meaning no disrespect, sir, but people such as yourselves don't really know what goes on in places like this.'

The Doctor sensed Sam bristling again. Those who questioned her self-image of streetwise rebel usually received short shrift. Hastily he said, 'Perhaps you would care to enlighten us then, Sergeant?'

Tompkins harrumphed and, discomforted by the Doctor's scrutiny, looked down at the open ledger, his already ruddy cheeks turning an even deeper shade of red. He appeared to chew on the ends of his heavy ginger moustache for a moment, and then he said, 'Well, sir, miss, it's like this. It may sound harsh, but if I sent my men down to the river every time some vagabond fell in, they'd spend all their time fishing, if you see what I mean.' He held up a chunky hand to forestall any protestations. 'Now I'm not an uncaring man; far from it. But I am a practical one. And from the way you described this fellow to me, sir – thin and ill and the like – well, a man like that wouldn't have a deal of fight left in him, do you see? If he fell into the river in the middle of the night with the water so cold, you can guarantee that he will have dropped like a stone. Now, I can send a couple of men down there with lanterns and boathooks if it will ease your minds, but I can tell you now they would be wasting their time. We won't see that fellow again until the river decides to give him back to us.'

The Doctor sighed. 'You're probably right, Sergeant. All the same, we would like you to send some of your men down there – just, as you say, for our peace of mind.'

'As you wish, sir,' the Sergeant said heavily. He called over one of his constables and gave the order.

'Now, sir, miss,' he said when the constable had gone to do his bidding, 'perhaps you would be kind enough to satisfy my curiosity on one or two matters?'

'If we can, Sergeant,' said the Doctor wearily.

'Thank you. Your co-operation would be much appreciated. Now, I hope you won't think me impertinent, but I'd be grateful if you could tell me exactly what the two of you were doing, walking along that towpath in the early hours of the morning. It strikes me as rather a curious occupation for persons such as yourselves, if you don't mind me saying so.'

The Doctor gave a grin which seemed to light up his face. 'I'm an inventor, Sergeant,' he said smoothly.

'A what, sir?'

'An inventor. I invent things. Slide fasteners, the cylinder phonograph, the pneumatic tyre.'

Tompkins blinked. 'You invented all those things, sir?'

'Well... no,' the Doctor admitted. 'But a number of my friends did. Some of them without my help.'

Tompkins looked at the Doctor stolidly for a moment as if he expected him to elaborate on his extraordinary claim. Eventually he said, 'Well, that's all very impressive, I'm sure, sir, but I don't see what relevance –'

'It's all to do with ideas, Sergeant,' the Doctor interrupted, and dropped his voice as though to impart a secret. 'I always have my best ideas when I'm walking in the dark and I can hear the gentle lap of water somewhere close by. Concentrates the mind wonderfully.'

'I see, sir,' said Tompkins, who evidently didn't see at all. 'And the young lady is...?'

'My niece,' said the Doctor quickly.

'Your niece?' Tompkins sounded doubtful.

'Yeah, but I'm going to be an inventor too,' Sam chipped in, determined to get her own back on the Doctor. 'We wander along, bouncing ideas off each other. Don't we, Uncle?'

'Er... yes,' said the Doctor.

'Penicillin,' blurted Sam.

'I beg your pardon, miss.'

'Penicillin. Haven't you heard of it, Sergeant?'

'Can't say as I have, miss.'

'I'm not surprised,' said the Doctor hastily. 'It hasn't been invented yet. You will keep me informed if your men find anything, won't you, Sergeant?'

Thrown by the Doctor's abrupt change of subject, and feeling he had somehow lost the initiative, Tompkins stammered, 'Er... yes, sir, of course... I'll, er, I'll need a few particulars from the both of you first though, sir.' It was only as he said this that he realised he knew nothing at all about this strange young couple. So far the gentleman had somehow managed to neatly sidestep all of his requests for personal information.

Now, however, the Doctor said promptly, 'My name is Dr John Smith and this is my niece, Miss Samantha Jones.' Raising his voice above Sam's muttered response of, 'Smith and Jones. Nice one,' he said, 'As for our address, we're from out of town – as you so correctly surmised, Sergeant. We're currently staying with a friend of mine.'

'I see, sir. And would this friend of yours have an address by any chance?'

'He would indeed,' said the Doctor, and smiled again. 'Four Ranskill Gardens.'

At first the sound seemed to form part of Litefoot's dream. He was taking tea with his father, who kept referring to Litefoot as 'sir', and insisted on standing ramrod-straight in his brigadier general's uniform. Inordinately distressed by this, Litefoot was saying, 'For goodness' sake, do sit down, Father.'

'Yes, sir,' his father barked, but remained standing.

That was when the hammering began.

'Come in,' Litefoot called, but then the dream began to fall apart, to break away from his waking mind in shards like pieces of a broken mirror. His eyes opened and flooded with darkness, and he sat up in bed, uncomfortably aware of his pounding heart. Blinking away sleep that filled his eyes like grit, he groped at the objects on his bedside table and found his box of lucifers. He extracted and struck one and applied it to the wick of the candle he always carried up to bed with him. Instantly the room was bathed in a flickering mustard light.

Litefoot reached for his timepiece, consulted it squinting, and was outraged to discover it was almost 3.20 a.m. Gad, who could be making such an infernal racket at this hour of the morning? Whoever it was, he'd soon give the bounder what for!

Energised by his anger, he jumped out of bed, shrugged himself into his maroon velvet dressing gown, stepped into his slippers and rushed downstairs, the flame of his candle flapping in the breeze. Grabbing his cane from its stand in the hallway as the hammering came again, he stomped to the front door. The dim light from the gas lamps shining outside enabled Litefoot to make out a vague shape through the frosted-glass panels. Putting down the candle, he unlocked the front door and yanked it open.

A young man with long, curly hair and an even younger woman whose blonde hair was cropped shockingly close to her scalp were standing on his steps. At the sight of him, the man's lips curled upward in a delighted grin.

'My dear Litefoot!' he exclaimed. 'How marvellous to see you!'

Litefoot's eyes widened. Confound the man's insolence! 'Who the Dickens are you, sir?'

'You don't recognise me?' the young man said, surprised, and then his face cleared. 'No, of course you don't. How silly of me.'

'Perhaps you'd care to explain yourself, sir,' Litefoot said, tightening his grip on his cane.

'Yes. Yes, of course.' The young man leaned forward and murmured confidingly, 'I believe you were once acquainted with a colleague of mine. A man who called himself the Doctor.'

'The Doctor?' Litefoot spluttered, his anger evaporating. A little weakly he said, 'You know the Doctor?'

'Oh yes,' the young man said. 'He and I are very close.'

'Well... 'pon my soul. Perhaps you had better come in, sir, and tell me what I can do for you.'

The young man grinned and was about to cross the threshold when the young woman hovering behind him cleared her throat.

The man turned, looking momentarily blank as if he hadn't realised the girl was there. Then he said, 'Ah yes, introductions. Professor, this is Samantha Jones, my... er... niece. Samantha, this is Professor Litefoot. He's a great friend... um, of a friend of mine.'

'Hiya, Professor,' the girl said, striding forward, grabbing Litefoot's right hand and giving it a firm shake. 'Pleased to meet you.'

Litefoot, startled both by the girl's peculiar greeting ('Higher'? Higher than what?) and her lack of etiquette could only murmur, 'Er... yes. Charmed, I'm sure. Well... won't you come in?'

The two of them entered, Litefoot closing the door behind them. Holding up the still-burning candle, he led the way along the hallway and into a darkened sitting room. He waved the strange young couple to a pair of overstuffed armchairs covered in heavy fabric, then bustled about, lighting yet more lamps. Though the fire in the grate had died, the coals were still glowing brightly. Litefoot scattered some kindling on top of them and shovelled more coal on top of that. Within minutes flames were dancing merrily in the grate.

'Now,' he said, 'can I offer either of you a drink? A brandy perhaps for you, sir? And how about some cocoa for you, Miss Jones?'

'No thank you, Professor,' said the young man, absently staring into the flames.

'I'll have a G and T if you've got it,' Sam said. And then, catching the Doctor's eye, 'Or perhaps I won't. And by the way, call me Sam. If you keep calling me Miss Jones, I'll feel like I'm in an episode of *Rising Damp*.'

Litefoot gaped at her; he couldn't have been more bewildered if she had spoken to him in Swahili.

'Sam,' the Doctor warned under his breath, 'behave. Remember where you are.'

Sam gave him one of her cool looks. With a little more maturity the look alone would surely prove a quite devastating put-down. The Doctor, however, merely gazed unblinkingly back at her, his blue eyes somehow managing to be both implacable and intense, and eventually she looked away.

Litefoot watched this exchange, looking a little perplexed, though of course far too polite to pass comment on it. Instead he said uncertainly, 'You don't mind if I imbibe?'

The Doctor wafted a hand. 'It's your house, Professor.'

Litefoot poured himself a generous measure of brandy from a crystal decanter, then plumped down heavily on a wooden dining chair. 'I hope the two of you will forgive my singular lack of decorum. I have to confess, this entire situation has me rather rattled.'

Sam grinned, thinking how easy it was going to be to knock people off their stride in this day and age. The Doctor, however, smiled sympathetically. He appeared perfectly relaxed, his features bathed in firelight. 'As far as I'm concerned, Professor, your decorum has always been impeccable.'

'Always?' said Litefoot. 'You speak as though we're well acquainted.'

The young man leaned forward a little. Though he seemed an agreeable enough young fellow, Litefoot had to admit that the intensity of his gaze was a little unsettling.

'Forgive me, Professor,' he said. 'It's just that I feel as though I do know you very well. The Doctor often talks about the Weng-Chiang business and the gallant part that you played in it.'

'Does he?' said Litefoot, evidently flattered.

The 'Weng-Chiang business', as the young man had termed it, had taken place some five years previously, though Litefoot still recalled it as though it were yesterday. It had been a relatively brief but extraordinary affair. He, together with the Doctor, the Doctor's charming but equally perplexing companion, Leela, and a local theatre owner, Henry Gordon Jago, had become involved in the evil machinations of a masked criminal named Magnus Greel, who was passing himself off as an ancient Chinese god known as Weng-Chiang. The Doctor had described Greel as a 'foe from the future', and, though even now the idea seemed preposterous, Litefoot had seen enough evidence to believe that what the Doctor had told him might very well have been the truth.

As for the Doctor, he had been, in his own way, just as

mysterious a character as Greel himself. Dear Henry, who had since become a firm friend, had described him as a super-sleuth who was held in the highest esteem at Scotland Yard. However, although as a police pathologist Litefoot had many significant contacts within the force, subsequent inquiries had unearthed no information whatsoever about the fellow. If the police did know of his existence they were keeping very quiet about it. The last Litefoot had seen of the Doctor and Leela was when they had stepped into a tall blue box which had emitted an appalling bellowing sound before vanishing into thin air!

'What's the Weng-Chiang business?' Sam asked now.

'I'll explain later,' the Doctor said.

'I'll hold you to that.'

'I know.'

The Doctor turned back to Litefoot. 'Tell me, Professor, how's Mr Jago?'

Litefoot smiled. With his grey hair and moustache, beaky nose and twinkling eyes, Sam thought that he resembled a kindly uncle. 'Actually, he's been rather dyspeptic of late. I prescribed him a tonic and a healthy dose of sea air. He's currently spending a few weeks with his sister in Brighton. But Henry's an old war horse. He'll bounce back. Outlive the lot of us, I'll wager.'

'I dare say,' the Doctor murmured.

'But if you'll permit me, sir, I have a number of questions that I would rather like to ask you.'

'People always do,' said the Doctor.

Litefoot gave him a quizzical look. 'Quite,' he said and took another sip of brandy. Then he admitted, 'Although to be frank, sir, it's hard to know where to begin. When the Doctor... disappeared, he left so many questions unanswered, so much unexplained.'

'Yeah, he's like that,' Sam put in, relishing the moment. 'Untidy. Forgetful. Thoughtless. Downright annoying sometimes.'

Litefoot chuckled. 'Do you know, he once drew a map on my best linen tablecloth. Dashed impudent. Ingenious, though.' He stared into the fire as though lost in his own thoughts for a moment, and then said, 'Perhaps the best place to begin would be if you, sir, were to explain how you and our mutual friend, the Doctor, happen to be acquainted.'

The Doctor steepled his fingers to his lips. After a moment he murmured, 'He and I are in the same line of business. We're... partners, you might say.'

'Indeed? And what, may I ask, might that line of business be?'

'We're investigators. Of a sort. We attempt to keep events on the right path.'

'Me too,' said Sam, and pointed at the Doctor. 'I work with him. Indispensable sidekick. He'd probably have snuffed it more than once if it wasn't for me.'

Litefoot looked at her dubiously. 'You are employed by the police then, I take it?'

'Not if we can help it,' said the Doctor.

'I see,' said Litefoot wearily, 'or rather, I don't.'

He took a sip of his brandy. The Doctor watched him do so with genuine affection. Litefoot must be almost sixty now, and though he had a few more wrinkles and a slightly wider girth than the last time they had met, he was still basically the same old Litefoot. Despite his gentlemanly appearance and rather formal behaviour, by Victorian standards he was actually something of a rebel. He had outraged his parents by leaving the army, in which his family had a long and honourable tradition, and becoming a doctor in one of London's poorer

39

hospitals in the East End. For the last twenty years of his life, his father had refused to speak to him, a situation which Litefoot regarded as eminently regrettable, but which nevertheless had not swayed him from his chosen path.

To compound his family's shame, Litefoot had never married, and therefore had no children to continue the family name. Furthermore, although he lived comfortably enough and had a handsome private income, he flew in the face of convention by refusing to flaunt his wealth and surround himself with servants and material possessions. Most men of his standing had a butler, a housekeeper, a cook, a nanny for the children, and several maidservants, but Litefoot, who preferred his privacy, was content enough with a single housekeeper, Mrs Hudson, who came in from outside to cook and clean every day except Sunday. He had no private carriage (and therefore no groomsman), and although, by modern standards, his house was cluttered with furniture and ornaments (many of which reflected his upbringing in Peking), compared with those of his neighbours, the number of his personal effects was relatively small.

'I'm sorry, Professor, for being so obtuse,' the Doctor said. 'What I... er, we actually do, what we actually are, is a little too complex to explain.'

'Top secret too,' said Sam importantly. 'Need-to-know, all that kind of thing.'

'Ah,' said Litefoot. 'Then perhaps I ought not to pry, after all. Though answer me these questions, if you will. How are the Doctor and Miss Leela? What, sir, is your name? And what brings the two of you here at such an unsociable hour?'

'The Doctor is fit and well,' said the Doctor, grinning at Sam. 'Leela is married, with children I believe. My name... well, this is where it does get a little complicated. You see,

40

Professor, in our… um…'

'Department,' supplied Sam.

'Yes, department, we are all known as the Doctor. It's a sort of… codename.' He pulled an apologetic face.

Litefoot raised his eyebrows and shook his head. 'Indeed? I must say, sir, this state of affairs gets queerer by the minute.' Then suddenly he was smiling mischievously. 'Jolly intriguing, all the same.'

'Isn't it?' the Doctor agreed, his grin reappearing. 'As for our appearance here tonight, I can only apologise, Professor, on behalf of myself and my niece, for turning up unannounced on your doorstep like this. The fact is, we're working on rather a hush-hush case, and came to London at short notice. The Doctor gave us your address and assured us that we would be certain of a warm welcome.'

'And so you are, both of you,' Litefoot said with sudden bonhomie. 'As friends of the Doctor's you are welcome to stay here for as long as you like. I must confess, my life has been singularly lacking in excitement these past few years.' Then he added ruefully, 'My only hope is that if events turn out anything like as perilous as the last time, my poor old heart will be able to stand the strain.'

At the stroke of seven a.m. Emmeline Seers was woken as usual by a timid knock on her bedroom door. The moment she opened her eyes she felt fresh and alert. 'Come in, Mary,' she called.

The door opened and Mary Dobbs, the housemaid, entered with the tea tray.

'Good morning, Mary,' said Emmeline. 'How are you today?'

'Very well, thank you, Miss Emmeline,' said Mary demurely. She was eighteen, two years younger than Emmeline herself.

Emmeline had been exhorting the housemaid to call her by name ever since the girl had joined the family four years ago, but it was only recently that she had begun to do so, and then only when the two of them were alone together. Mary was small and slim, with pale, smooth skin that would have made many girls of Emmeline's age and status green with envy. Indeed, many of Emmeline's acquaintances – she hesitated to call them friends – sipped vinegar and even arsenic in an attempt to achieve an alabaster complexion. Emmeline, however, who was nevertheless tall and slim and rather beautiful, had no time for such silly vanity. She had far more important concerns.

She wanted to become a solicitor, an ambition which her father, kind and understanding though he was (or at least had been up until a few weeks ago), regarded as 'preposterous'. Certainly she wanted more than simply to be a wife and mother. The thought of doing nothing but sitting at home sewing, planning meals, and taking tea with other ladies filled her with dread. With the formation of the Women's Franchise League in 1889, Emmeline fervently believed that the woman's role in society was changing for the better, and that it surely would not be very much longer before women were allowed to vote in both local and general elections. Wasn't the country ruled by a woman, after all, and had it not been so very successfully for almost six decades? Was it, therefore, too fanciful to hope and believe that one day Great Britain would have not only a female monarch but a female prime minister?

With Mary's help, she washed and dressed, favouring her royal-blue suit edged in white, with its tight waistband, puffed sleeves, floor-length skirt and bustle. Though her mother liked her to wear ringlets, Emmeline preferred her deep chestnut hair combed back into a bun – a practical, no-nonsense style.

'How is Mama this morning?' Emmeline asked. Of late her father, once so gentle and loving and attentive, had become hard and cold, almost cruel at times in his offhandedness. Not only that but he had taken to staying away from the house for long periods, sometimes remaining at the factory for days and nights at a time. It was a transformation which had upset her mother greatly, and though Florence Seers had done her utmost to keep the situation and her own distress from her servants, Emmeline knew that the recent disruptions to household routine could not have escaped their notice.

Mary looked hesitant, as though afraid of being caught out. 'I'm not sure it's my place to comment, Miss Emmeline.'

Emmeline smiled warmly. 'Oh come now, Mary, I'm not going to punish you for using your eyes and ears.'

Mary, nevertheless, looked as though she was having to gather her resolve. Finally she said, 'Well, Miss, I must confess that Mrs Seers does not seem quite herself this morning.'

'Nor many mornings of late,' Emmeline said, and sighed. 'Where is she, Mary?'

'In Mr Seers's study, I believe, Miss Emmeline.'

'Then I must go to her,' said Emmeline. 'But first, Mary, tell me, what is your opinion of my father's demeanour these past weeks?'

Mary's white skin reddened with a blush. 'I'm sure I don't know, Miss Emmeline.'

'I'm sure you do,' Emmeline said, not unkindly. To Mary's surprise, she reached out and took the housemaid's hand. 'I assure you, I'm not trying to get you into trouble with Mrs Brandon. I simply want your opinion. What you tell me will go no further than this room.'

Mary glanced around the room in question as though to make certain of its parameters, and then said hesitantly, 'Well,

Miss Emmeline, I have always found your father a most kind and gracious employer. But of late…'

'Go on,' coaxed Emmeline.

'Of late, he has seemed… troubled. I must confess, both Lottie and I are a little afraid of him.'

Emmeline patted the hand she still held, then released it. 'Thank you, Mary, for being honest with me. It's certainly true that all is not well with him at present. But try not to worry. I intend to rectify the situation.'

'You, Miss Emmeline?' Mary said, unable to keep the doubt from her voice.

'Yes. Now I think I will go and see Mama. You may return to your duties, Mary.'

'Yes, Miss,' Mary said hastily. She picked up the tea tray and left the room.

Emmeline went downstairs, maintaining her poise despite her anxiety. The house in which she lived with her mother and father was in a fashionable terrace in the West End. It had four floors and a basement, and was made from yellow London stock bricks partly coated in white stucco. The road in which the house was situated was blocked off by gates, which were manned by a gatekeeper who let callers and tradesmen in, but who refused entry to so-called 'undesirables'.

Emmeline heard her mother before she saw her. Although the door to her father's study was of stout wood, and her mother was doing her utmost to be discreet, her sobs were nevertheless audible.

Emmeline tried the door, which was locked, and then tapped on it. 'Mama,' she called, 'it's Emmeline. Please let me in.'

There was a sudden silence, which seemed to fill the house. Emmeline had the momentary and no doubt ludicrous notion

44

that all of the servants were crouched in the kitchen below stairs, holding their collective breath, loath not only to intervene but even to be seen going about their daily duties. She pressed her ear to the door and through the silence heard a number of stifled sniffles. She was about to call again when her mother's voice, evidently trying not to sound tearful, said, 'I'll be out presently.'

'No, Mama, I wish to see you now,' Emmeline said firmly. 'I know very well that you've been weeping. The entire house can hear it.'

There was another short silence, and then in a faint voice her mother said, 'Very well.'

A key grated in the lock and the door was opened. As Emmeline entered the study, her mother was already walking away from her. She was a stout, handsome woman with hair the same colour as her daughter's. Her velvet and satin dress, edged with lace, shimmered purple as she crossed the room, the long train trailing behind her. Only when she reached the over-stuffed leather armchair by the roaring fire did she turn and face Emmeline. She looked forlorn, lost, confused. Emmeline's heart leapt with sorrow at the sight of her.

Her mother lowered herself wearily into the armchair as Emmeline closed the door. She had always liked her father's study, had always found it a magical place with its stuffed animals and exotic insects in glass cases, and its many books, but now it seemed merely to accentuate the gulf that had developed between her father and the rest of the household.

She eyed the writing bureau with its secret compartments, the heavy oak desk, its worktop inset with a rectangle of stretched red leather.

'Have you been going through Father's things, Mama?' she asked.

Her mother looked at once both shocked and full of guilt. 'Why do you ask that?' she said.

'It is what I would do,' Emmeline replied, 'if a husband of mine was acting as father is.'

Now her mother looked defeated, but relieved. 'You must understand, my dear, that I am at the end of my tether.'

Emmeline crouched down, took her mother's right hand, cool despite the warmth of the fire, in both of hers, and said, 'I understand perfectly, Mama. Did you discover anything?'

Florence Seers cast her eyes downwards. A tear dropped from one of them into her lap. 'Nothing,' she whispered. 'Nothing at all.'

Emmeline closed her arms around her mother's shoulders, and after a moment's resistance the older woman allowed herself to be comforted.

All at once Emmeline said, 'I intend to go to the factory today and speak to Father.'

Her mother stiffened. 'No, dear, you mustn't. He will not thank you for it.'

'Nevertheless, I intend to do it. We must find out what is troubling him so.'

Florence Seers shook her head. 'Believe me, I have tried,' she said. 'I have done little else but try.'

'Then I will make him tell me,' Emmeline said with fierce determination. 'I promise you, Mama, I will not rest until he is back with us and we are content once more.'

The Doctor and Litefoot were enjoying a breakfast of kedgeree, grilled sheep's kidneys, toast, marmalade and tea when a knock sounded at the front door. The two of them heard Mrs Hudson bustle along the hallway to answer it. A few moments later she tapped on the dining room door and entered, a dough-faced woman with black button eyes and an expansive bosom.

'There's a gentleman from the police to see you, sir.'

'Thank you, Mrs Hudson,' the Doctor said before the professor could answer. He jumped up and hurried out into the hallway. Litefoot dabbed his lips with a napkin, then followed at a more sedate pace.

Another clone, the Doctor thought, at the sight of the stout, bewhiskered constable standing on the doorstep.

'Good morning, Constable,' he said heartily. 'You have news, I take it?'

'Yes, sir. That is... you *are* the Doctor, sir?'

'Indeed I am,' the Doctor confirmed, 'and this is my friend, Professor George Litefoot.'

'Yes, sir,' the policeman said politely, 'the professor and I are acquainted.'

'What can we do for you, Constable?' Litefoot asked.

'This is a matter that concerns both of you, sirs. It seems a body was fished out of the Thames this morning, and we have reason to believe it may be that of the man you was inquiring about last night, Doctor. We'd like you to carry out a post-mortem, Professor, if you would?'

'He'd be delighted,' the Doctor said before Litefoot could reply. 'He'll be with you directly. He'll just get his coat and hat.'

'Just what I was about to say,' said Litefoot ruefully. As he shrugged himself into his heavy overcoat, he was struck by a thought. 'I say, shouldn't we rouse Miss Samantha?'

The Doctor glanced a little guiltily up the stairs, as if expecting to see his latest protégée standing at the top, scowling at him. 'Better let her sleep,' he said. 'No doubt she'll hate me for saying so, but there are some sights she needn't see, if it can be avoided.'

'Quite so,' said Litefoot approvingly. 'Well, Doctor, shall we go?'

The Doctor nodded vaguely and turned to Litefoot's housekeeper, who was hovering behind them, waiting to see them out. 'Mrs Hudson, will you explain to Sam that the professor and I had to leave on a matter of the utmost urgency, and that there was really no time to wake her? Tell her I'll be back as soon as I can.'

'Don't you worry, sir, I'll look after her,' Mrs Hudson promised.

The Doctor thanked her and hurried down the steps after the top-hatted professor, whose breath was vaporous in the crisp morning air.

'*Déjà vu*, eh, Professor?' the Doctor said, catching him up.

Litefoot raised his eyebrows. 'Whatever do you mean, Doctor?'

'The post-mortem. Didn't you meet the Doctor – the other Doctor – in similar circumstances?'

Litefoot chuckled. 'Yes, I believe I did.'

'Time has a marvellous way of revisiting itself, don't you find?'

Litefoot looked as though he didn't know quite what the Doctor was talking about, but was too polite to say so. 'I suppose so,' he said.

The two of them climbed into the waiting cab as the police constable who had summoned it paid the driver. The driver cracked his whip and the cab rattled away up the road.

It was not too long before the clean, tree-lined streets, long gravel drives, large gardens and elegant villas began to peter out, giving way to streets stinking of ordure and disease, crammed with narrow, scabrous buildings. Barefoot, hollow-eyed children congregated in doorways watched them pass;

adults, equally shabby, lowered their gaunt faces as though ashamed of their reduced circumstances.

'Poor wretches,' Litefoot said, lighting his pipe as much to combat the stink as anything. 'Almost every day I travel through districts such as this, and yet my despair at the poverty I continually witness around me never lessens.'

'One should never get used to the suffering of others, Professor,' the Doctor said quietly.

'Oh, quite agree. One does what one can, of course, but it never seems enough.'

The cab stopped outside a long, low building in a dingy street. A brass plaque beside the main door identified it as the Limehouse Mortuary and Coroner's Court. The two men alighted and, after Litefoot had tipped the bowler-hatted cab driver, entered the building.

The smell of disinfectant hit them immediately, though it seemed to conceal an altogether more unpleasant odour that may simply have been the pervasive stench of the surrounding streets. The interior of the place, consisting – the Doctor recalled – of one large room partitioned into smaller sections by the use of screens, was basic, clinical. Both walls and floor were tiled, the walls in gleaming white, the floor in a muddy brown. There was a minimum of furniture, and that which the place did contain was battered and roughly hewn. In the first 'room', little more than a reception area, a red-faced constable, whose moustache was trimmed a little closer than most of his colleagues', was sitting behind a desk on which a candle burned, writing laboriously in an enormous leather-bound ledger. As the Doctor and Litefoot entered, he jumped up, his chair juddering backwards over the tiles with a screech. The Doctor half expected him to salute, but he didn't.

'Good morning, Professor. Sir,' he said, nodding at the

Doctor. 'You're here for the post-mortem, I take it.'

'Good morning, Constable Butler. We are indeed,' Litefoot said, already stripping off his coat and hat.

'A mysterious one, this, sir,' Butler said. Looking pointedly at the Doctor, he added, 'I'm afraid it's not for the squeamish.'

The Doctor looked at the constable with a deadpan expression. For a moment Butler had the unsettling notion that the cool blue eyes of the young man, whom he had assumed to be one of the professor's students, were boring into his mind.

Then the Doctor blinked and said gently, 'There's no need to worry, Constable. Your wife will recover.'

Butler flinched, startled. A chill passed through him. 'I beg your pardon, sir?'

'She's been ill, hasn't she? You've been putting on a brave face for her sake, but you've been more worried than you'll dare admit to yourself.' He grinned suddenly and clapped the policeman on the shoulder. 'But cheer up, Constable. Any day now you'll see a marked improvement in her condition. By this time next week she'll be back to her old self. Now, how about leading us to the body?'

'Er... yes, sir. This way,' Butler said, bemused. His mind was brimming with questions, but something about the odd young gentleman's manner prevented him from asking them. Everything the fellow had said was true. His wife, Abigail, *had* been ill, and he had been more concerned than he had led anyone to believe. Although astounded, even a little frightened, by the young man's proclamation, Butler found that his overwhelming feeling was one of relief. For some reason, he felt greatly reassured by the man's words, felt as though he could believe them without question.

Dazedly he led the way behind the screens into the inner

'room'. This was the mortuary proper, harsh flares of light from the profusion of gas lamps and strategically placed candles bouncing off the tiled walls. Along one wall were a sink, a set of glass-fronted cabinets containing medical textbooks and large bottles of different-coloured chemicals, and a bench cluttered with a tangle of test tubes, vials and ampoules. A number of metal trays covered with white linen cloths on which a variety of surgical instruments had been carefully laid out awaited Litefoot on a small table. The mortuary slab itself was little more than a large wooden table in the middle of the room which was regularly scrubbed. A sheeted form, which appeared disconcertingly diminished, lay on the slab. A mop and bucket lolled against the wall in the corner, the mop-head stained an ominous pink.

Stripped down to his shirtsleeves, Litefoot donned an apron and a pair of protective oversleeves which stretched from his cuffs to his elbows. Watched by the Doctor, who stood silently at his shoulder, hands clasped behind his back, the professor reached out and peeled the sheet from the body as carefully as if he were unveiling an important archaeological find.

The body under the sheet had appeared diminished because a good half of it was missing. Its legs were gone, and its left arm. Indeed, most of the left side of its torso and what it had once contained was simply no longer there. It was as if the man were a fruit out of which an enormous bite had been taken, or a bag which had been punctured, freeing its slippery contents.

Because of the loss of blood, the flesh of what remained of the body was fishbelly-white. Furthermore, the face was bloated with water, squeezing the features into slits. All the same, the Doctor recognised the man immediately.

'Is this the chap you told me about, Doctor?' Litefoot asked.

'Yes,' the Doctor said quietly. He had told Litefoot a little more than he had told the police, had told him that after hearing the man scream the two of them had seen 'something big but indistinguishable' through the fog.

'An animal, do you mean?' Litefoot had asked, a little incredulously.

'Perhaps. I don't know,' the Doctor had lied, flashing a warning glance at Sam. 'It was too dark and murky to tell, and it had gone by the time we got there.'

Now Litefoot said, once again adopting that faintly incredulous tone, 'The fellow looks as though he's been devoured by an alligator!'

'Oh, something far bigger than that,' the Doctor replied almost airily. He gestured at the ragged stumps that were all that remained of the man's limbs. 'Look at the way the flesh and bone have been sheared through. The teeth of a creature able to do that would have to be… what? A foot long?'

'Good Lord,' Litefoot said faintly. 'What are you suggesting, Doctor?' Then his eyes widened. 'You're surely not intimating that that old rogue Magnus Greel is up to his tricks again? Perhaps this time he's using his devilry on alligators rather than rats.'

The Doctor shook his head, speaking almost soothingly. 'No, no, this is nothing to do with genetic disruption.' He lapsed into silence, staring thoughtfully at the body.

'Well, if you're certain…' Litefoot ventured.

'Nothing is certain, Professor.' Turning to Constable Butler, who had been standing with his back to the screens in a respectful silence, the Doctor asked, 'Do we know who this man is, Constable?'

'Yes, sir,' Butler said, producing and consulting a notebook. 'The deceased's name is Thomas Daniel Donahue, of no fixed abode. Until recently Mr Donahue had been residing at number forty-two Market Street, Whitechapel. Seems he fell on hard times after losing his job at Seers's bottle factory –'

The Doctor held up a hand, his blue eyes suddenly intense, staring straight ahead. 'The devil himself. Back there at the factory,' he murmured. 'Eyes glowing like lanterns.'

'Beg your pardon, Doctor?' asked Litefoot, perplexed.

'Something Mr Donahue said when we met. Where is this factory, Constable?'

The ear-splitting roar of machinery was a sound that filled the heads and lives of factory workers around the country. It was a sound they could never escape from, for even in their sleep the echoes went on and on, permeating their dreams. For many, the sound was almost a physical burden; it weighed them down, bowed their heads, slumped their shoulders. Many were pummelled into deafness by it, and a not inconsiderable number even driven insane. For the factory owners, the businessmen and the politicians, this, however, was the roar of progress. Their workers were the fuel for the great machine that powered the British Empire, and as such should surely be nothing but proud of the fact, proud to be part of the most powerful and prosperous nation in the world.

After alighting from his cab, having first absent-mindedly tried to pay the driver in a Delphonian coinage known as dur'alloi, the Doctor walked through the wide-open gates of Seers's Superior Bottles and across the cobbled, deserted courtyard. The factory, built of red brick now blackened by grime, consisted of several massive, dour buildings inset with rows of small windows. Two enormous chimneys belched black smoke into air already so polluted it had a dark, gritty taste. Even here, the Doctor could hear the churning bellow of the machines, and reflected that the cacophony was not that unlike the powerful but primitive engines of many spacecraft he had encountered.

He headed towards what appeared to be the main building, and entered via one of several doors. He found himself walking directly on to the shop floor, where the roar and the heat and the smell of hot metal swept over him in a wave. Though Seers's factory, compared with others, was as clean as it could be, and its workers well catered for, it still seemed like a living depiction of one kind of hell. The machines, dominating ninety per cent of the floor space, were a dark, oily mass of pistons, pulleys, levers and cogs. The workers, standing in their narrow aisles, tending the machines, were thin and shabbily dressed, their pale, blank faces shiny with sweat, their eyes wide and staring. As a slab of daylight accompanied the Doctor into the building, shining through his long, curly hair in a glowing corona, one woman nearby turned and glanced at him for a moment, then looked almost fearfully away.

The Doctor closed the door behind him and approached the woman. Though she did not acknowledge his presence directly, he saw her shoulders tense as he stepped up behind her.

'Excuse me,' he bellowed into her ear.

She flinched and half turned, her eyes flickers of fear, and he saw her mouth form the words, 'Yes, sir?'

'I'm sorry to trouble you. I wonder if you can help me. I'm inquiring about a man named Tom Donahue. I believe he worked here up until a few weeks ago. Did you know him, by any chance?'

The woman's eyes now seemed to be wanting to retreat like small, scared animals into the dark hollows of her eye sockets.

She shook her head slightly. 'No, sir.'

'Do you know of anyone who might have known him?'

'No, sir.'

'Then I won't trouble you any further. Many thanks for your help.'

The Doctor moved on, leaving the woman – who evidently was not used to being treated with such politeness and respect – gaping incredulously after him.

For the next few minutes the Doctor strolled along the aisles, questioning men and women at random. Nearly all reacted with the same fearful caution, and, though some were a little more forthcoming, he could find none who would admit to knowing Tom Donahue.

He had spoken to some two dozen people, and was currently questioning a youth of perhaps seventeen with a cluster of sores on his lips, whose gaze remained fixed on the pattern of the Doctor's waistcoat, when he became aware of someone standing at his shoulder. He turned and saw a squat, red-faced man whose sandy moustache and tousled hair were dark with grime. The man, who had evidently left his post, was glancing nervously around him, twirling a ragged cap in his stubby hands.

'Hello,' said the Doctor reassuringly. 'Can I help you?

'Understand you was asking about Tom Donahue, sir?' the man shouted, just loud enough to be heard above the roar of the machines.

'Indeed I was. Did you know him?'

The man nodded. 'Reckon I did, sir. It was him what got me this job here. But if you've come looking for him, sir, he ain't here. He had an accident a few weeks back, just before Christmas, and Mr Seers dismissed him on account of the fact that he was unable to work.'

'Ah,' said the Doctor. 'It was his hand he injured, wasn't it?'

'Yes, sir. Proper mess it was. I was one of the ones who took him to the hospital, sir. There was blood all over the place.'

The Doctor thought of the bloodless, mangled corpse back at the Limehouse mortuary. 'What kind of a fellow would you say Tom Donahue was, Mr…?'

'Whitney, sir. But I'm not sure as I get your drift.'

'Well, would you say, for instance, Mr Whitney, that Tom Donahue was given to flights of fancy? Would you say that he was… unstable in any way?'

Whitney pushed out his lips, causing his moustache to bristle. 'No, sir. Leastways, not that you'd notice.'

'So if Mr Donahue were to tell you that he'd seen the devil here at this factory in the dead of night, what would your reaction be?'

Whitney looked uncomfortable, and twirled his cap faster between his fingers. 'I'm sure I don't know, sir. I believe I might think he was pulling my leg.'

'You would have no reason to believe, then, that he might be telling you the truth?'

Now Whitney looked not only uncomfortable, but confused and troubled. 'I…' he mouthed, before shaking his head and glancing around once more.

The Doctor presumed that Whitney was keeping a watch-out for overseers. In this din he couldn't possibly be worried about eavesdroppers. Pressing home his advantage, the Doctor leaned forward as though to impart a confidence. 'What I mean to ask, Mr Whitney, is this: has anything – shall we say – unusual been happening here lately? Anything at all? I would urge you to think very, very hard. The smallest detail may be of vital importance.'

Whitney looked as though he was wishing he hadn't

become involved in this conversation, after all. 'Forgive my impudence, sir,' he said, 'but may I ask who you are to have the right to be asking such questions?'

'I'm the Doctor,' shouted the Doctor, as if this made everything perfectly clear. He crooked a finger, beckoning Whitney to incline his head even closer. When the man had done so, he shouted, 'I'm afraid I'm investigating Tom Donahue's death.'

Whitney jerked back as though he had been burnt, and the Doctor saw him mouth, 'Tom, dead?'

The Doctor nodded sadly. 'Murdered. His body was fished from the river this morning.'

'Oh Lord,' the Doctor lip-read Whitney saying 'Poor Tom. God rest his soul.'

'So if there's any way you can help me, Mr Whitney...' the Doctor coaxed.

Whitney looked agitated for a moment, and then seemed to come to a decision. 'You might do well, sir,' he confided, 'to talk to our employer, Mr Nathaniel Seers.'

'Really?' said the Doctor, adopting a wide-eyed, ingenuous expression. 'And why's that?'

Whitney had another quick look around. 'Mr Seers has been... vexed lately, sir.'

'Vexed? In what way?'

'He hasn't been himself, sir. I'd venture there's something troubling him. Troubling him bad.'

'Have you any idea what that might be?'

'No, sir. At least...'

'Go on,' the Doctor encouraged.

'Well, sir, it's a queer thing, but Mr Seers won't let none of us go down in the basement no more. He says the foundations is no longer safe. Now, I'm not saying that's a lie, sir, but it's just that he seems so… vigorous about it. It seems to have become something of a fixation with him.'

'You think there's something in the basement he doesn't want you to see?'

'I don't know about that, sir. All I know is it struck me as queer, the way he keeps on about it. You did say, sir, to let you know of anything out of the ordinary taking place, no matter how small.'

'Yes, I did,' said the Doctor thoughtfully. 'I wonder, Mr Whitney, could you – where are you going?'

Whitney did not answer. A moment before, his eyes had opened wide and he had begun to back away from the Doctor. Now he turned and fled, back to the machine he should have been attending.

The Doctor swivelled on his heels to see what had alarmed the man. On the far side of the factory a black iron stairway led up to a railed catwalk. On the catwalk, leaning over the railings like a huge black vulture, glaring down at him, was who the Doctor could only assume was Nathaniel Seers.

He was a tall, rather spindly man in his late forties, wearing a black suit and tie, and a white, wing-collared shirt. He seemed to be trying to compensate for the fact that he was going a little wispy on top by sporting heavy mutton-chop whiskers. At the moment his pale, rather delicate face was twisted with rage, his teeth clenched, his eyes stretched wide. A lesser man might have quailed at the burning intensity of those eyes, but the Doctor merely grinned, waved and bellowed, 'Hello there! Nathaniel Seers, I presume?'

He saw Seers's hands tighten on the railings, his knuckles turn white. Then Seers turned his gaze away from the Doctor for a moment, pinpointed someone on the factory floor away to the Doctor's left, and raised a hand to gesture angrily at the

Doctor. He looked to the Doctor's right and repeated the action. The Doctor now presumed that two factory overseers were heading towards him, intending to cut him off in a pincer movement. He sighed and began to stroll casually along the narrow aisles between the machines, heading for the iron staircase. Some of the workers ignored him studiedly, keeping their eyes downcast as he passed them by, while others gaped at him, as though unable to believe his gall.

'Hello there,' said the Doctor cheerfully when one of the overseers caught up with him. The man, wearing a frock coat, striped trousers, and a top hat, had a mean, predatory face. His teeth, most of which were brown and broken, looked too big for his mouth, and seemed to push his lips forward in a sneering pout.

'Who the devil are you?' the man barked, and grabbed hold of the Doctor's arm.

'I'm the Doctor. It's awfully nice to meet you, Mr…?'

'Doctor? We didn't call for no doctor. There's nobody ill here.'

'Just as well,' said the Doctor. 'I don't make house calls as a rule.'

The overseer thrust his face forward. 'You're no doctor. Where's your bag?'

The Doctor was saved from having to answer by the arrival of the other overseer. He was a porcine man with a sweaty bald head and ginger side whiskers that made his employer's look puny by comparison. He barrelled over and grabbed the Doctor's other arm, even though the Doctor was making no attempt to struggle from the first man's grip. His thick sausage fingers dug in, squeezing the flesh and grinding against the bone.

This was evidently intended to be painful, judging by the

nastily expectant look in the man's eyes and his clenched teeth. The Doctor, however, merely smiled beatifically and said, 'It's so frustrating when you put in so much effort for so little reward, don't you find?'

The porcine man snarled and shouted across to his companion, 'Who is he?'

'He says he's a doctor,' the first man replied.

'A doctor, does he? Then where's his bag?'

The Doctor raised his eyes heavenwards. 'Gentlemen, this is getting monotonous.'

The porcine man swung his face towards the Doctor. 'What's your business here?' he bellowed. 'What were you talking to the workers about?'

'Oh, this and that,' said the Doctor. 'Slugs and snails and puppy dogs' tails. String and sealing wax and other fancy stuff. Just passing the time of day really. I'm an inveterate gabbler, you see. Always have been and always will be.'

'Don't try my patience, sir,' said the man with the brown teeth.

'I wouldn't dream of it,' said the Doctor.

'I could break your arm, tear it from its socket,' the porcine man growled, twisting the Doctor's arm behind his back to demonstrate the efficacy of his threat.

'Look, do you think we could skip all the bluster and the chit-chat,' said the Doctor reasonably, 'and get on to the bit where you say, "You'll have Mr Seers to answer to"?'

The porcine man looked at the Doctor incredulously for a moment, and then said to his companion, 'What shall we do with him, Mr Beech?'

'Let's throw him in the Thames, Mr Stoker,' said Beech.

'It would seem the answer to my question is no, then,' said the Doctor. 'Ah well, it's been nice meeting you, gentlemen.' He suddenly seemed to twist and spin, and a moment later was striding away from the two overseers, who were no longer clutching his arms, nor even his coat, but each other's hands, like young lovers.

The two men gaped at each other, astonishment turning to embarrassment, and then to fury. They each tore their hands from the other's grip and blundered after the Doctor.

The Doctor, however, was too far ahead of them now. Without seeming to hurry unduly, he nevertheless moved swiftly along the aisles and between the machines, and reached the bottom of the metal stairway with the overseers still a good ten yards behind him. He glanced back, smiled, and then ascended the stairway so quickly and effortlessly he seemed almost to flow. The two overseers clattered up the steps behind him, the porcine man pouring with sweat and puffing out his rapidly reddening cheeks. However, if the object of their pursuit was to prevent the Doctor from reaching their employer, then it was doomed to failure. The Doctor was at the top of the steps long before they managed to catch up with him.

'Good morning, Mr Seers,' he said, his voice riding above the din of the machines. 'I've been looking forward to meeting you.'

'Have you indeed?' Seers said frostily. 'And who might you be, sir?'

'I'm known as the Doctor. I'm investigating the death of one of your former employees.'

'On whose authority, may I ask?'

'My own mostly,' said the Doctor, then added, 'I'm helping the police.'

Seers stared at the Doctor for a moment with cold, hard eyes. He seemed to be weighing up the situation in his mind.

At that moment the two overseers reached the top of the stairway and rushed forward, panting. Mr Beech reached out to grab the Doctor, but Seers, his eyes suddenly blazing, lunged forward and stayed the man with a hand on the shoulder.

'This man is from the police,' he said, his clipped, almost hissing voice audible even above the machines. 'Afford him some courtesy, if you will.'

Beech retreated, cowed. 'Sorry, Mr Seers, sir. He didn't tell us that.'

The Doctor shrugged and grinned. 'I like to keep people guessing.'

'Which of my former employees' deaths are you investigating, sir?' Seers asked when the two overseers had slunk resentfully away.

'You mean there are several?' said the Doctor.

'I mean, sir, that I have many former employees. I surely cannot be expected to continue to provide for them all?'

'Of course,' said the Doctor. 'How silly of me.' He rubbed his forehead with the fingers of his right hand and adopted a pained expression. 'Do you think we might talk somewhere a little quieter? This constant noise is giving me a headache.'

Seers hesitated.

'Your office, perhaps? I take it you *do* have an office?'

'Certainly. Follow me, please.'

Seers led the way along the catwalk and stopped at a wooden door inset with two frosted-glass panels. His name was painted on the door in elaborate gold script. He hesitated again, as though trying to remember something, then pushed the door open. The Doctor noted that Seers's gaze swept quickly around the room as the two of them entered, almost as if he was checking to make sure that everything was in place.

Seers waved the Doctor to a seat, and sat down himself,

behind a large, heavy desk. The office was panelled in dark wood. There were charts and maps on the walls, a glass-fronted cabinet full of books and ledgers, a hat-and-coat stand over which Seers's overcoat and top hat were draped, and various other freestanding cupboards and cabinets, on top of one of which was a large globe of the world, and on another a marble bust of Queen Victoria.

Gas lamps gave the room a cosy glow, but the Doctor noticed that the fireplace contained nothing but pale grey ashes.

'Brr,' he said, rubbing his arms. 'It's chilly in here. Don't you keep a fire burning?'

Seers glanced at the fireplace. 'I do not feel the cold,' he muttered.

'Most convenient,' said the Doctor. 'Must save you a fortune in fuel bills.'

Seers failed to respond to the Doctor's flippancy. In his clipped, cold voice he said, 'I trust you did not wish to waste both our times questioning me about my personal habits, sir?'

'No,' said the Doctor. 'Time is money, eh?' He jumped up from the chair he had barely settled into, crossed the room and began to spin the globe idly on its axis. He closed his eyes, stabbed a finger at the globe as it was spinning, then opened them. 'Paraguay,' he said. 'Do you know, I don't think I've ever been there. Must rectify that some time. Tell me, Mr Seers, what do you remember about Tom Donahue?'

The question had come unexpectedly, almost as a natural extension of the Doctor's ramblings. However, if he was hoping to catch Seers off guard he was to be disappointed.

The factory owner, his hands clasped on the desk in front of him, allowed himself a pause for thought, and then said evenly, 'I don't recall the name.'

The Doctor swung round. 'Oh, come now, Mr Seers, you must do. He was one of your employees.'

'I have many employees,' Seers repeated stubbornly. 'I cannot be expected to remember –'

'He cut his hand. Badly. A few weeks ago. Blood all over the place. You dismissed him. Rather mean of you, wasn't it?'

'If you are going to become abusive, sir, then I think I am entitled to ask you to leave.'

The Doctor crossed the room and sat down again. He leaned forward, gazing earnestly into Nathaniel Seers's grey, almost silvery, eyes.

In a gentle, coaxing voice, he said, 'Something's troubling you, isn't it, Nathaniel? Why don't you tell me what it is? I can help you.'

Seers stared back. The Doctor thought how incredibly still and composed he was for a human. Like a lizard on a leaf. When he spoke, the only part of him that moved was his mouth.

'You are not only abusive, sir, you are presumptuous,' he said quietly.

'Yes, I'm sorry about that,' said the Doctor with a disarming grin. 'Terrible habit of mine. I really must do something about it.' Then abruptly becoming serious once more, he said, 'Tom Donahue was seen running from here last night. He was terrified out of his wits. He claimed that he'd seen something awful at the factory, something that had caused him to flee. You wouldn't know anything about that, I suppose, Mr Seers?'

Seers gazed back at the Doctor, his features cast in stone. 'I would not, sir.'

'And then this morning his body was found in the Thames. He had been torn apart, almost completely devoured by some unknown creature. I don't suppose you would know what kind of creature would be capable of doing something like that to a man?'

'Of course not. I have no knowledge of such matters.'

'No, no, of course you don't,' said the Doctor as if he had been foolish. 'After all, why should you have?' He paused and then added, 'You don't seem very shocked by Tom Donahue's death, Mr Seers.'

'Why should I be? People die all the time. The fellow may have been in my employ, but as I have already told you, I did not know him personally.'

'But the manner of his death. Don't you feel compassion for the way he died? As a fellow human being?'

'Naturally,' said Seers with no feeling whatsoever.

'Naturally,' repeated the Doctor quietly. He stared hard at Seers's intertwined hands on the desk top. Throughout their exchange, not even one finger had given the minutest twitch.

'I wonder if I could have a look in your basement, Mr Seers?' the Doctor said with a winning smile.

This, at least, provoked a reaction, though not an extreme one. Seers's shoulders stiffened almost imperceptibly, his face adopting a wary expression.

His voice, however, was unchanged, each word like a chip of ice. 'May I ask why?'

'Of course you may,' said the Doctor. 'Basements are very interesting things. Architecturally, culturally, criminally…'

'Criminally?' repeated Seers.

'Oh yes. All sorts of dark secrets are kept hidden away in basements. Secrets you wouldn't believe… or perhaps you would.'

'What are you implying, sir?'

'Only that you seem like an open-minded kind of chap. Now, about this basement of yours…'

'I'm afraid that it is out of the question. The foundations are unsafe,' said Seers quickly.

'Oh, well, that's a pity. I'll just get my men to pop over instead then, shall I? Give the place a thorough going-over? Would this afternoon be convenient for you, Mr Seers?'

'Are you possessed of cloth ears, sir? As I informed you mere seconds ago, the foundations of the place are unsafe.'

'Yes, but my men are experts, Mr Seers. Used to working in dangerous environments. They won't put themselves at risk, I assure you. And if there's anything to be found down there, they'll find it.'

Seers hesitated, trying to hide his obvious annoyance. Finally he said, 'I am an extremely busy man, Doctor. Perhaps it might be more prudent, after all, if you were to investigate the basement now – accompanied by myself, of course.'

'Of course,' said the Doctor graciously, and jumped up from his chair once again. 'Shall we go?'

Seers led the way out of his office, back out on to the catwalk, and down the metal stairway to the factory floor. His employees seemed to be engrossed in their tasks as he passed by, but the Doctor could tell by the way they stood that not only were they aware of their employer's presence, they were also afraid of him.

The two men crossed the floor to the far side of the factory and came to a halt before a door that was barred and padlocked. Seers produced a heavy ring of keys on a chain that was attached to his waist. The keys clinked and jangled as he selected the right one and inserted it into the padlock. The padlock sprang open with a twist of the key. Seers removed both padlock and bar and pushed the door open.

Beyond the door the Doctor saw stone steps descending into blackness. On the topmost step were several candles in simple brass holders and a box of matches. Seers squatted down on to his haunches, lit two of the candles, and thrust one roughly at the Doctor.

'Thank you,' said the Doctor, sounding as delighted as if Seers had given him a rare and precious gift.

The two men started down, holding their candles out in front of them at head height. The steps were a little slippery, the walls rough and cold to the touch. A gentle but chill breeze wafted up and over them from the depths below. From deeper still, beneath the building it seemed, the Doctor could hear the muffled gushing of water. As the two men descended, the yellow candlelight caused their gigantic shadows on the wall beside them to twitch and shudder, as if trying to tear themselves from the bodies that had cast them.

At last they reached the bottom of the steps and found themselves in a huge dank room with walls that glistened with moisture. The room was empty save for a few old barrels, some lengths of rotting timber, and several items of rusting machinery.

On the far side of the room, close to a large grating which, from its smell, presumably led down to the sewers, was an arch inset into a supporting stone wall, revealing only blackness beyond.

'What's through there?' asked the Doctor, the echo of his voice almost immediately dampened by the heavy atmosphere.

'Why don't you look for yourself, Doctor?' Seers's eyes glittered orange in the candle light.

The Doctor approached the arch, holding his candle out before him as he stepped through. Hallowe'en light bloomed in the darkness, slithering up the walls and across the ceiling and floor.

There was nothing to see. This room was smaller than its counterpart, little more than an alcove, in fact. Water dripped from the ceiling and trickled down the walls. There was another cluster of barrels in the corner, their wood dark green, spongy with rot.

The Doctor pursed his lips thoughtfully, then went back into the main room where Seers was waiting for him. The flickering light from his candle transformed his face into that of a bloodless ghoul.

'Are you satisfied, sir?' Seers asked, clearly intimating that he had far better things to do.

'Rarely,' murmured the Doctor, and looked around again. There was something very wrong here. Perhaps not here specifically, but in the factory.

He sighed and said, 'Your basement seems to be devoid of secrets, Mr Seers. Obvious ones, at least.'

'Covert ones also, I hope you'll agree. Now, if you'll excuse me, I have a great many business concerns to attend to.' Seers gestured towards the steps.

'Of course,' the Doctor conceded, and began to move across the room. Suddenly he stopped and stamped his foot down hard on the floor.

'Whatever are you doing, sir?' Seers asked impatiently.

'Testing your foundations,' said the Doctor, and smiled. 'You know, Mr Seers, they seem perfectly sound to me.'

After the Doctor had gone, Seers returned to his office and closed the door behind him. He crossed the room and sat down in the chair behind his desk, his hands clasped in front of him, his face thoughtful. After a moment he produced the set of keys he had used to open the door to the basement and selected a different one, a smaller one. This he used to unlock the bottom right-hand drawer of his desk. He pulled the drawer open and moved aside a sheaf of notes.

Beneath the notes was a creature not unlike a small jellyfish. A delicate pink-grey in colour, its body resembled a translucent lens. Feathery frond-like tentacles fanned out from the body, quivering and twitching like nerve ends in receipt of constant stimuli. Seers reached into the drawer and picked the creature up. It sat in the palm of his hand, a soft, gel-like blob.

Tentatively at first, it curled its tentacles around Seers' hand and wrist, tightening them until it resembled a strange inverted watch. Seers extended the forefinger of his free hand and caressed the creature gently. The creature responded, first flushing a brighter pink, then extending a fringe of bristly appendages, like the antennae of a snail. Seers ran his finger gently over the appendages in an almost ritualistic pattern. The lens became a metallic silvery colour, and then, astonishingly, the creature emitted a crackle like radio static.

Suddenly, from the midst of the static, came a sibilant voice, a voice that seemed almost to generate a hissing echo of itself.

'Yesss, Commander?'

Seers raised the creature to his lips and spoke into it, as if it was not a living thing at all, but merely an artefact, a form of communicator.

'The Doctor is suspicious, and unusually intelligent. I want him followed. I want his movements monitored.'

'Yesss, Commander,' the voice said again, its warbling sibilance filling the room.

'But do not use Beech or Stoker. The Doctor knows them. Use… use Hetherington,' Seers ordered.

'I shall prepare him now, Commander,' the voice concurred.

'Good,' said Seers. 'Keep me informed.' He touched the silver lens and the creature shuddered, loosening its tentacles from around his wrist. The metallic sheen faded from its body and it became translucent once more.

CHAPTER 3
LAIR

Finally managing to shake off the attentions of the revolting Mr Stoker, Emmeline ascended the metal stairway to her father's office. She had always found Stoker a somewhat unwholesome man (the way he looked at her with his hungry eyes discomforted her greatly), but it was only recently that he had become arrogant and forceful. Today he had all but blocked her path, claiming that her father was too busy to receive her. It was not until Emmeline had reminded him, in no uncertain terms, who she was that he had stepped aside and allowed her to pass.

Now she marched up to her father's office and rapped on the door. Though the grinding roar of the machines was loud even up here, she heard what sounded like a drawer slamming inside the room, and then a voice that barely sounded like her father's barked, 'Who is it?'

Emmeline put her face up close to the wood. 'It's me, Father. Emmeline. May I come in?'

'Just a moment,' came the brusque reply.

Emmeline waited for considerably longer than a moment, and was about to knock again when the door opened. Her father stood there, or at least a cold, imperious version of him did. Emmeline could not believe how much he had changed in so short a time. Where had his warmth and affection gone, his smile, which had never been far from his face and which he had used to offer her whenever she came into his sight?

'Emmeline,' he said, speaking her name – the name he and Mama had chosen for her – in a voice that sounded almost contemptuous. 'What do you want?'

'I wish to speak with you, Father,' she said firmly.

However, just as Mr Stoker had planted himself in her path on the factory floor not ten minutes before, so her father did now, stepping forward and spreading himself to fill the doorway to his office.

'I'm very busy,' he said.

'Too busy to spare a few moments of time for your own daughter? I have given up my morning to come to see you, Father.'

'I didn't ask you to come,' he said.

'Nevertheless I am here, and I do not intend to leave until you have heard what I have to say.'

Her father's eyes were suddenly ablaze with such anger that it took all of Emmeline's resolve not to quail beneath it. 'Impudent female,' he snarled. 'You will return home this instant!'

'No, Father, I will not!' she responded, trying to force as much defiance as she could into her voice.

He took a quick step towards her, half raising his hand.

Still forcing herself to stand her ground, Emmeline said, 'Are you going to strike me, Father? Has it come to that?'

Though her words stayed him, his face – with its burning eyes and clenched teeth – contained such hatred that Emmeline felt no sense of relief or gratitude, but merely loss, despair. Slowly he lowered his hand and half turned away from her. 'Say what you have to, but be quick about it,' he snapped over his shoulder.

With a heavy heart she followed him into his office, closing the door behind her, cutting off the clamour from the factory. She watched him as he stumped to his desk and sat down behind it, and tried to compose herself. She did not wish to argue with him; that would achieve nothing. Her own anger, quick to surface though it sometimes was, would only provide further fuel for his.

She walked as calmly as she could to the chair facing him and sat down.

'Well?' he barked immediately, and she realised that this was going to be even more difficult than she had envisaged.

She sighed and said, 'Please don't be angry, Father. I have come here in the hope that we can help each other.'

'I don't need your help,' he said.

'I think that you do. I know that something is troubling you greatly, something that you are keeping from Mama and me. Perhaps you feel that you are protecting us by keeping it to yourself, but you are not protecting us, Father. On the contrary, your recent behaviour is causing us great pain and distress. Mama, in particular, is at her wits' end. This morning, not for the first time, I discovered her weeping, unable to comprehend why you have abandoned your household duties of late.'

In the cab on the way to the factory, Emmeline had played this scene over and over in her mind, had imagined her father softening at her words, an expression almost of enlightenment overcoming his face. 'My dear, I never realised...' he would say, reaching out to take her hands. He would apologise for his behaviour, open his heart to her, perhaps even travel home with her to see Mama...

However, as she stumbled to the end of a speech that now seemed ill-prepared, Emmeline realised that this was not going to be the case. Her father simply sat there, as haughty and unmoved as before, his face like granite.

At last he said, 'Have you finished?'

Unable to think of any other response, she nodded dumbly.

'Then I believe you can go,' he said, half rising from his seat. As an afterthought, he added, 'Give your mother my regards.'

Emmeline simply sat there, momentarily dumbstruck. Finally she spluttered, 'Is that all you have to say, Father?'

He looked at her completely without expression. 'I have already said and heard more than I would wish to,' he replied evenly.

'But do you not *care* about Mama?' she exclaimed, unable to prevent her voice from rising. 'Have you no explanation for your actions?'

'There is nothing I wish to discuss,' he said acidly.

'But there is much *I* wish to discuss,' Emmeline retorted.

Her father had rounded the desk now and was standing above her, so that she had to tilt her head up to look at him. She was all at once aware of his tightly clenched fists, the way he held himself, rigid and straight-backed, giving the impression that the real force of his anger was still coiled inside him like a spring.

For the first time, Emmeline suddenly realised that she was actually *afraid* of her father, afraid of what he might do. However ludicrous she tried to convince herself that this notion was, the fear would not go away.

In his cold, clipped voice, he said, 'I have no time for this nonsense. Good day, Emmeline.'

He strode away from her then, towards the door, evidently intending to open it for her, not as a gesture of courtesy, but of dismissal.

A thought fluttered across her mind: he doesn't even move like Father! He moved with a fluid, effortless grace, but with something quick and darting about it. Like a lizard, but like a predator too. Silent.

She tried to use her fear, to turn it into anger, but her blurting voice came out somewhere in between. 'It is not nonsense!'

He turned to her. Did his eyes flash with a momentary orange light? Before the thought had even fully formed, she had dismissed it.

'Please leave now,' he said.

'Father, what has happened to you?' she pleaded desperately.

'Nothing has happened to me. I am perfectly fine. Everything is fine.'

'Then why don't you come home? Come back with me now and speak to Mama, comfort her.'

For a moment it seemed as though he was not even going to grace her with a reply, and then he said, 'Your mama is unstable and over-emotional. I suggest that what she needs is a physician.'

'There is nothing wrong with her!' Emmeline cried. 'You are the one with the affliction, Father! You are the one who should see a physician!'

'Leave now!' he snarled again, and yanked the door open so violently that she was afraid he might tear it off its hinges.

She stood up, her legs shaky, smoothing down her long skirt with trembling hands. She was angry and upset, but trying not to show it. 'I will go, Father,' she said, 'but I will not allow this situation to prevail for many more days. In spite of what you say, I know you are deeply troubled, and however you have behaved these past weeks, Mama and I still love you dearly.' She crossed to him and leaned forward to kiss his cheek. He, in turn, leaned back, preventing her from doing so, a look of distaste on his face.

Hurt and confused, Emmeline left the office, the door of which was immediately slammed behind her. She hurried along the catwalk and down the metal stairway, fighting to hold back tears. Keeping her head bowed so that the brim of the hat she wore, with its blue ribbon and jauntily angled feather, covered her face, she hurried towards the nearest door. She half expected Stoker to appear in front of her, blocking her way once again. Well, woe betide him if he did. Despite her distress, he would soon feel the sharp edge of her tongue.

The overseer, however, was nowhere to be seen, and a moment later Emmeline was stepping out of the hot factory into the cool air. She paused a moment to compose herself.

Though the air was by no means fresh, she took great gulps of it. Her head was spinning. She felt ashamed and angered by her failure. Whatever would she tell Mama? More importantly, what more could she do to recapture the affections of her father? She wished she knew what it was that ailed him so. If she could find that out, then perhaps she would be able to help him. But how could she find out?

She began to stroll across the cobbled yard towards the gates, her mind a turmoil of thoughts and emotions. She was so deep in reverie that when a voice called out, 'Excuse me? Miss Seers!' she jumped, startled.

She turned, half expecting to see sweating, red-faced Stoker clumping across the yard, but in fact the man hurrying towards her was a complete stranger. Where he had appeared from she couldn't begin to guess. Surely he had not been concealing himself, waiting for her to emerge?

The man was young, with startlingly long hair, albeit well dressed. He had a quirky mouth that seemed used to smiling, and frank, clear eyes of the most incredible blue. In spite of her reservations, Emmeline found herself instinctively warming to the man; even in this first instant of their meeting she sensed a calm, knowing manner about him.

He halted a few feet away from her. 'You are Nathaniel Seers's daughter, I take it?' he asked gently.

'I am, sir,' said Emmeline.

'I thought so. I saw you arrive.'

'Indeed?' said Emmeline. 'And who, may I ask, are you?'

The man smiled at her. 'I'm usually referred to as the Doctor.'

'The Doctor?' said Emmeline, bemused. 'I see. And what, *Doctor*, do you want with me?'

'To talk,' the Doctor said. 'I have a cab waiting outside the gates. I'd be honoured if you would share it with me.'

Emmeline bridled a little. 'I am not usually in the habit of sharing cabs with strangers, sir.'

'Of course you aren't,' said the Doctor soothingly. 'Very wise. It's just that... I wanted to talk to you about your father.'

'My father?'

'Yes. I'm a friend and associate of his, you see. And just lately, well... he's changed. He's not the man he was at all. And I for one am gravely worried about him.'

Hetherington watched as the Doctor and Emmeline turned and walked across the yard towards the gates, deep in conversation. He had been trailing the Doctor for a little while now, had watched the man poking around the factory and the outbuildings, rattling locked doors, peering through windows. He had not been unduly worried by the Doctor's inquisitiveness; he knew that the man would find nothing untoward. As the Doctor and Emmeline strolled out of the gates, Hetherington rose up from behind his hiding place – a water barrel beside one of the factory's outbuildings – and hurried towards the stable block.

He procured one of the horses and carts belonging to the factory and set off in pursuit of the Doctor and Emmeline, the cart rattling and jouncing over the cobbles. He realised how conspicuous he would be until they reached the more busy thoroughfares, but he was banking on the fact that the Doctor and Emmeline would be inside the carriage that she had waiting for her outside the gates, and so would neither see nor hear him, and that the cab driver would simply assume he was making a delivery. As the horse trotted out of the gates, Hetherington, a weaselly man wearing a heavy topcoat and a bowler hat, turned his head to look both ways, and saw the hansom cab fifty yards away to his left. With a flick of the reins he urged his horse onward, and had soon made up the distance between the two vehicles.

He tugged on the reins and his horse slowed a little. He was ten yards behind the cab now, keeping pace with it. Glancing around to ensure there were no onlookers, Hetherington slipped his hand into his coat pocket and withdrew a strange insect that was about the size of a tarantula, and, indeed, looked like a cross between a large spider and a jellyfish. It had a shimmering, gelatinous body and bony, jointed legs. It was shrimp-coloured, apart from the clusters of black, bead-like eyes on what passed for its head. As Hetherington held it delicately by its body, the creature moved its legs slowly up and down, trying to gain purchase on something. Hetherington glanced around again, and then, with a sudden flick of his wrist, tossed the creature through the air, towards the Doctor's cab.

It struck the back of the cab, but, rather than bounce off, attached itself instantly, its bony legs somehow clamping themselves to the smooth, painted wood. It quivered for a moment, and then scuttled like the large pink spider it resembled around to the carriage window and slipped inside.

Hetherington nodded in satisfaction and produced yet another of the creatures from his pocket. He flipped it upside down, and ignoring its wildly perambulating legs, dug his fingers into its jelly-like flesh and peeled back part of its stomach. Beneath the outer layer of flesh was a smooth lens, not unlike that possessed by the creature that Seers had taken from his desk drawer, inset with pulsing black blood vessels. On the lens was a fuzzy image of the Doctor and Emmeline inside the cab. The creature, its legs moving feebly now, resonated with the Doctor's and Emmeline's voices, which, though tinny, were audible enough. Above the rattling of the two carts, Hetherington heard the Doctor say, 'I'm not sure yet…'

'…but I intend to find out.'

Emmeline looked at the Doctor, doubt and hope mingling on her face. 'How?' she asked.

The Doctor glanced out of the cab window. 'I have my methods,' he murmured.

Emmeline regarded this mysterious, clean-shaven, long-haired man, and wondered, not for the first time, why she had poured her heart out to him, why she was now bestowing him with such faith and trust. Despite her youth and inexperience, she was neither naïve nor foolish. Was it simply desperation, then, a need to share her problems, her fears?

He was certainly a good listener. It had not taken her long to recount the sorry tale of her father's recent transformation from loving husband and father to cold-hearted stranger. After she had finished, the Doctor had asked her a number of succinct and pertinent questions, which she had done her utmost to answer, and had then lapsed into contemplation.

The silence had stretched between them for several seconds, before Emmeline had asked, with an uncharacteristic tentativeness, 'Doctor… what do you think is troubling my father?'

The Doctor had looked at her, his face serious, thoughtful. 'I'm not sure yet,' he had said, 'but I intend to find out.'

Now, having asked him how, only to receive an equally vague reply, Emmeline was beginning to become impatient.

'May I ask, sir, what your exact connection with my father is?'

'I've told you, I'm a friend and business associate.'

'And what, pray, is the manner of your business?'

'Distribution,' said the Doctor. 'Distribution and export.' Then, abruptly, he shook his head. 'No, I'm lying. I don't know your father at all. I only met him for the first time today. I can see you becoming alarmed, Miss Seers, but don't be. I'm telling you the truth because I want you to trust me. Believe me, my sole aim is to help you and your father. I think there is something very wrong at your father's factory, very wrong indeed. I think your father is acting as he is because he is under some form of… influence.'

The Doctor looked earnestly into her eyes. Emmeline, who was still struggling to take all of this in, said weakly, 'Influence?'

'Your father is being controlled, Miss Seers. By whom, I don't know. Yet.'

'But… but why? For what purpose?'

'I don't know that either. It will be something nefarious, though. You can count on that.'

Emmeline looked shocked. She didn't know what to say.

In a gentle yet compelling voice the Doctor said, 'This is a dangerous situation, Miss Seers. One man – a former employee of your father's – has died already, in mysterious and rather grisly circumstances. I don't want to alarm you any more than I have to, but it is imperative that you stay away from the factory until further notice. And on no account must you confront your father. Do you understand?'

'But…' Emmeline said before her voice petered out. She licked her paper-dry lips and cleared her throat, and forced herself to say, 'But my father would never harm me.'

'Your father is not himself.' The astonishing blue of the Doctor's eyes seemed to flood her mind, to make his words boom with incredible import and authority. 'He is not responsible for his actions. Please promise me that you'll stay away from him.'

Emmeline found herself nodding slowly, dazedly. 'I promise.'

'Good,' said the Doctor, settling back into his seat. 'And I promise you, Miss Seers, that I'll do my utmost to get to the bottom of this mystery, and restore your father to you.'

The carriage rattled on its way, through the poorer parts of London. The streets were busier now, full of people and traffic.

Presently the Doctor said, 'This is where I get off. But before I do, allow me to give you this.' He held up his hand, and as if by magic a small white business card appeared in it, which he handed to Emmeline.

She read the name and address on the card, which meant nothing to her. 'What is it?' she asked.

'It's the address of where I'm staying,' replied the Doctor. 'If you need me, any time of the day or night, don't hesitate to call.'

Then he smiled at her, and despite everything that she had seen and heard this morning, Emmeline could not help but smile back.

Later, in his office, Seers listened grimly to Hetherington's report of the exchange between the Doctor and Emmeline, the weasely man's voice issuing from the jellyfish-like communications device that Seers held in his hand.

When Hetherington had done, Seers said, 'This Doctor is even more intelligent and resourceful than I thought. He cannot be allowed to interfere with our plans.'

'Shall I terminate him, Commander?' Hetherington asked eagerly.

Seers turned the matter over in his mind. Finally he said, 'No. I will deal with the Doctor myself. I will deal with the Doctor *and* the girl.'

'Careful,' hissed Jack Howe as Albert's spade slid through the last thin layer of dirt and clunked against the coffin lid. 'We don't want to bring the peelers down on us.'

Albert Rudge cringed, his eyes like saucers above the manure-smeared rag he wore over his thin, lugubrious face.

'Sorry, Jack,' he said in a hushed voice. 'I never realised I was so close to the wood. I thought we had a ways to go yet.'

'You wants to keep your mind on the job and not on the money,' Howe said. 'I don't want to get my neck stretched just because you wasn't paying attention.'

'Sorry, Jack,' Rudge repeated. 'It won't happen again.'

'It had better not,' Howe warned, 'or there'll be a fresh body in that box to replace the one we're taking with us.'

Rudge quailed, and bent to his task with renewed concentration, taking extra care not to make a sound as he scraped the last of the dirt from the roughly hewn coffin. Despite the claims of his companion, it hadn't been the money he had been thinking of. Of course, he couldn't claim that the money was anything other than a godsend, but that still didn't prevent him hating every minute of what he and Jack had to do to earn it. It wasn't the cadavers that bothered him particularly – he had seen so much death in his forty-one miserable years that it had long ago become a familiar if unwelcome acquaintance. No, it was the fear of getting caught, of having a noose placed over his head, of dropping through a hole in the floor and his neck breaking like a stick. Would he hear the crack of his own bones? he wondered. Would he die at once or hang there in the darkness for a while, twitching in agony? He knew that Jack thought himself invincible, knew too that greed was making his companion fearless, but Albert had fear enough for both of them; that, and a clear enough mind to realise that if they continued to do what they were doing night after night after night, then sooner or later their luck was going to run out, and when that happened no amount of money in the world was going to save them.

Each morning, waking up in the hovel that he called a home, Albert decided that this would be the day he would tell Jack that he no longer wanted to be part of the grisly task that his colleague had bullied and cajoled him in to, that he no longer wanted to spend his evenings touring the cemeteries of East London, that he no longer wanted to be privy to the nightly assignations with their mysterious employer. And each day

Albert's resolve would be fierce right up until the time he actually saw Jack, and then it would melt away, like ice in a sudden thaw, and he would think: I'll tell him tomorrow. I'll tell him tomorrow, for sure.

The thing was, Jack was not a man to trifle with. Aside from being physically big, he was unpredictable and possessed of a vicious temper. Albert had seen him break men's heads without a qualm, even when sober; had seen him hold a man down by his throat and grind jagged glass into his eyes, blinding him permanently. He had even once seen him bludgeon to death a young child who had been too persistent in begging for a morsel of bread. Violence for Jack Howe was not, therefore, a rare occurrence, but something he meted out every day, to friends and enemies alike. Thus far, Albert, who was careful not to bait Jack, had received no more than a few hefty cuffs, an occasional black eye or burst lip. If he should reveal his intention to abandon Jack to his grave-robbing, however...

He shuddered, hardly daring to ponder on what the consequences might be.

So here he was, caught between the devil and the deep blue sea. It was after midnight. The moon was wrapped in cloud, making it dark as Newgate's knocker. He was standing chin-deep with Jack in yet another cold grave, his back and arms aching with fatigue. His head was swimming with the stink of manure, which, though disgusting, was at least preferable to the stink of the dead. All he could see around him were tombstones and crooked, leafless trees swathed in fog. Sometimes, in his more fanciful moments, he imagined that the trees were the twisted, angry souls of those whose graves he and Jack had defiled. This, however, was not what caused his heart to beat far too rapidly inside his chest. No, that was due to his constant expectation that any moment he would see the yellow lights of lanterns bobbing towards them through the fog, coming from every direction, closing in on all sides…

'I wonder who he really is,' Jack murmured, breaking into his thoughts.

'Eh?' Albert said, momentarily confused. 'Who?'

Jack gave him a withering look. 'Our employer. Our benefactor. And not only does the question of his identity vex me, but so too do his reasons for acquiring all these cadavers. What does he want with them, I wonder? Is he a sawbones, do you suppose?'

Albert did not like the faraway expression that had suddenly appeared on Jack's face. Such an expression, Albert knew, did not bode well for his future peace of mind. Despite his social standing (which in the great scheme of things was sorely negligible), his frequent drunkenness and his propensity for casual violence, Jack Howe was not a stupid man. He knew his numbers, he could speak in the plummy tones of a gentleman when it suited him, and he even read a little.

Furthermore, his mind was forever lively with schemes and ideas for improving his lot in life. Even when he was on to a good thing, he was always striving for that little bit more.

Albert sensed such a scheme brewing now, and he strove to quash it quickly.

'I don't know, and I care even less,' he said. 'We are well-paid, Jack, and that's all that should concern us. It strikes me that questioning our employer's motives may prove an unhealthy occupation.'

'Albert, you have all the ambition of… of this worm,' Jack said, reaching down and nipping a fat, pink, wriggling earthworm between the stubby thumb and forefinger of his right hand. He tossed the worm at Albert, who flinched as it struck his cheek – a brief, cold, slithering kiss from the grave.

'At least my caution keeps me alive,' Albert muttered.

'Life? You call this miserable existence of yours a life? You live in filth, you sleep in filth, you eat filth, you drink filth –'

'And what of you?' Albert retorted, momentarily roused. 'You dine on quail and caviar, I suppose, and lay your head on feather pillows?'

Jack grinned savagely, showing his brown and broken teeth. 'At least I dream of it,' he said, and his voice dropped to a murmur. 'One day I shall be celebrated in Threadneedle Street. A plaque will be erected in my name…'

More likely a tombstone in this sorry excuse for a graveyard, or one very like it, Albert thought, but this time wisely kept his opinions to himself.

Jack's glazed eyes became shrewd again. 'Have you no interest at all in the identity of our employer?'

'None,' replied Albert. 'He could be Old Nick himself for all I…' His voice tailed off as he thought of their employer's cold grey eyes and watchful manner. He shivered.

'He's a wealthy man, there's no mistaking that,' Jack mused. 'You only have to set eyes on him to know it.'

'What of it?' Albert said uneasily.

'Is your mind completely addled? Think on it, Albert. A gentleman – of some standing and refinement, I'll be bound – keeping his identity a secret, procuring corpses for what must surely be questionable purposes. There's money to be made here. If our elusive employer's dealings should ever become public knowledge…'

'You're not talking about blackmail?' said Albert, horrified.

Jack looked indignant. 'Blackmail? Certainly not. Blackmail is a dirty word. It pains me, Albert, that you, of all people, could ever think me capable of even contemplating such a foul deed. No, no, I was thinking more in terms of a… business arrangement. Between gentlemen, as it were.'

Albert looked around. The fog was growing thicker, the night colder. Those bobbing lights he so feared would be more difficult to spot in a fog like this. The lantern-bearers would be almost upon them before they even had chance to throw down their shovels.

'Let's open this box and be away from here, Jack,' he said. 'We've spent far too much time here already.'

Jack grinned. 'Afraid of the wraiths and the hobgoblins, are you?'

'No, just the rope,' Albert said.

Jack chuckled, and the two men dropped into the narrow trench they had dug by the side of the coffin and set about opening the box. It did not take long: the wooden lid was already so soft with rot that they found they could tear it off in chunks with their bare hands.

Inside the coffin was the corpse of a woman wrapped in a winding sheet. Her skin, which was the texture of old fruit about to dissolve to mush, had turned a ghastly blue-black. Her jaw yawned open, her withered eyes had sunk deep into their sockets, and there were beetles and grubs in her hair.

'Not as fresh as most,' Jack said with a sigh. 'Still, it'll have to do. We'll put it at the bottom of the pile, and maybe he won't notice.'

The two men manhandled the corpse out of the grave and dumped it unceremoniously on the damp grass. Insects, their feasting interrupted, scuttled hither and thither. As they began to refill the grave, Jack said, 'I propose we follow him tomorrow evening after he's taken his leave of us and see where he goes.'

Albert groaned inwardly, but was quick to spot a potential flaw in Jack's plan. 'We'd never keep up with that cart of his.'

Jack heaved dirt effortlessly into the grave. He was not even short of breath, unlike Albert, who was wheezing like a grampus.

'Don't concern yourself with that. I'll provide the transport.'

'You?' Albert said, surprised. 'And what transport do you have all of a sudden?'

'I'll borrow Ned Cockles's old nag. It might look clapped out, but it's a sturdy enough beast.'

Albert's heart was sinking slowly into his boots. 'I still think it best to leave well alone, Jack.'

Jack looked up at Albert and winked. By contrast to his colleague, he was in an uncommonly good mood. 'You just leave the thinking to me, Albert,' he said, 'and I'll make both of us rich.'

Albert, however, could not find it inside himself to look even remotely convinced.

'This is madness,' said Litefoot. 'Utter madness!'

'Yeah,' said Sam with a grin. 'Fun, isn't it?'

It was one o'clock in the morning. She had just about forgiven the Doctor now for leaving her behind some sixteen hours earlier while he went off gallivanting with the professor, though she wasn't about to let *him* know that. To his credit, the Doctor had been profusely apologetic, had told her that his intention had been to attend the post-mortem with Litefoot and then to pop back for her, but that events had 'sort of spiralled'.

'They always do,' Sam had snapped. 'You should have known that they would.'

The Doctor had sighed, giving her what she sometimes thought of as his regretful, puppy-dog look. 'I'm truly sorry, Sam,' he said again, 'but there really was no time to wake you. Our presence was required urgently.'

'Two minutes,' said Sam. 'That's all it would have taken me. I'm an up-and-at-'em girl. You should know that by now, Doctor. I'm not one of your fluffy-bunny, screaming types.'

'I know, I know,' the Doctor had said, holding up his hands. 'I suppose I thought…'

'Thought what?'

'Well, this was no picnic. It wasn't fun or exciting or dangerous. It was a post-mortem, Sam. A post-mortem on a half-eaten corpse which had been in the water for several hours. There are some things that you don't... well, anyway...'

Sam had felt anger rising in her, tightening across her shoulders, cramming the back of her throat. In a strained voice she had said, 'I don't want you protecting me, Doctor. And I certainly don't want you deciding what I can and can't see or do. I can make my own choices, you know. I thought you respected that, I thought you respected *me*. I have enough sexist crap without –'

'This has nothing to do with your gender,' interjected the Doctor, quietly but firmly.

'Sure,' Sam said.

'It hasn't, Sam. It's just... well, you're seventeen –'

'Ageist as well as sexist now –'

'Listen to me.'

There was not exactly anger in his voice, but his tone nevertheless had the same effect as his banging the flat of his hand down hard on an unyielding surface. Sam clammed up and looked at him.

Quietly he said, 'Sam, you're young. That is a fact. And however tough you may think you are, however much you may think you can take, you are not a superwoman: you are a thinking, feeling, caring human being, and therefore not immune to the psychological effects of extreme trauma. This isn't a failing, Sam. I've seen hardened, combat-trained soldiers weeping, catatonic, driven half mad by the nightmares of what they've seen and experienced on the field of battle. You wouldn't be a properly functioning human being if you didn't have such emotions.'

'Yeah, I know all that, Doctor, but I also know better than you what my limitations are. I mean… I've seen bad stuff. I've been bitten by vampires. I've even *killed* a vampire. I've seen people die.'

'I know that,' the Doctor said quietly, 'but that's because you happened to be there. It was unavoidable. Travelling with me is not some kind of endurance test, Sam. You don't get points for the number of atrocities you can witness before teatime.'

'I know that. Don't insult me, Doctor.'

'I'm not insulting you. I'm just trying to make you understand.'

'I do understand. Besides, that isn't the issue. I'm not saying I really, really wanted to be at the post-mortem. I'm just saying that in the future I want to be given the choice, that's all.'

He had agreed, wearily, that from that moment on he would not wilfully exclude her from anything. Then he had told her about his day, relating his conversations with Nathaniel Seers and his daughter, Emmeline, with a thoroughness that Sam couldn't help but find impressive. Later, over supper, he had announced his intention to return to the factory in order to take another look in the basement. When Litefoot had realised that the Doctor actually intended to break in to the premises that very evening he had been horrified.

'You can't do that, Doctor. If the police discover you, they'll view your behaviour as nothing more than the actions of a common criminal.'

'Then I'll have to make sure I don't get caught, won't I?' said the Doctor facetiously, grinning at Sam.

When Litefoot's only response was a disapproving shake of the head, the Doctor exclaimed, 'Oh, come on, Professor! Surely you can see that it's in a good cause? One man has already died in terrible circumstances and I aim to find out why.'

'We,' said Sam firmly. 'You're not leaving me behind this time, Doctor.'

'I don't intend to,' the Doctor said. 'In fact, I'll need your help.'

'Outrageous,' spluttered Litefoot. 'What you are proposing, Doctor, is bad enough, but to inveigle Miss Samantha into your foolhardy venture –'

'He's not inveigling me,' said Sam. 'I want to go.'

Litefoot sighed. 'In that case, you leave me no alternative. I shall have to accompany you – under protest, of course.'

The Doctor laughed. 'You old rogue. You're itching to get going, aren't you?'

Litefoot had looked indignant, though Sam had thought she could detect a twinkle in his eye. 'Certainly not. My sole intention in this venture is to keep you both out of trouble.'

Now, three hours later, the three of them were creeping round the back of the factory, cloaked by the dark and the freezing fog. Litefoot was wearing his overcoat and top hat, together with a muffler and a pair of kid gloves. He was also carrying a cane, which he had insisted to Sam was purely to steady himself on the slippery cobbles. To his consternation, both the Doctor and Sam had refused his offer of protective garments. Sam had said that she liked to keep her arms relatively free just in case she had to throw any punches.

''Pon my soul,' Litefoot had remarked. 'Did the Doctor find you floating down the Amazon in a hat box too, my dear?'

The Doctor had laughed, but Sam had merely curled her nose up. 'What you on about, Professor?'

Now the Doctor pointed to one of several windows above his head. 'Here we are.'

Litefoot peered up at the dark pane. 'Don't quite see what you're getting at, Doctor.'

'The catch inside is loose. I noticed it this morning. Give us a bunk up, someone.'

Before Litefoot could react, Sam had stepped forward and made a stirrup of her hands. The Doctor stepped into them and used his elbows to haul himself up on to the windowsill. He began to thump at the frame with the heel of his right hand, trying to dislodge the catch from its mooring inside. Litefoot winced at each thump and looked around anxiously, clearly expecting the full force of the law to descend upon them from all sides at any moment.

'I usually… prefer… more subtle… methods,' the Doctor gasped as he hung there, 'but sometimes… brute force… is the only… way!'

He gave one final thump, and with a splintering sound and a scrape of metal the window swung open. With remarkable agility, the Doctor slithered up and over the sill, his legs together like those of a swimmer diving into water. Sam watched the soles of his shoes disappear. A moment passed.

'Doctor,' she hissed. 'Are you all right?'

His face appeared at the window, grinning down at them. 'Wait there,' he said. 'I'll find something.'

He disappeared again. This time he was gone for almost a full minute, though it seemed like longer. Sam jumped back as something came flying out of the window towards her. She had adopted a defensive stance, fists bunched, before she realised it was a rope.

The rope swung back, slapping against the factory wall. There was a noose tied in the end.

'Put your foot in the loop and I'll pull you up,' the Doctor said, popping up like a jack-in-the-box. 'You first, Sam. Then we can drag the professor in together.'

Sam did as instructed, and felt herself being hauled upwards at an alarming speed. It was as if there was not just the Doctor, but a ten-man tug-of-war team heaving on the other end. She was level with the window within seconds, reaching out to grab the sill and pulling herself inside. Moments later it was Litefoot's turn. He looked distinctly uncomfortable as he placed his foot in the loop and began to rise slowly but surely into the air. As he came level with the window he took off his top hat and tossed it through the gap, then gamely grabbed hold of the windowsill like Sam before him and dragged himself inside. His probing foot found the topmost of several wooden crates, which the Doctor had stacked beneath the window, and he clumped down on to it, flushed and gasping.

The Doctor pulled in the rope, panting a little from his exertions, while Sam rushed forward to help Litefoot down on to the factory floor. Once there, he produced a large white handkerchief which he used to mop his sweating brow.

'I've a feeling I'm getting a little too old for all this,' he said, then managed a weak smile. 'Rather exhilarating all the same.'

'This is nothing, Professor,' said Sam airily. 'You want to see us when we really get going.' She picked up the professor's hat and placed it on her head. 'How do I look?'

'Very fetching, my dear,' said Litefoot diplomatically.

The Doctor was peering into a murky darkness in which the now silent machinery was nothing more than a black silhouetted mass of jutting angles and irregular shapes. 'This way,' he muttered.

He led them unerringly across a factory floor which even in the cooling darkness still smelled of metal and oil and human sweat. A minute or so later they were standing outside the door that led down to the basement.

'Locked,' Sam said wearily, eyeing the padlock and bar. 'How predictable.'

'We can either go for the direct approach here or the more subtle. Which shall it be?' mused the Doctor.

'Direct,' said Sam.

'Subtle, I think,' said the Doctor as if he hadn't heard her. 'After all, we don't want to draw attention to ourselves.'

He rummaged in the pocket of his long-tailed frock coat and produced what appeared to Litefoot to be a metal wand with a red, egg-shaped bulb on the end.

'Whatever is that, Doctor?' Litefoot asked.

'Sonic screwdriver,' said the Doctor, 'but it doesn't exist in this century, so it might be best if you forgot all about it.'

Litefoot's wordless response was an expression of weary disbelief.

'Don't worry,' Sam said, smiling mischievously. 'You'll get used to it.'

The Doctor crouched down, running his fingers over the padlock, looking not unlike a master safe-cracker about to start work. 'This may take a few minutes. These primitive locks can be a bit tricky.'

To Litefoot's astonishment the sonic screwdriver began to emit a high-pitched warbling noise, and the bulb in the end started to burn with a light almost too fierce to look upon. The Doctor began to sweep the bulb slowly back and forth across the padlock. Too fascinated by what was happening to worry about the sound the device was making, Litefoot leaned forward, gloved hands on knees. 'Incredible.'

'It's simply a case of finding the right frequency,' the Doctor said, as if talking to himself. His thumb manipulated a tiny yet intricate array of controls set into the handle of the screwdriver and immediately the warbling changed in pitch, becoming shriller, more frantic.

Three minutes later the padlock sprang open. The Doctor switched off the device and stepped back. 'Eureka,' he said.

After the trilling of the screwdriver the silence was deafening. Sam, who was sitting cross-legged on the floor, massaged her ears. 'About time. That was like listening to a Smurfs cover of a

Prodigy song. We would've made less noise if we'd kicked the door in.'

The Doctor gave her a look, removed the padlock and bar and opened the door. From the pitch blackness beyond, a breath of freezing cold air wafted over them.

'Ever see that film, *The Beast in the Cellar*?' whispered Sam.

Litefoot gave her a curious look. 'Film?' he inquired.

'There are candles in here,' the Doctor said. He edged forward in to the darkness and crouched down, groping to his left. 'Here they are.'

A moment later his face bloomed from the darkness, washed by the pale, yellowish light of a candle flame. The flame wavered, tugging at the shadows around his nose and mouth, as if trying to drag his features askew.

He passed the candle in its brass holder to Sam and lit another for Litefoot. After lighting a third for himself he said, 'Watch these steps, they're slippery,' then began to lead the way down.

Sam, in the middle, watched their shadows balloon and jitter on the wall beside them, animated by the flapping candle flames. Though she had already faced all manner of terrifying situations with the Doctor, she felt increasingly nervous as they descended, a fact which irritated her no end. Licking her lips, she whispered, 'And to think I joined you so that I could see all the exotic places in the universe.'

The Doctor half turned, smiling. 'With me, I'm afraid you have to take the rough with the smooth.'

'I wouldn't mind that,' Sam said, 'if the rough didn't outnumber the smooth by about nine to one.'

The Doctor chuckled. A moment later they were at the bottom of the steps.

'Not much in here,' said Sam, holding up her candle and

looking around.

'May I ask what it is you're hoping to find, Doctor?' Litefoot inquired.

'I'm not sure,' the Doctor said. 'Help me move these, would you?'

His footsteps echoed hollowly as he crossed the stone floor to the barrels and lengths of timber and bits of old machinery. The three of them rolled the barrels across the floor, Sam pulling a face at the white mould furring the damp wood, Litefoot wearing an expression of weary indulgence.

The Doctor peered at the floor where the barrels had been. As far as Sam could see, there were only a number of dark slimy circles populated by a great many fat and confused woodlice. At the Doctor's behest, they moved the timber next, then the machinery. A spider roughly the size of Venezuela crawled out of the machinery and scuttled over Sam's hand. To her shame, she was unable to suppress a cry of alarm, but at least she didn't drop what she was holding.

There was nothing underneath the timber or the machinery. The Doctor moved across to the arch on the far side of the room, holding his candle above his head like a tour guide.

'Here we have the spacious master bedroom,' Sam said, squeezing into the alcove behind him. She eyed the walls distastefully. 'Plenty of running water, though unfortunately no taps.'

'More barrels,' the Doctor said apologetically. 'Professor, would you mind?'

Litefoot had stuck his head through the arch behind Sam and was looking up at the seeping walls warily, as if afraid something unpleasant was going to plop down on to his top hat and ruin it. 'I must be quite mad,' he decided, but propped his cane against the wall. Together he and the Doctor shifted the barrels from one side of the alcove to the other.

'Aha,' the Doctor said, and placed his candle on the floor next to what had been revealed.

'What is it?' Sam breathed, cautious of getting too close.

Set into the stone floor was what appeared to be an upside-down crab, its jointed legs tightly meshed.

'It's a lock,' the Doctor said.

'A lock?' exclaimed Litefoot, his voice echoing in the confined space.

'It looks alive,' said Sam.

'Well it is, in a manner of speaking.' The Doctor crouched down and peered at the 'crab', his face only inches from its bunched legs. 'Organic technology,' he murmured. 'That narrows it down a bit.'

'Whatever are you talking about, Doctor?' Litefoot asked.

The Doctor looked up at him. 'I'm afraid this is going to be rather hard for you to accept, Professor, but the mechanism you see here doesn't originate on this planet.'

'Doesn't originate…? What the Dickens are you trying to say?'

'Aliens,' said Sam, not without some degree of relish.

'*Aliens?*' repeated Litefoot. 'Beings from outer space, do you mean?' He started to laugh, then abruptly stopped when he realised that no one was laughing with him. 'I do believe you're serious.'

'Oh, we are,' said the Doctor. 'Deadly.'

'I *am* mad,' said Litefoot faintly.

'Nonsense, Professor,' said the Doctor, producing his sonic screwdriver once more. 'You're as sane as I am.'

'Very reassuring,' said Litefoot doubtfully. He looked at the alien lock again. The Weng-Chiang business five years ago had broadened his horizons considerably, but creatures from another planet? The idea was preposterous!

'No, I'm sorry, Doctor,' he said, 'but I simply can't accept what

96

you say. It must be some sort of trick.'

'Must it?' said the Doctor as if the idea had never occurred to him.

'Well… of course. It stands to reason, surely? I mean, beings from other worlds are a fantasy. They simply do not exist.'

'Don't they?' said the Doctor, all innocence, and switched on his sonic screwdriver. Sam grinned in anticipation.

He pointed the screwdriver at the alien lock, the red bulb almost touching the 'stomach' section between the meshed legs. The effect was instantaneous and spectacular. The legs began to writhe like those of a crab which had been flipped on to its back and was frantically trying to right itself.

'Great Scott!' exclaimed Litefoot.

'Gross,' said Sam.

The Doctor half turned, and was about to say something when his face fell. 'Oh dear.'

'What's the matter, Doctor?' asked Sam, then realised that he was looking not at her, but beyond her. She twisted round, holding up her candle. Something was moving in the darkness by the door, just beyond her candle range.

It was big. Nowhere near as big as the creature they had encountered on the towpath, but big all the same. As it emerged from the shadows, Sam got a confused impression of a silvery, fish-scale body, a long neck and a head containing rolling eyes and slavering fangs.

Then the creature let out a thundering bellow and charged towards them…

CHAPTER 4
DEVIL INCARNATE

Sam froze. The candle holder slipped from her nerveless fingers and clattered on the floor, the candle going out. Though it must have been no more than a split second, she seemed to be standing there for a long time, watching the vast bulk of the creature ploughing through the darkness towards her. *I wonder what being eaten will feel like*, she thought almost abstractedly. Then someone shoved her roughly to one side.

It was the Doctor. He leapt forward, holding his sonic screwdriver out before him like a weapon. The bulb on the end was glowing a fierce cherry-red. Sam clapped her hands over her ears as the Doctor manipulated a control, and the device suddenly emitted a high-pitched screech. Beside her, Litefoot screwed his face up and also pressed his fingers to his ears. The effect on the creature was far more dramatic.

It released a groaning bellow of pain and skidded to a halt, its head weaving from side to side like a boxer trying to shake off the effects of a powerful, dizzying punch.

'Quickly,' the Doctor shouted. 'Make for the steps while it's disorientated.'

Sam felt him grab her arm with his free hand and propel her forward. 'It's all right, I can manage,' she gasped, and stumbled towards the creature, skirting round it and heading for the steps. The sound from the sonic screwdriver was like a drill trapped in her brain. She reached the steps and staggered up them, feeling as though she was going to fall flat on her face at any moment. She was vaguely aware of Litefoot just behind her, the Doctor bringing up the rear. Then she was stumbling out of the door and on to the

99

factory floor, whereupon her legs promptly turned to jelly and she dropped to her knees.

Litefoot appeared, wheezing, having lost his candle, cane and hat, and half collapsed against the wall. Finally, out catapulted the Doctor. In a bewildering blur of movement, he switched off and pocketed his sonic screwdriver, slammed the basement door, and replaced the bar and padlock.

'Gad,' Litefoot gasped. 'What was that thing?'

'Well, I don't think it was the factory cat,' said the Doctor, and flipped a thumb at the door. 'The creature will recover quickly, and this door won't hold for long. I suggest we make ourselves scarce.'

Litefoot nodded and pushed himself away from the wall, his face a pale oval in the darkness. Sam heard the Doctor coming towards her and forced herself to stand up before he had to help her. She was aware she had reacted badly, and was annoyed with herself for having done so. That, she promised herself, was the last time she would ever freeze. From now on, she would remain alert, would force herself to keep thinking, whatever the situation.

When the Doctor came up beside her and asked her if she was all right, she forced herself to grin and hoped the lack of light would mask the true expression in her eyes. 'Never better,' she told him, but her voice was too loud and too raw in the dark and silent factory.

Emmeline awoke with a jolt, her heart pounding. She lay for a few moments in the darkness, wondering what had woken her. The house seemed silent, and her sleep, as far as she could recall, had been dreamless. Presently she closed her eyes again, though now she did not feel the slightest bit tired. Her mind kept turning over that morning's events, particularly the awful and upsetting conversation she had had with her father.

What was it that strange man, the Doctor, had said? He had told her her father was being controlled. But what precisely did that mean? Was her father being blackmailed or threatened in some way? Or was it something more than that?

She thought of how her father had seemed when she had spoken to him. It had been like speaking to a completely different man, like an impostor wearing her father's body. It was not simply his manner that was different: it was the way he moved, the expression in his eyes…

Everything.

But what could change a man's character so comprehensively? Was her father being forced to consume some kind of… chemical compound or narcotic mixture? Something that altered his mind, reduced him to little more than a slave, a puppet?

Such a notion did not bear thinking about. Indeed, the very idea of it made her sick to her stomach.

She pushed aside her bedclothes and swung her legs to the floor, deciding to go down to the kitchen and make herself some hot milk. Mama, she knew, would have woken a servant for that, but Emmeline was thoughtful enough to allow them what little sleep they managed to get. Besides, she wished to be alone to think, to plan her best possible course of action. Despite the Doctor's warning, she had no intention of abandoning her father to whatever devils were plaguing him.

She pulled a dressing gown over her long nightdress, stepped into a pair of slippers, and crossed the room to the door. Outside in the corridor she paused once again to listen, but aside from the sonorous ticking of the clock in the hall downstairs she could hear nothing. She crossed the landing, her feet sinking into the thick, heavily patterned carpet, and listened at the door of the master bedroom where once again her mother was sleeping alone. She half expected to hear stifled weeping penetrating the stout oak, or the sound of her mother moving about restlessly inside, but all was silence. Satisfied that her mother was sleeping soundly, Emmeline went downstairs, walking on the outside of the stair-rods to prevent the stairs from creaking.

Though it was dark, she noticed immediately that the parlour door was ajar. This was unusual, as Mama always insisted that all the doors be closed at night to keep the heat in. Quietly, Emmeline crossed the hallway, passing the grandfather clock, the stand full of canes, the pictures crammed together on the wall around the elaborately framed mirror, and paused outside the parlour. She raised a hand to the door. 'Mama,' she called softly. 'Mama, are you in here?'

There was no reply. Emmeline gave the door a little push and it swung open. She licked her lips, then stepped smartly into the room, which was in darkness. She stood for a moment, trying to identify the shapes that were lamps and chairs and ornaments, side tables, vases and pot plants. On the far side of the room, close to the windows now covered with their long, thick velvet drapes, was a high-backed armchair, which Emmeline, screwing up her eyes, was almost certain contained a dark and bulky mass that may or may not have been a figure.

'Mama,' Emmeline said again, her voice wavering a little, 'is that you?'

The mass in the armchair did not respond, nor even stir. Perhaps it was simply a stack of cushions, or her own eyes playing tricks on her, conjuring shapes from the night that were not really there.

Tightening her lips, Emmeline took a slow, measured step forward, then another and another. A chill breeze slipped like a breath across her cheeks, making her shiver inside. She had the impression that the darkness was drawing her in, engulfing her, wishing her to become a part of it. Her eyes were adjusting now, the various darknesses dividing into subtle gradations, acquiring sharper lines of definition.

There was certainly a figure sitting in the chair. If she concentrated hard, Emmeline could see its outline – the dark bulb of its head, its shoulders and arms, the mass of its torso, the curve of its lap, the bend of its legs.

'Who's there?' she demanded sharply. Again the figure did not respond. Emmeline hesitated, then crossed to the mantelpiece, groping for the box of lucifers that she knew to be there. She found them and extracted one with fumbling hands. Above the mantelpiece was a large mirror, on each side of which was a gas lamp. Emmeline struck the match, and, forcing her hand to remain steady, lit the lamp that was closest to her.

A soft orange glow suffused the room.

Emmeline turned – and a shock so great it stopped the scream in her throat slammed into her.

It *was* her mother sitting in the armchair, after all. Or rather, not sitting, but slumped. The reason for this was not because she was sleeping but because she was dead. Emmeline could tell that from her ghastly pallor and glaring eyes, the look of awful terror frozen on to her face. And there was something else too, something that Emmeline's spinning, horror-filled mind could make no sense of. In her mother's throat were several ragged puncture wounds, out of which was dribbling not blood but a viscous green slime.

Emmeline backed away on legs so rickety it seemed they would snap like dry sticks at any moment. Still unable to scream, she was making breathy, high-pitched mewling sounds. She dropped the box of lucifers, which struck the hearth and burst open, scattering its contents. The long velvet drapes covering the window billowed as though buffeted by a strong wind.

Then a figure stepped from behind them.

It was her father, his hands reaching out as though to draw her into an embrace. Only it was not her father at all, for his eyes were burning with a hideous orange light. Emmeline looked at his hands, and saw that on his palms were a number of suckers, like small puckered mouths, from which protruded long thorn-like spikes. From the tips of the spikes green slime was oozing, the same green slime that was leaking from the holes in her dead mother's throat.

Awkwardly, moving like a child learning how to walk, Emmeline turned and blundered from the room. She wanted to scream, not only in terror of her life, and in horror at what she had seen, but also to rouse the servants, procure help. However, shock still clamped the sound down inside her somewhere, refusing to let it out. With hands that no longer seemed part of her, she grabbed the door as she exited the room, slammed it behind her, then raced along the corridor towards the front door. She had no plan, no strategy: she just wanted to get away, get out of the house.

Behind her, she heard her father give a hideous hissing gurgle that did not sound even remotely human. Then he ripped the parlour door open and came tearing down the corridor after her.

'Cyborg,' said the Doctor.

'I beg your pardon?' replied Litefoot.

'That was what attacked us. A cyborg. Part animal, part machine.' He leaned back in his chair and smiled. 'I've always found biotechnological species fascinating.'

Sam looked at him almost with resentment. Here they were, barely an hour after having almost been gobbled up by some massive monster with metal teeth, and the Doctor was sitting back, perfectly relaxed, talking about their ordeal with all the boyish enthusiasm of a schoolkid discussing an earthworm experiment.

Though she tried to hide it, Sam was still furious with herself for having frozen back there at the factory. What was more, she couldn't stop the shiver of reaction deep in her belly, which was still juddering away like a little motor despite her having drunk two brandy-laced coffees.

She wondered if she ought to bring the subject up with the Doctor, apologise or something, assure him that it wouldn't happen again, that her behaviour back there had been nothing more than a momentary aberration. She wanted to be an asset, not a liability; she'd hate it if the Doctor thought he had to protect her all the time.

Maybe later, when the time was right. For now, trying to sound smart, she said, 'That was why the sonic screwdriver was able to scramble its synapses.'

The Doctor nodded. 'I gave it a brainstorm, though the effect was only temporary. I suspect these creatures have a built-in protective response to sonic attack.'

Litefoot was looking from Sam to the Doctor, trying in vain to hold on to the conversation. 'I'm afraid you've lost me,' he admitted. 'Do I take it, Doctor, that the animal that attacked us was *built*, that it was some form of machine?'

'Not built exactly,' said the Doctor. 'Grown outside the womb in a controlled environment, engineered, augmented...'

'By spacemen?' said Litefoot.

'Aliens, yes,' said the Doctor.

Litefoot let out a long sigh. 'I don't mind admitting I'm somewhat out of my depth. If I hadn't seen what I've seen with my own eyes I'm sure I would think you both quite deranged.'

'Do you know who the aliens are then, Doctor?' Sam asked.

'There are several possibilities.' The Doctor held up a hand, thumb extended, evidently to reel off a list of alien races that would mean nothing to either Sam or the professor, when he was interrupted by a pounding on the door. 'Expecting company, Professor?' he asked.

'Not at this hour,' Litefoot replied, but the Doctor was already jumping to his feet. Sam saw him reaching into his jacket pocket in search of his sonic screwdriver, and eager to make amends for earlier she shoved herself out of her seat and went after him.

'Wait a moment, Doctor. I'll bring my revolver,' Litefoot called, but the Doctor was already running out of the door and into the hallway. Sam was only a few paces behind him, but she faltered slightly when she saw the dark silhouette of a figure pressed against the glass on the other side of Litefoot's front door, arms held upright in a cruciform position.

Then the figure drew its fists back and pounded on the door again. A female voice cried, 'Let me in! Let me in!'

'Careful, Doctor,' warned Sam, but the Doctor had already pocketed his sonic screwdriver and was unlocking and unbolting the front door. As he pulled the door open, the figure on the other side of it lunged towards him.

The Doctor caught the girl as she fell, and half-dragged, half-carried her into the house. Sam rushed forward to close the front door through which a chill winter wind was blowing.

'Good Lord!' exclaimed Litefoot, appearing from the sitting room brandishing a revolver. Quickly recovering his composure, he put the weapon down on the lid of a wicker laundry basket that was sitting in the hall and hurried to help the Doctor. He glanced at the girl's dirty, scratched feet and shins below her nightdress with alarm and concern. Then he manfully took hold of the girl's ankles and lifted her feet clear of the floor. Together, he and the Doctor carried her through to the sitting room and laid her gently down on a chaise longue.

'Sam, would you fetch me a blanket, a towel and a bowl of warm water? The professor will show you where everything is. Professor, would you make Miss Seers a hot drink?'

'Certainly, Doctor,' said Litefoot. 'You know this young lady, then?'

'Emmeline Seers. Her father owns the factory where Tom Donahue worked.'

'Ah,' Litefoot said sagely. He and Sam left the room to do the Doctor's bidding.

'Emmeline,' said the Doctor gently. Since tumbling into the house, the girl appeared to have retreated into herself. Her eyes were glassy with shock, and her breathing was quick and stertorous, as if she was on the verge of hyperventilating. Gently the Doctor pushed aside a curtain of sweat-damp, fog-smelling hair that was plastered to her forehead. 'Emmeline, can you hear me?'

Her eyes flickered, then she reached out and clutched the Doctor's sleeve. 'Please, keep him away,' she hissed.

'Who?' the Doctor asked. 'Your father? Is that who you mean?'

'He is not my father.' Her body tensed, and the Doctor placed his hands lightly on her shoulders as though to hold her down in her seat. 'He is the devil incarnate.'

The Doctor put his arm around her, tried to comfort her, though her body was ramrod-straight, the muscles in her back and shoulders so tensed they seemed hard as concrete. He was still in the same, slightly awkward position when Sam and Litefoot re-entered the room. Sam was carrying a tin bowl from which steam was rising. She had a towel draped over her right arm and a woolly blanket slung over her left shoulder. The professor was carrying a tea tray on which was a delicate china cup and saucer, two jugs, and a sugar bowl protected by a weighted lace doily.

'You two look cosy,' Sam said, her tone more truculent than she would have liked.

The Doctor looked up, but gave no indication he had heard either her words or the manner in which she had spoken them. 'Ah,' he said, and took the blanket from Sam. He encouraged Emmeline to sit up, then wrapped the blanket around her so that only her head was visible. Emmeline hardly seemed to notice what he was doing. She continued to stare ahead, white-faced.

The Doctor instructed Sam to place the bowl of water on the floor, the towel beside it. Then he took the tray from Litefoot, poured cocoa into the cup from one jug, added hot milk from the other, and sweetened the mixture with sugar. As he held the cup to Emmeline's lips, imploring her gently to drink, Sam could not help but appraise the new arrival. Physically, she and Emmeline could not have been more different. Whereas Sam was small and wiry, almost boyish, with cropped blonde hair, Emmeline was tall and willowy, her dark hair long and lustrous. Sam watched as Emmeline took dainty sips from the cup, and she found herself wondering how this girl would have reacted to the creature in the basement of her father's factory. She would probably have thrown a screaming fit or dropped to the floor in a dead faint, she told herself, ashamed of her vindictiveness even as the thoughts crossed her mind.

The Doctor put the cup aside and pulled the bowl of warm water towards him. 'Emmeline,' he said, his voice soft as velvet, 'are you able to tell us what happened?'

Emmeline gave a slight nod and began to tell her story, speaking in an oddly detached voice as if the cold force of her shock had frozen solid her emotions. As the tale unfolded, Sam found her capricious resentment evaporating, to be replaced by compassion, horror, and not a little self-loathing. As the girl described how she had slammed and locked the front door with the slavering, burning-eyed creature that was masquerading as her father mere inches behind her, Sam clenched her teeth and had to repress an urge to move forward, put her arms around the girl and comfort her as the Doctor had done.

'I fled into the night,' Emmeline said. 'I barely knew what I was doing. And then I recalled the card you had given me, Doctor, and without even thinking about it, the address simply sprang into my mind. I knew this street to be less than half a mile from my own home, and so I ran here without looking back. Even now I am uncertain whether that creature was pursuing me.'

There was a moment of silence, then Litefoot said, 'Astonishing. You ran all this way with nothing on your feet?'

Emmeline looked down at her bare feet, which the Doctor was now tenderly bathing with warm water. 'I suppose so,' she said. 'I'm afraid I don't recall. I was overwhelmed by panic and confusion.'

'Of course you were, my dear,' Litefoot said, and then inadequately added, 'Try not to upset yourself. You've undergone a most appalling ordeal.'

As if he had reminded her of something she had momentarily forgotten, Emmeline said quietly, 'I cannot comprehend what has happened. Mama is dead, Father is lost to me…'

'There, there,' the Doctor soothed. 'We'll look after you. You can stay here with us. Can't she, Professor?'

'What? Er… oh yes, of course. Though I rather think it's time we called the police in to deal with this sordid – not to say perplexing – affair.'

'You're not thinking clearly, Professor,' the Doctor said. 'Who's going to explain to them about the cyborg, the aliens?'

Litefoot looked momentarily nonplussed, then said, 'But surely, Doctor, they won't be able to dismiss the evidence of their own eyes? Even if the creature itself is no longer present in the factory, we can still show the police the peculiar artefact in the basement.' He leaned forward, lowering his voice. 'And then, of course, there is Miss Seers's poor, unfortunate mother. I'm sure her corpse –'

'Will have disappeared by now,' the Doctor interrupted. 'And I guarantee, if we went to the police with our story we wouldn't even get within spitting distance of Seers's factory.'

'Nah, they'd lock us in the funny farm and throw away the key,' said Sam.

'Besides,' said the Doctor, not even giving Litefoot time to draw breath, 'the Great British constabulary, wonderful institution though it is, would be no match for aliens equipped with the technology we've seen.'

'So you see, Professor, we're on our own,' said Sam, taking up the mantle once again. 'Me and the Doctor, we operate above the law. We're used to dealing with stuff like this. We don't want a load of coppers clodhopping all over the place, getting themselves killed and mucking things up. Isn't that right, Doctor?'

'Hmm,' the Doctor said noncommittally.

Litefoot sighed. 'In that case, may I ask what our next move should be?'

The Doctor gently towelled Emmeline's feet dry and straightened up. 'I'm certain the aliens' base is beneath the factory. Somehow I have to bypass the cyborg and get in there, find out what we're up against.'

'Sounds incredibly dangerous,' said Sam. 'Count me in.'

Litefoot gave her a despairing look, but for the time being seemed to have given up trying to dissuade her and the Doctor from putting themselves in peril. 'May I ask how you propose to implement this scheme of yours, Doctor?'

'I aim to approach from below,' the Doctor replied. 'The grille in the basement must lead to a sewer outlet, which is how the cyborg got in. It's almost certainly situated on the bank of the Thames.'

'Great,' said Sam sardonically. 'I've always wanted to wallow knee-deep through –'

'Shh,' said the Doctor, holding a finger to his lips.

Sam grinned. 'Couldn't you just give this cyborg thing another blast from your sonic screwdriver?'

The Doctor shook his head. 'As I said, the effect is short-lived. Besides, any interference in the cyborg's brain patterns will alert its masters to our presence. We might just as well knock on the door and announce our arrival.'

'So when are we off, then?' Sam asked.

'There's no time like –'

'The present?' suggested Sam.

'Exactly! Let's go.' The Doctor jumped to his feet and headed for the door.

'Doctor, I really must protest –' began Litefoot.

The Doctor turned back, wearing the expression of a small boy who has been forbidden to play outside. 'Oh, must you?'

Litefoot set his face sternly. 'I'm afraid so. I really don't see that the situation has altered overmuch from earlier this evening, and as such I would not feel comfortable allowing you and Miss Samantha to embark on this hazardous expedition without my assistance.'

'But Professor, you have a vital role to play here,' said the Doctor persuasively. 'Looking after Emmeline, keeping the wolves from the door – or one particular wolf, at least.'

'I am well aware of that, Doctor, in which case I rather think –'

'I would like to come too, if I may,' said Emmeline suddenly.

All three turned to look at her. She was shrugging off her blanket, a determined expression on her pale face.

'Well, I'm not sure –' the Doctor began, but now Emmeline interrupted him too.

'Sir, my mother is dead and my father possessed by I know not what. Now, I have heard much of what you have said, and though I do not profess to comprehend it all, I do know that you intend to hunt down and expose the evil protagonists of these awful crimes. With this in mind, I would ask that I be permitted to accompany you. Surely I, more than anyone present, have a great deal of hurt to repay?'

Sam felt like applauding, but contented herself with a hearty, 'You tell 'em, girl.'

The Doctor sighed, recrossed the room, crouched down in front of Emmeline, and took her hands. 'What we are about to do, Emmeline, will almost certainly entail an appalling risk to all our lives. There's really no need for you to expose yourself to that.'

'I understand what you are saying, Doctor,' Emmeline said, 'and I appreciate your concern, but I still wish to accompany you.'

'The Doctor's right, my dear,' said Litefoot. 'Considering your delicate state, perhaps it might be best if you were to remain here.' Reluctantly he added, 'I will keep you company if you wish.'

Emmeline, however, shook her head. 'No, sir. It is a kind offer, but my mind is made up. I believe it is my duty to avenge my mother's death. As I say, I would wish to accompany you, but if you will not allow me to do so, then I will be obliged to go alone.'

'Oh no, Miss Seers, I cannot permit you to do that!' exclaimed Litefoot.

'Sir, I do not need your permission to do anything. I believe I am free to act as I please.'

'She's right,' said Sam. 'You can't stop her from doing what she wants.'

'Then you *will* allow me to accompany you?' said Emmeline.

The Doctor wafted a hand wearily. 'It's a free cosmos.'

Sam grinned and turned to Emmeline. 'Don't worry, Em, you just stick with me. You'll be all right.'

Emmeline looked up, her gaze lingering on each of them in turn, before pushing herself to her feet. 'Yes,' she said, her voice as determined as it had been since she had entered the house, 'I am sure I shall.'

CHAPTER 5
IN THE BELLY OF THE BEAST

Forty minutes later, the four of them were standing on a thin, muddy strip of riverbank behind and below the factory, which they had reached via a narrow set of slippery stone steps leading down from the towpath. Behind them, lapping almost at their heels, was the Thames, its black skin leavened by the occasional glint of light; directly in front of them was a high stone wall crusted with silt. Sure enough, as the Doctor had predicted, there was a waste pipe inset into the wall. Nothing more than a stone-lined tunnel some seven feet in diameter, the section of wall beneath it was caked with a thick, evil-smelling sludge.

Sam peered into the tunnel, but the blackness beyond the first few feet appeared absolute. She glanced behind her at the Thames, thinking about the cyborg that had killed Tom Donahue, and the one that had attacked them in the factory earlier, wondering how many more of them there were like it. If one of those creatures should rise from the water behind them now, they wouldn't stand a chance. But life with the Doctor was like that, she thought, a mad dash from one life-threatening situation to the next, relieved only by the occasional tea break. She had more or less grown used to the constant adrenaline rushes, though every so often the excitement caught up with her and she ended up having to sleep for twelve or fifteen hours.

She gave Emmeline an encouraging smile. Professor Litefoot had managed to find the girl some clothes; in fact, he claimed they had been part of a job lot bought for the 'other' Doctor's companion, a girl called Leela, but that she had departed suddenly without claiming, or even wearing, them.

Litefoot peered dubiously into the tunnel, sniffed, then pulled a face. 'Incredible as these cases always turn out to be, Doctor, why is it that somewhere along the way there is invariably a sewer pipe involved?'

'We're just lucky, I suppose,' said the Doctor solemnly, then stepped up and heaved himself into the pipe. The sludge squelched and slurped around the soles of his shoes. 'Come on in,' he called, his voice echoing off the curved walls, 'the water's lovely.'

Sam climbed into the pipe after him, and turned to give Emmeline a hand, leaving Litefoot to bring up the rear. On the way over here, Sam had tried to explain to Emmeline what to expect, but the girl had seemed confused, unable to grasp the concept of aliens with organic technology and giant lizards that were part machine.

Oh well, Sam had thought, hopefully she'll pick it up as we go along. She was worried, though. Spirited though Emmeline undoubtedly was, her imagination seemed pretty limited. There was simply no way of knowing how she would react should her narrow world-view be not only challenged but blown apart, as it almost certainly would be before much longer.

The four of them began to plod forward, heading into the darkness, the gunk that was either raw sewage or industrial effluent (or perhaps both) clinging to their feet as if attempting to drag them back. As her eyes began to get accustomed to the dark, Sam expected to see rats, but didn't; she also expected the sludge to become abruptly wetter and deeper, but that didn't happen either. 'You all right?' she asked, turning back to see how Emmeline was taking it. Despite all she had been through, Emmeline's face was set, her eyes on her booted feet. She nodded grimly.

'I say, Doctor,' called Litefoot from the rear, 'how do you know this tunnel will lead to the grille in the basement?'

'Educated guess,' replied the Doctor. 'I'm hoping we'll come across a vertical shaft that will lead us up there.'

'What if a load of crap comes down on top of our heads while we're climbing up?' said Sam.

'We hold our breath and pray that we get the chance to have a hot bath later.'

'Great.'

The Doctor chuckled. 'Don't worry. The plumbing won't be back in operation for several hours yet. Our only worry is if the aliens get wind of our presence and decide to drench us with boiling oil or sulphuric acid or something.'

'Doctor, sometimes you say the most reassuring things,' Sam told him.

'I aim to please,' the Doctor said.

'Pardon me, but surely there's a rather more urgent probability that we appear to have overlooked,' called Litefoot.

'What's that then, Professor?' asked Sam.

'The creature. Is it not reasonable to assume that it will still be present in the cellar, guarding the peculiar artefact that we earlier uncovered?'

'Good point,' said Sam, but ahead of her she could just make out the Doctor shaking his head.

'I'm banking on the fact that the creature will have been given the run of the factory in order to prevent us or anyone else breaching the security of the building in the way that we previously did.'

'And if you're wrong? If the aliens have already worked out that this time we might try and get in through the sewers?' said Sam.

'Then we'll be in trouble. But if they don't kill us immediately, they'll probably take us into their base so that their leader can have a good gloat, which is where we want to be anyway.'

'Yeah, but if that happens, it'll be on their terms, not ours.'

'Ah well,' said the Doctor, 'you can't have everything.'

Their journey was a short one, no more than a few hundred yards. Suddenly the Doctor cried, 'Aha!' and next moment appeared to Sam to be rising into the air in front of her. She took a few more squelching steps forward and found herself standing at the foot of a metal ladder, which the Doctor was already half way up. Thinking ruefully of the clots of sewage that would almost certainly drop off his heels and splat down on to her head, she began to climb up after him.

Pushing aside the metal grille at the top of the ladder was a struggle, but eventually they were climbing out into the basement that they had left with such haste less than two hours before. After the pipe it was almost a relief to be here. Sam looked around nervously, peering into the darkest shadows for the cyborg, but the basement appeared to be empty. As the Doctor gave Emmeline and then Litefoot a helping hand, Sam stamped her feet and scraped her boots on the rough walls to try to get as much of the gunk off as possible. Much to her amusement, Litefoot solemnly produced a small clothes brush and applied it vigorously to his overcoat. With a twinkle in his eye he told her, 'Standards must be maintained, particularly if one is about to be introduced to foreigners.'

The Doctor was already crossing the room to the small recess, sonic screwdriver at the ready. When the others caught up with him, he was crouching down beside the inverted crab that he had referred to as a lock. As before, he pointed his sonic screwdriver at the thing's exposed 'belly' and turned it on. The bulb glowed red, the device's high-pitched trilling filled the air, and the tightly meshed legs once again began to thrash and writhe.

'What is the Doctor doing to that creature?' Emmeline asked.

Sam looked at her. Her eyes were wide, full of concern. Sam realised that to Emmeline the Doctor must resemble a boy torturing something he had found washed up on the beach.

'Well, it's not really a creature,' she said. 'It's a sort of lock. It was built by the aliens I told you about.'

'It was the Doctor who informed you of this?'

'Well… yeah.'

'How does he know such things?'

'Ah well, he's knocked about a bit. And he's basically just a know-all.'

All at once there was the grating of stone on stone and a whole section of floor slid back.

'*Voilà!*' said the Doctor.

'Good Lord!' exclaimed Litefoot.

It was not so much the movement of the floor but what was revealed beyond it that had astonished the professor. He and the others found themselves staring into the mouth of a glowing, pulsing chute, its fibrous, pumpkin-coloured walls shot through with filaments of red that looked alarmingly like blood vessels. A little uneasily, Sam couldn't help wondering whether the chute was not actually a chute at all, but part of some animal even more gigantic than the cyborgs. What she was looking at now was most probably the inside of some sort of feeding tube; perhaps she and the others were little more than plankton gazing down the throat of the whale.

Unsure exactly how to react, she looked to the Doctor for guidance. He did not seem in the least bit surprised by what he had uncovered, but then again, neither was it possible to tell whether he had been expecting it. Sam wanted to ask him whether he had ever seen anything like this before, but she kept her mouth shut. She would rather die of curiosity than betray her ignorance and inexperience in front of Emmeline and the professor.

Litefoot had taken a tentative step forward and was crouching down to examine the glowing chute more closely, his professional interest piqued. 'This is quite astounding,' he said. 'I'd swear this was living tissue.'

'It is,' said the Doctor. 'That is, it's manufactured living tissue. It's part of a large, organic construction which possesses not even one iota of what you or I would consider sentience.'

Litefoot looked at him. 'Preposterous.'

'Yes it is, isn't it?' said the Doctor with a smile. 'I'll go first, shall I?'

He sat down on the lip of the chute, dangling his feet over the edge.

'Wait a moment, Doctor,' said Litefoot hastily. 'Do you think it's quite safe?'

'Oh, I shouldn't think so for a minute,' the Doctor replied, then gave a little wave and levered himself over the edge of the hole with his arms.

For perhaps the first eight feet he dropped like a stone. Then he struck the edge of the chute where it began to curve out of sight, and although the pulsing walls stretched and gave like rubber, he managed to come to a skidding, arm-pinwheeling stop. Sitting on his backside, momentarily arresting his progress by digging his heels into the fleshy walls, he looked back up at the others. He was grinning, his teeth seeming luminous in the strange light. 'You ought to try this,' he said. 'It's fun.'

Feeling like someone who wanted to be next in line for a parachute jump because she was afraid her nerve might fail if she waited any longer, Sam stepped forward. 'Out of the way, Doctor, I'm coming down,' she called.

The Doctor waved and slid-scuttled down on his backside. Sam sat on the edge of the hole. When the Doctor was out of sight she said with a cheeriness she didn't feel, 'Well, here goes,' and pushed herself out into space.

Though the speed of the drop was fast enough to make her feel that she had left her stomach behind, the initial fall into glowing space seemed endless. From above, the chute had looked narrow, but now it appeared so wide that she didn't think she would be able to touch the walls at either side even if she stretched out her arms.

Just as she was beginning to think that something had gone wrong, that some trap had been sprung and she was going to fall for ever, her body encountered a spongy obstruction. Unprepared for it, she bounced, and, rather than use her arms and legs to skid to a stop as the Doctor had, she found herself flipping over, rolling and spinning, unable to stop her momentum. For a few seconds panic gripped her; she was completely disorientated, and she was still falling and bouncing at such a speed that there seemed little prospect of the situation improving. Different parts of her body collided with the rubbery wall, but the separate impacts were so fleeting she was unable to use them as reference points.

Then, quite suddenly, she began to slow down. The steep angle of the chute appeared to be lessening, levelling out. She felt her shoulder strike the wall of the chute, but this time, instead of bouncing, she simply rolled, as though down a gentle slope. As her senses, which had seemed jarred from her head, began to settle into place again, she managed to use her arms and legs to halt her progress.

Next moment she was motionless, lying on her stomach, panting hard, her heart thudding away. She blinked, and though she had kept her eyes open the whole time, only now did she realise she was looking back up the chute again.

She couldn't see the top, however. It curved away above her, out of sight. As the more petty concerns of life began to filter back into her consciousness, she found herself hoping that

Litefoot and Emmeline had seen little of her graceless descent.

'That didn't do much for your image, did it?' said a voice behind her, as though stealing her thoughts.

Sam pushed herself up on to her elbows and looked round. The Doctor was just a few feet below her, leaning back against the wall with his hands behind his head, looking so relaxed she wanted to hit him.

'I missed my footing,' she said huffily.

'Several times,' said the Doctor, nodding. He shoved himself away from the wall, his redistribution of weight causing the surface of the chute to ripple like the skin of a trampoline. 'Are you all right?' he asked, now displaying what sounded like genuine concern.

'Yeah, I'm fine,' she said. 'I bruised my ego, that's all.'

'That'll mend,' he said. Lolloping past her, he called up, 'Who's next?'

There was a short pause, then Sam felt the membranous surface beneath her shiver as something above impacted with it. Next moment Emmeline appeared, and – much to Sam's chagrin – slid gracefully to a halt beside them, as though she had been doing this kind of thing all her life.

Litefoot's descent was more uncoordinated, but still not as undignified as Sam's. He appeared without coat, hat, or cane (which he had left in a neat pile on the basement floor as though fully intending to pop back for them later), on his stomach, facing back the way he had come, arms stretched out, hands splayed. He looked, thought Sam, trying not to laugh in case the Doctor mentioned her own shortcomings, like Wile E. Coyote vainly trying to prevent himself sliding down a cliff face. She almost expected to see vertical lines in the soft tissue where he had tried to dig in his fingernails.

He came to a gentle stop and rose shakily to his feet, blinking around. With a dignity that made Sam feel a sudden burst of affection for him, he tugged down his jacket, which had ridden up almost to his armpits, and smoothed his hands over his wayward grey hair. His cheeks were flushed but his eyes were sparkling. 'What a way to travel!' he exclaimed. He examined the glowing, pulsing walls closely, running his fingers over the fleshy surface. 'This is a rum place, Doctor. I feel rather like Jonah in the belly of the whale.'

'Pongs a bit,' said Sam.

'Pongs?'

'Smells'

'Ah.' Litefoot sniffed the air. 'Indeed. Though oddly the odour is not unfamiliar.' Then his face cleared. 'Ah, I have it! It is an odour very reminiscent of… Oh dear, but I'm afraid I'm rather forgetting myself.'

'Why?' asked Sam.

Litefoot looked embarrassed. 'Well, my dear, it's simply that the topic is not really an appropriate one for discussion in… um, polite company.'

Sam rolled her eyes. 'Oh God, not all that sexist nonsense again. It's all right, Professor, we girls are tougher than we look. Aren't we, Em?'

Emmeline nodded, though her face was deadpan; in fact, she looked as though she had not heard what Sam had said at all. Once again, Sam felt a pang of anxiety. Despite Emmeline's earlier insistence on coming, Sam couldn't help wondering whether all this was getting a bit much for her. After all, this evening she had already seen her mother killed by the slavering monster that her father had become; that alone would have been enough to send anyone into the deepest shock. True, for the moment she was still responding, still functioning, but aside from the odd flutter of curiosity she was doing so mechanically, without any real emotion. Sam only hoped that she wasn't going to suddenly freak out at some stage and put them all in jeopardy.

Putting aside her worries for the moment, Sam turned back to Litefoot. 'See?' she said. 'So come on, Professor, tell us what this smell reminds you of.'

Litefoot flashed a pleading glance at the Doctor, who shrugged. 'You'd better tell her, Professor. She won't leave you alone until you do.'

'Very well,' Litefoot sighed, and pursed his lips. He thought for a moment and then finally he said, 'As you know, my dear, my work as police pathologist brings me into contact with a wide variety of... um... how shall I put it?'

'Stiffs?' Sam suggested.

Litefoot looked startled. 'If I take you to mean cadavers, Miss Samantha, then yes, quite so. 'Pon my soul, what a colourful turn of phrase you have.'

'I just say it like it is,' said Sam. 'So that's what this smell's like then, is it? Dead people?'

'Well, I was thinking more specifically of their stomach contents, after several days of... um' – he leaned towards her and lowered his voice – 'putrefaction.' He straightened up and sniffed once again. 'Yes, I must say that the air here is most redolent of that singular odour.'

Sam tried not to pull a face. 'Right,' she said. 'Nice one.' Turning to the Doctor, she asked, 'Doctor, you don't think we're making a big mistake here, do you? I mean... you don't think we're anything's lunch?'

'Only one way to find out,' said the Doctor maddeningly. 'Come on.'

He turned and began to head downwards again. Sam glared at his back for a moment, then – because there was really no other

122

alternative – whispered an oath and followed. At the moment they were on a kind of plateau, able to walk in single file, but it was not long before the chute began to slope downwards again, whereupon they had to negotiate it as before, on their backsides, using their hands, elbows and feet for purchase.

It was a long and exhausting journey, with no change in their surroundings. Sometimes the gradient was steep, sometimes gentle, and sometimes it levelled out altogether. However, the trend was always downwards, and after a while Sam began to wonder whether the chute was in fact burrowing deep into the earth. If it was, it made no discernible difference to the supply of light and air. True, the inside of the chute was uncomfortably warm, but then it had been so from the outset. It was true also that after a while Sam began to feel sick and a little dizzy, but that, she assured herself, was because of the constant unpleasant smell and not because she was suffocating.

At last she saw the Doctor, some eight or ten feet in front of her, dig in his heels to make himself stop, and raise a warning hand. She slid a little closer to him, then stopped herself. Palming sweat from her brow, she asked, 'What is it?'

'Shh,' said the Doctor, the raised hand curling into a fist aside from an extended forefinger which jabbed the air in emphasis. 'I think we're there.'

'Where?'

'Where we're going.'

Sam huffed in exasperation. 'Yeah, but where's that?'

The Doctor glanced at her, then silently pointed in front of him. Sam scrambled up behind him and peered over his shoulder. Some twenty or thirty feet below them the glowing, pulsing walls of the chute ended in a dark circle. Sam screwed up her eyes, but the glare from the walls around her prevented her from seeing anything except vague, lumpy shadows.

'I wish we knew what was down there,' she said, and then, as the Doctor opened his mouth to reply, 'Yeah, I know – there's only one way to find out.'

Litefoot and Emmeline had joined them now. 'You all right, Em?' Sam asked for what seemed like the hundredth time.

Emmeline nodded.

'The moment of truth, eh?' hissed Litefoot excitedly, and reaching into his jacket pocket produced his revolver. 'With your permission, Doctor, I think perhaps I had better take the lead at this juncture. That way I can protect the ladies, if needs be.'

Sam opened her mouth to protest, but the Doctor effectively plugged it with a jelly baby which he produced out of nowhere, simultaneously closing his other hand around Litefoot's revolver.

'That won't be necessary, Professor,' he said mildly. 'We come in peace.'

'Yeah,' said Sam, chewing, 'but do they know that?'

The Doctor smiled. 'Let's see, shall we?'

He slid-crawled down the last thirty feet of chute, paused a moment at the circular mouth to glance around, then dropped into the shadows. Sam followed suit, unable to fully shake off the notion that any second now she would drop into a vast stomach and immediately begin to liquefy in the acidic digestive juices that churned down there.

She gritted her teeth as she reached the end of the chute and dropped into darkness as the Doctor had done. Even though she bent her knees to cushion her body from the impact of landing, the unexpectedly short fall jarred her legs and caused her to lose her balance. However she managed to convert her momentum into a forward roll and sprang immediately to her feet in what she hoped looked a professional and athletic manner.

Even as Litefoot and Emmeline were being helped out of the

end of the chute by the Doctor, Sam was looking keenly around at her surroundings.

Her first thought was that the four of them had emerged in a hobbit hole – or at least some kind of weird root system. The walls, floor and ceiling of the circular chamber they stood in appeared to be composed of a mass of orange and green fibres, so densely packed that it did not look possible to force even a coin between one strand and the next. There were no straight lines or sharp angles visible anywhere, and though the chamber was sparse it was certainly not featureless. Twisted nodules and protuberances jutted seemingly haphazardly from every surface, some of which resembled strange roots, some giant fungi, some monstrously deformed pieces of exotic fruit, and some fleshy, bell-shaped flowers without bloom.

There was some light here too, though not much. What there was seemed to come from the walls themselves, the entwined fibres releasing a greenish glow like rotting swamp moss. More light, of a more luminous green, was provided by a viscous substance which moved sluggishly through what appeared to be rope-thick, pulsing veins which criss-crossed the walls, floor and ceiling.

Aside from the mouth of the chute, the only other means of access to and from this chamber was an arched, tunnel-like opening covered by some kind of opaque, crystalline membrane in the opposite wall. As Sam noticed this, she became aware for the first time that the chamber was not silent. From all around them, from within the walls themselves, there was a constant burbling-shushing noise, rhythmic, almost soothing.

It's like being inside a giant womb, she thought wonderingly. She was about to turn and share this observation with the others when a muffled but distinctive roar from somewhere beyond the arched opening froze the words in her throat.

Cyborgs! There were cyborgs down here! Sam suddenly had the horrible feeling that she and her friends had emerged in the equivalent of the lion enclosure at London Zoo. At least the Doctor had his sonic screwdriver, but how effective would that be if half a dozen of the things suddenly came at them? She turned to say something, but the Doctor was already at her shoulder. Absently he patted her arm. 'Brave heart, Tegan,' he murmured.

She didn't have time to ask him what he was talking about, because he was already past her, moving towards the opening. She hurried to catch up with him. 'Doctor, what are you doing?' she hissed.

'Exploring.'

'Yeah, but that noise –'

'Oh, don't worry about that,' he said airily. 'The cyborgs may have the brawn but we have the brains. It's no contest.'

Sam wasn't so sure about that. She looked back at the others. Emmeline was still moving like a sleepwalker, barely even looking around her. Litefoot's eyes, by contrast, were everywhere, drinking in his surroundings. He would have looked the perfect image of the innocent abroad, if it wasn't for the revolver which he clutched firmly in his right hand.

'Fascinating. Absolutely fascinating,' he muttered. 'I say, Doctor, have you ever seen anything remotely like this before?'

'Yes, I have,' said the Doctor.

'What a surprise,' said Sam. 'Perhaps you'd like to let the rest of us in on it, then? Arm us with a bit of information. I mean, you never know when it might prove useful.'

'Organic crystallography,' said the Doctor.

'I beg your pardon?' said Litefoot.

'That's the term for the technology you see around you.

Peculiar to a particular star cluster in the Biphaelides System.'

'You know who the aliens are then?' said Sam.

'I have a very strong suspicion. And if you would just care to follow me…'

He stepped forward and with a beelike buzzing the crystalline membrane covering the arch slid up into the roof, allowing the Doctor to step through.

'…I'll take you on a little guided tour.'

He turned and strolled off down the corridor that lay beyond the arch, looking for all the world as if he owned the place. The others followed, Sam glancing around tentatively. The walls, floor and ceiling of the corridor were made of the same root-like material as the chamber they had just left. She heard another roar, which, although it sounded closer this time, could have come from anywhere. She gritted her teeth, but said nothing, deciding to put her faith in the Doctor. Although he could be ridiculously reckless, he had managed to keep her alive so far.

This corridor curved round a corner and ended in another crystalline door. The Doctor walked towards it unhesitatingly. Once again, it slid up and into the roof at his approach.

The room they now found themselves in had more features than those they had seen so far. On one wall was a kind of control panel that looked to have been hewn from a gigantic crystal and then partly engulfed by a fungal-like growth. Instead of knobs and levers and switches, the panel was covered with a profusion of the fleshy nodules and protuberances that jutted and bulged from every surface around them. Beside the control panel were an irregular row of what appeared to be convex screens shuttered with thick curtains of membrane.

Confidently the Doctor walked over to the control panel and was just reaching out his hands to the alien controls when his head jerked up and he looked towards the door through which they had entered.

'What's the matter?' asked Sam.

'Quick,' said the Doctor, ushering them into the narrow gap between the control panel and the wall. 'Everybody hide.'

He dived behind the control panel himself just as the crystalline door slid open with its familiar buzzing sound. Squashed against Emmeline, head hunched into her shoulders, chin resting on her upraised knees, Sam heard movement as something, or several somethings, entered the chamber. She heard the arrivals move across the floor towards the row of screens, and when she felt it was safe enough she slowly craned her neck and peered around the edge of the control panel. What she saw seemed to suck the air out of her lungs, and she had to clap a hand over her mouth to prevent herself gasping for breath.

Three aliens had entered the chamber, one of which Sam assumed to be male, the others female. The 'male' was the most fearsome in appearance. Squat and powerful, it was fiery orange in colour, with a huge, domed head that sprouted direct from its broad shoulders. Its deep-set eyes were glints of dark malevolence beneath its vast brow. It had an almost ferret-like snout and a tiny, down-turned mouth. A row of suckers, like small funnels, ran from the centre of its brow, up over its head, and down its back in a Mohican-like crest. There were more rows of suckers running down its chest and arms and legs, and congregating in tiny barnacled clusters on its torso.

The 'females' were smaller and slimmer than their companion, still with the same domed head but with perfectly smooth, maggot-white skin. Their hands and feet were small and dainty, and in contrast to the prowling male they moved with an almost balletic grace. Sam drew her head back down behind the panel and looked at her companions. Evidently due to the expression on her face, Litefoot gave her a quizzical look. Sam responded by

128

grimacing and rolling her eyes.

The question burst out of her the instant the aliens had gone. 'Doctor, what were those things?'

'Zygons,' the Doctor said, and nodded, seemingly unconcerned.

'I thought as much.'

'You've come across them before, then?'

'Yes, though only a small warrior faction. I encountered them about ninety years from now, give or take a decade or so. They had crash-landed on Earth centuries before. I knew very little about them at the time, but I've read various texts since. They're a fascinating species, a hermaphrodite race. Each adult is able to produce and self-fertilise its own eggs, which it lays in clusters of between five and twenty, three or four times a lifetime. Their society is divided quite rigidly into warrior-engineers, scientists and civilians. However, to become a warrior-engineer, which is considered a great honour, a Zygon must first undergo the ritual of sterilisation. This has the effect of drawing out their fierce but latent aggressiveness and, supposedly, making them more single-minded in battle.'

'Stupid, you mean,' said Sam, 'like most men.'

'Interestingly,' said the Doctor, ignoring the interruption, 'an added effect of sterilisation is that it alters not only the Zygon's personality, but also its appearance. In its natural state a Zygon has smooth, creamy-white skin and is dainty, almost feminine, in appearance. After sterilisation, however, its body fills out, its skin colour deepens to a reddish-orange as it becomes suffused with blood, and it develops body armour, rather like a porcupine raising its quills, in the form of suckers which, if a Zygon is attacked, release a deadly poison.'

'Sounds delightful,' murmured Litefoot.

'Is there anything else we should know?' asked Sam.

'Plenty,' said the Doctor, and began to count facts out on his fingers as he listed them. 'Every Zygon has a "sting", again poison-based, which it can use to stun, paralyse or kill its victim. They have the technology to transform their physical appearance – literally to alter the colour, shape and texture of their flesh – in order to imitate individuals of particular species, based on that individual's mind and body print. They use their cyborgs – which are called Skarasen – both as milk-cows, living on their lactic fluid, and as devastatingly effective weapons of destruction. Oh, and they're very partial to board games.'

Sam pursed her lips thoughtfully. 'Doctor, you said the other mob, the ones you met in the future, had crashed centuries before. But they were all warriors, so they couldn't lay eggs, right?'

'Right.'

'So that must mean they live for a very long time.'

The Doctor nodded. 'Compared with humans they do. A Zygon's average life span is around seven hundred to a thousand years.'

Sam whistled. 'That's old.'

'Do you mind?' said the Doctor indignantly. 'If I were a Zygon, I'd be –' Then he caught Litefoot's bemused expression. 'Never mind.'

'So where do these Zygons come from?' Sam asked.

'Originally a planet called Zygor, but that was destroyed by a stellar explosion. They're homeless now.'

'Maybe they could get jobs flogging *The Big Issue*,' said Sam.

The Doctor gave her a withering look and moved back across to the control panel, flexing his fingers. He began to tweak and twist the alien controls seemingly at random, though only a few seconds later Sam was stepping back and Litefoot stifling an exclamation as the membranes slowly peeled back like eyelids.

Now they could see that the screens were in fact observation windows, looking down on what appeared to be a swamp. The surface of the swamp was wreathed with a drifting green mist, and as Sam looked closer she realised that what she had instantly taken for moss-covered trees and bushes and rocks were in fact peculiar tangled structures, made of some furry green substance she couldn't identify, but whose shapes reminded her of vast wax sculptures that had been exposed to too much heat and had drooped and sagged and partly melded together.

So incredible was this sight that she didn't notice the Skarasen until they started to move. Then she realised that there were two of them, massive reptiles each thirty to forty feet long, weaving through the scum and the mist, eyes rolling in their savage, blunt-snouted heads, their silver-scaled bodies possessing an unnatural metallic sheen.

All at once the two Skarasen began to thrash and writhe in the scummy water, apparently squabbling over a chunk of meat. One of the cyborgs had the meat clamped in its jaws and the other was lunging forward, attempting to tear it from its companion's grasp.

Litefoot stiffened. 'Gad,' he murmured.

'What's up, Professor?' asked Sam.

He turned to her, his nostrils flaring with distaste. Evidently making an effort to control the horror he was feeling, he said, 'I believe you would be well advised to avert your gaze from the distressing scene below, Miss Samantha.'

Immediately Sam looked down into the swamp with renewed interest. 'Why?' she said. 'I don't see what –' And then she *did* see. 'Oh my God!'

The two Skarasen were not merely tearing at a chunk of meat, but at a partly devoured human corpse. The legs of the corpse were already gone, and even as Sam watched, a good portion of the torso disappeared with a rending of flesh and a crunching of bones. The Skarasen that was still clinging to its prize, shook the corpse in its jaws, like a predator subduing its prey. Sam saw an arm and a head flop like those of a rag doll. Then the Doctor's hand curled around her shoulder and he drew her gently away.

'That was… *horrible!*' she said, putting her hand to her mouth.

'Yes,' said the Doctor gently, 'it was. But if it's any consolation, I don't think the poor chap was eaten alive.'

'The scoundrels murdered him first, do you mean?' exclaimed Litefoot.

The Doctor shook his head. 'No, I think it's more likely that the body was stolen from its grave. To feed the Skarasen the Zygons would need an almost endless supply of bodies. I think dozens of murders in such a short time in so small an area would be bound to attract attention, don't you?'

Litefoot glanced down into the swamp once more. 'I've never seen creatures of such size,' he marvelled.

'Oh, those are just babies,' said the Doctor, 'like the one that attacked us in the cellar. Even the one that killed Tom Donahue still had quite a bit of growing to do. I suspect the Zygons are pumping the meat full of hormones to speed up the creatures' growth rate.'

'Whatever for?' asked Litefoot.

'Oh, invasion. Colonisation. Something boring like that.' The Doctor gave Sam a reassuring squeeze, then turned back to the control panel. He tweaked a few more ganglions and the membranous shutters slid back across the eyelike windows.

'How are we all feeling?' he asked, looking at Sam.

'Fine,' she said defiantly.

'Splendid. Then we'd better move on. Places to go, people to see and all that.'

'Forgive my curiosity, Doctor,' Litefoot said, 'but what precisely, now that we *are* here, is our plan of attack?'

The Doctor shrugged. 'I thought we'd introduce ourselves,

have a little chat, perhaps some light refreshment.'

'You're not serious,' said Sam.

'I'm always serious,' said the Doctor. He led them across the observation chamber and through another of the crystalline doors.

For a while they weaved through the Zygon ship, Sam feeling like a little kid walking through a haunted house, waiting for something nasty to leap out at her. However, even after passing through myriad rooms both large and small, most of which contained more of the Zygons' peculiarly organic technology, the place remained seemingly deserted.

Eventually they entered a room that contained a mass of fleshy vines hanging from the ceiling like loops of intestine. When he saw it, the Doctor tutted. 'Very nasty, that. They'll need a trilanic flange oscillator with detachable spirons to fix that little lot.'

Sam smiled at Litefoot's baffled expression and said, 'There don't seem to be many Zygons around, Doctor.'

'No, it *is* odd,' the Doctor mused. 'Especially when the indications are that this is quite a sizeable community.'

'When you say "sizeable", Doctor, to how many of these creatures are you referring?' inquired Litefoot.

The Doctor spread his hands. 'Well, it's difficult to say exactly. Five hundred? A thousand? Something along those lines?'

'Maybe they're all playing Monopoly,' suggested Sam.

The Doctor smiled. 'Maybe.'

They filed through yet another door and found themselves in an observation area very similar to the one overlooking the swamp that had contained the Skarasen. In fact, it was so similar that Sam said, 'Oh no, we've come in a circle. We're back at Pets' Corner.'

'I don't think so,' said the Doctor, and walked over to the control panel, which perched beside a row of shuttered windows almost identical to those in the previous chamber. He flexed his fingers and manipulated a number of the controls. As the shutters peeled away, a peculiar purplish light filled the chamber from the room beyond.

Bracing herself, Sam stepped forward and looked into the room. Almost immediately she gasped, though not with horror but awe. The room she was looking into was vast, as big as an aircraft hangar; she could barely see the opposite wall, lost as it was in a thick soup of plum-coloured shadow. Covering every square inch of floor was a grid-like construction resembling a gigantic honeycomb, though made not of wax but of a lumpy, glassy substance. And within each of the honeycomb's individual compartments were clusters of creamy-white, perfectly round eggs.

'It's... incredible,' she murmured, feeling the hair tingling on her scalp.

'Incubation area,' said the Doctor almost matter-of-factly. 'There are thousands of eggs in there. A potential invasion force. Our friends have been busy.'

'And you, Doctor, have been extremely foolish,' Emmeline said, her voice strangely harsh, brittle. Sam turned to look at her and couldn't believe what she was seeing. Emmeline's body was encased in a shimmering red aura, her clothes and flesh bleeding into a single jelly-like mass. Her features were changing, softening, running like tallow.

'Oh, Christ,' said Sam softly as she realised what was happening.

Before their very eyes, Emmeline was turning into a Zygon.

CHAPTER 6
BALAAK

'A trap,' said the Doctor with almost child-like wonder. Then he nodded. 'I thought it might be.'

Beside him, Litefoot instinctively raised his revolver. Before he could do anything so foolish as fire, however, the Doctor twisted it from his grasp and tossed it to the floor.

'We're not here to fight, Professor,' he said mildly. 'We're here to talk.'

Litefoot looked at him, wild-eyed, then he swallowed and seemed to recover a little. He nodded quickly. 'Yes, of course, Doctor. Forgive me. It was the shock of seeing such a fearsome… that is to say, monstrous…'

'I'd shut up now before you offend somebody,' hissed Sam.

The shimmering aura around Emmeline's body evaporated and now a fully fledged Zygon warrior stood before them.

They had barely got over the shock when doors opened at either side of the chamber and more of the creatures appeared. Most were warriors, though there were a number of white-skinned scientists hovering at the back of the group. Sam tried to adopt the Doctor's expression of scientific interest, though found it difficult. Her heart was pumping not only with apprehension but with sheer physical revulsion. The thought of one of these creatures actually touching her made her skin crawl.

The creatures crowded closer, the Zygon warriors advancing with ponderous menace, the scientists moving with an almost mincing step.

'Hello,' said the Doctor warmly, raising a hand in greeting. 'May

I say what a pleasure it is to encounter your charming species once again. As... er... Emmeline here will tell you, we've come to have a chat about things, see if we can't come to some mutually beneficial –'

'Silence, human,' the Zygon that had been impersonating Emmeline said in a hissing, gurgling voice.

'I'm sorry, I was only –'

'Where is the sonic device that you used to incapacitate our Skarasen?' one of the Zygon scientists asked, gliding forward. Its voice, in contrast to that of the warrior that had spoken, was soft, fluting, akin to the voice a songbird might possess if it could speak.

'In my pocket,' said the Doctor.

'Make him produce it,' the Zygon scientist said to the warrior that had been impersonating Emmeline.

Several of the Zygon warriors began to move forward. 'There's no need for that,' the Doctor said hastily. 'I'll happily show it to you.' He slipped his hand into his pocket and produced his sonic screwdriver, which he held up for all to see.

A couple of the Zygon scientists cringed. 'Make him drop it,' one of them squealed.

'Jesus! Doctor!' Sam warned, clutching his free arm. The Zygon warrior nearest to her had extended and opened its hands, unsheathing a number of thorn-like spikes from suckers on its palms.

Calmly the Doctor dropped the sonic screwdriver to the floor. Instantly one of the Zygon scientists darted forward and dropped what looked like a wriggling blob of slug-like flesh on to it. The blob of flesh adhered to the device, immediately extending antenna-like tentacles which it wrapped tightly around the handle. The Zygon scientist moved across the room and delicately tweaked a control that resembled a small green mushroom on the bottom left of the panel.

Immediately the blob of flesh began to glow and to emit a shrill whistling sound, like a note of distress. Barely a second had passed, however, before the sound was silenced by an intense flash of light that caused Sam and Litefoot to throw their arms up in front of their faces. As the light faded, Sam blinked the after-image of the flare away and peered down at the place where the sonic screwdriver had been. There was now nothing left of it but a blackened, twisted lump of smoking metal.

'I hate it when people do that,' said the Doctor ruefully. 'It took me long enough to get round to building a new one after the last time.'

'You will come with us,' the Zygon scientist who had destroyed the sonic screwdriver trilled. The creature turned and moved to the door on the far side of the chamber, which slid open to admit it.

As the Zygon warriors began to close in once again, the Doctor said, 'It's all right, you don't have to push,' and began to stride after the Zygon scientist, his coat flying behind him. Sam fell into step behind the Doctor, sticking close to him, while Litefoot, looking somewhat shell-shocked, brought up the rear.

The three of them were escorted through yet more rooms and corridors until they reached an area which contained a number of crystalline alcoves set into the wall. In each alcove was a motionless human body, held upright by an entwining mass of fibrous tentacles. Though the face of each human was partly concealed by a spongy, veinlike cowl of softly pulsing tissue, Sam recognised Emmeline and pointed her out. The Doctor nodded and indicated a tall man in a dark suit. 'This is her father,' he said, 'Nathaniel Seers. Owner of the factory above us.'

'What hellish treatment have these poor unfortunates been subjected to, Doctor?' Litefoot whispered.

'Their mind and body prints have been extracted by the Zygons,' said the Doctor. 'As long as they're hooked up to that brain-drain thingy there the Zygons can impersonate them at will.'

'Are they dead?' asked Sam.

'No, just unconscious. They'll probably wake up with a bit of a headache, though.'

'If this lot ever allow them to wake up at all,' muttered Sam.

The Doctor flashed her an encouraging smile. 'Don't worry, I'm sure we'll be able to sort something out.'

'You will each enter one of these cubicles,' hissed a Zygon warrior, indicating several unoccupied alcoves beyond the initial row of humans. Sam was not sure whether it was the Zygon that had been impersonating Emmeline that had spoken. Much as she hated to admit it, they all looked pretty much the same to her.

'Ah, well, that's very kind of you,' the Doctor said, 'but we'd really rather not if you don't mind.'

'You have no choice, human. Either you each enter a cubicle or you die.'

'Hang on, that means we do have a choice,' said Sam with a cheeky bravado that she didn't really feel. A Zygon swung round on her, hissing. 'All right, all right,' she said, holding up her hands and stepping hastily towards one of the alcoves. 'Just don't tell me it's only a shower, that's all.'

She stepped into the alcove and turned round. She felt sick with fear and her heart was racing in her chest, but she was determined to give the impression that all this was nothing more than a minor inconvenience. Beside her, Litefoot was stepping up into an alcove too. He gave her a quick, nervous smile.

'Bit of a bummer, eh, Professor?' Sam said loudly. 'I only hope this hairdryer thing won't give me split ends.'

'Quite,' Litefoot said, though Sam could tell he didn't know what the hell she was talking about. Then he stepped into the alcove and she could no longer see him.

The Doctor, meanwhile, was talking quickly and earnestly, willing the Zygons to listen to him. 'Look, all this is totally unnecessary. We came here of our own free will to speak to you, perhaps even to help you.'

'Zygons do not need the help of aliens,' one of the Zygon warriors said.

'Ah, now, well I'm afraid we all know that's not true, don't we? Why don't you just give me a chance, eh? I've met your people before, I understand your technology. I can help you, I promise. And I want to, believe me.'

'You wish to help us destroy your own species?' the warrior that had spoken before hissed mockingly.

The Doctor shook his head. 'No no no no. Look, you're a civilised, intelligent race. There's really no need for all this aggression.' He appealed to the Zygon scientists who were still fluttering about at the back of the group like ghosts. 'Surely you're interested in how I know so much about your people and in how I happen to own a sonic device that is far in advance of present Earth technology? Admit it: you must be just a teeny-weeny bit curious.'

The Zygon scientists looked at each other, as if each was waiting for one of the others to act as spokesperson. Finally one of them said in its soft, melodious voice, 'We do not need you to tell us anything. Once a print has been taken of your body and mind, all your thoughts, memories, and knowledge will belong to us.'

'I wouldn't be so sure of that,' said the Doctor. 'Look, I don't want to boast, and I don't wish to insult you, but bigger and nastier people than you have tried to suck my brains out before with no success whatsoever – well, not much anyway.'

The Zygon warrior that had done most of the talking suddenly lunged forward, reaching out hands that were vicious with spikes. 'I have heard enough,' it hissed. 'Enter the cubicle now, human, or die.'

The Doctor eyed a bead of green poison glinting on the tip of one of the spikes. 'Ah well, I suppose if you put it like that,' he said, backing into the alcove next to Litefoot. 'But I'm warning you, if this brain-sucking machine of yours breaks down, don't come crying to me.'

Once the Doctor was inside the alcove, one of the Zygon scientists hurried forward. It ran its slim, delicate fingers over a crystalline panel that was set into the wall beside the Doctor's cubicle, playing it almost as if it was a keyboard. Where its fingertips touched the panel, different-coloured lights within it flared then died. Finally it turned to a twisted knot of fleshy, trumpet-like growths jutting from the wall and began to squeeze and twist them in delicate, almost ritualistic movements. Instantly dozens of thick fibrous tentacles shot from apertures in the walls, ceiling and floor of the cubicle and entwined themselves tightly around the Doctor, holding his body rigid. The Doctor sighed, not even bothering to struggle, as the fleshy cowl, pulsing and veined like a flattened heart, came down from the ceiling and closed over his head. It was an unpleasant sensation: the cowl was cold and clammy, and moulded itself to the shape of his head, oozing down over his face to cover his eyes, cheeks, ears and the bridge of his nose. He could feel it pulsing against his eyelids. His nostrils twitched; it had the pungent, brackish smell of old, raw tripe. He hoped that Sam and Litefoot wouldn't find the sensation too unbearable.

'Try to relax,' he shouted for their benefit. 'Sam, George, don't struggle and try not to panic. Just close your eyes and relax. Empty your minds.'

He felt a tugging sensation, not on his head but inside it, as if the cowl was a giant leech that had gnawed through his skull into his brain. He gritted his teeth, fought back against the mental pressure, and instantly it went away. A moment later it was back, however, redoubled. The Doctor sent it away again. Over the course of the next few minutes the tugging sensation increased until it became uncomfortable, and then, as he continued to fight back, increased again, until gradually, inevitably, it escalated into tearing, white-hot pain.

And still the Doctor fought on, his body shuddering, drenched in sweat, his face contorted with agony. Now it felt as if his skull was open, as if hands were reaching into it, pushing thick, meaty fingers down the sides, trying to wrench his brain from its moorings. Not until he felt black speckles of unconsciousness creeping through his defences, however, did he accept that the battle – though not the war, *never* the war – was lost. He let go, mentally jumping feet first into the too-familiar long black tunnel. So many times throughout his long lives had he been rendered unconscious that he couldn't help but think he was about to reacquaint himself with an old but dubious friend.

Though he knew he was being foolish, Albert Rudge could not rid himself of the notion that their employer knew exactly what he and Jack were planning. Every time the man had looked at him this evening, Albert had felt sure he could feel those grey eyes boring into his skull. Once he had even found himself putting his hand up as if to shield his forehead; on another occasion the man had stared at him with such intent that Albert had had to bite his lip to prevent himself blurting out both a confession and a plea for forgiveness.

Now Albert was on his knees, scrabbling among the muddy cobbles for the coins that their employer had tossed carelessly, even contemptuously, to the ground, just as he did every evening. The sulphur-choked air was thick with drizzle, and though Albert's fingers and face were frozen, his heart felt like a red-hot poker stabbing repeatedly into his chest. He was alone for the moment, though a few seconds before he had still been able to hear the fading rattle of their employer's cart trundling over the cobbles. The instant the cart had disappeared into the mist, Jack had scampered hot-foot in the opposite direction, to retrieve the nag that he had bullied Ned Cockles into lending them for the night.

'Hurry it up there, Albert,' a voice hissed suddenly. 'We need to be away if we're not to lose our quarry.'

Albert jumped, certain for a moment that their employer had returned on foot to tear the truth out of him. Then the meaning of the words permeated his fear-sodden mind, and, looking up, he saw Jack emerging from the mist, his familiar meaty frame swathed in several layers of stained and ragged clothing.

Painfully Albert rose to his feet. As he eyed the horse that Jack was leading on a piece of rope, he gave an inward sigh of relief. In fact, so relieved was he that he couldn't prevent a chuckle escaping him.

'What tickles you?' Jack asked dangerously, rain dripping from the brim of his billycock hat.

'Forgive me, Jack,' said Albert, 'but it's this horse.'

'What of it?' said Jack.

'Well, it's nothing but a bag of bones and it sags in the middle. I doubt it could even support the weight of a saddle, never mind you and me.'

'You'd do well to shut that prattling mouth of yours and jump up here behind me,' Jack growled, hauling himself astride the animal.

Albert half expected the horse to fold in two beneath Jack's weight, but it stood surprisingly firm.

'Quickly now, unless you want to be dragged along by

your hair,' Jack said.

Hastily, with Jack's help, Albert scrambled up on to the horse. He wrapped his arms miserably around his companion's waist as Jack dug in his heels and urged the horse forward. Above the hiss of rain, the clop of hooves and the jangling of their night's wages in his pockets, Albert could still feel and hear the painful thud of his heart. Jack's voice was full of cheer, his talk full of the riches and opportunities that would soon be coming their way, but all that filled Albert's mind was the dread memory of a pair of staring grey eyes that had seemed to burn into his soul.

The Doctor licked his lips and murmured, 'Just one egg this morning, please, Matron. I'm not feeling terribly well.' Then his eyes sprang open and he sat bolt upright, looking around.

He was in what was evidently a cell on the Zygon ship. The fibrous, dimly glowing walls burbled around him like a giant digestive system. Above the door an eye-like camera on a quivering stalk monitored his every move. The Doctor waved to the camera and smiled. 'Any chance of a cup of tea?'

Moments later the door slid open and two Zygon warriors entered. Without a word, they each grabbed one of the Doctor's arms, hauled him to his feet and dragged him along a number of corridors. Eventually they reached a huge domed room packed from floor to ceiling with Zygon technology. Many of the weirdly organic control panels, manned by both Zygon warriors and scientists, stood around the floor in no particular pattern as though they had grown from seeds that had been scattered there. A screen like a gigantic veined lens dominated one wall, and above the Doctor's head, looping down from the ceiling, were thick furry lengths of vine. Clusters of glittering crystals set into the walls reflected the pulsing, greenish light.

'Ah, the nerve centre,' the Doctor said before being hurled

unceremoniously to the floor. Immediately he jumped up, dusting himself down. 'Very pretty.'

A Zygon warrior lumbered forward. It was bigger and more fearsome-looking than its fellows, with a scarred and puckered face that was almost on a level with the Doctor's. It regarded him for a moment, its deep-set eyes glinting darkly like a shark's, and betraying just as little emotion. Finally it rasped, 'I am Balaak, warlord of the Zygons.'

'Very nice to meet you,' said the Doctor politely, holding out a hand, which was duly ignored. 'I'm the Doctor – though I think I'd be right in saying that we've already met, haven't we?'

He was referring to his encounter with Nathaniel Seers earlier that day or the day before. Balaak, however, did not acknowledge the question. Instead the Zygon hissed, 'We know who you are. We know your every secret, Time Lord.'

The Doctor knew that Balaak's final words had been gauged to provoke a reaction – which was precisely why he didn't bat an eyelid. Instead he said in a reasonable voice, 'Ah, well, pardon me for contradicting you, but I don't think that's really the case is it? I mean, if it was, I wouldn't be standing here. I'd still be hooked up to your machine, having a little nap.'

He half expected the Zygon warlord to hiss angrily, perhaps to unsheathe the thorns in its palms and threaten his life, but instead it merely looked at him with a kind of shrewd malevolence. 'You have an astute mind, Time Lord, like most of your invidious race. Astute but diffuse, and therefore ultimately feeble.'

'Still managed to break your nasty little machine, though, didn't I?' the Doctor said, the acidity of his words belied by his polite tone and charming smile. 'If I hadn't you wouldn't have thrown me in the brig and waited for me to wake up. You'd have just got one of your chaps to plug into my mind print and soak up my memories and knowledge. That would have been much less bother than having the real thing running around, annoying people.'

Again Balaak paused before replying. The Zygon warlord was possessed of an unnerving stillness, like a scorpion preparing to strike. It opened its mouth, produced a gnarled, sucker-encrusted tongue, and ran it slowly over a double row of sharp, white, triangular teeth.

'It is true that our technology and your anatomy were... incompatible,' Balaak said at last. 'However, we were able to secure a partial mind print.'

'Not enough of one to be useful, though, I'll bet,' said the Doctor.

'Useful enough. We know that you possess a time craft.'

'But you don't know how to operate it, do you?' the Doctor said, smiling.

'Not yet. But you will show us.'

'And if I refuse? No, let me guess – you'll kill my friends.'

'Slowly,' said Balaak, drawing out the word so that it echoed sibilantly around the vast, high-domed room.

The Doctor sighed. 'Yes, that's usually the kind of deal I get offered. I don't suppose it'll help if I offer you and your crew a lift to anywhere at any time in the universe?'

Balaak's eyes glittered contemptuously. 'Zygons do not accept charity from aliens. Neither do we abandon a course of action once it has been initiated. Unlike the Time Lords, we are a proud race, Doctor.'

'Sometimes pride and stupidity are indistinguishable,' the Doctor murmured.

Again Balaak bared its teeth. The Doctor wondered whether the expression was intended as a snarl or a humourless grin. 'You walked like an innocent into our trap. You are our prisoner, to whom the only choice left is to serve us or die. Who is the stupid one, Doctor?'

The Doctor pursed his lips and frowned. 'Is that a trick

question?' Then he flapped his arms as though to wave Balaak to silence. 'No, no, hang on. You see, the thing is, Balaak, you're only looking at the situation from the most obvious angle. No offence, but it's a viewpoint typical of the military mind. What you're forgetting is that I might have a hidden agenda. The fact that I haven't is neither here nor there, but then again I might be lying about that, in which case – hello, Professor.'

The greeting was directed at the familiar figure of Litefoot, who had just strolled nonchalantly into the room. In this setting he looked grotesquely, even comically, incongruous. Litefoot glanced mockingly at the Doctor before turning to Balaak.

'It's all right,' the Doctor said, 'I know you're not really Litefoot. The walk's all wrong. Just give me a shout any time and I'll give you one or two pointers. I'm free most Wednesday afternoons.'

'Be quiet, Time Lord,' Balaak hissed. 'Your inane chatter is beginning to annoy me.'

Solemnly the Doctor ran his fingers over his lips in a zipping motion.

Balaak turned back to the Zygon that was wearing Litefoot's form. 'Give me your report.'

The Zygon spoke in Litefoot's clipped, plummy tones. 'Everything went smoothly, Commander. I performed the human's daily duties with ease. None of his fellow creatures suspected a thing.'

'Excellent. And the female? The housekeeper?'

'I informed her that the professor's house guests had departed. She accepted the information without argument.'

Balaak inclined its huge, domed head. 'You have done well, Veidra.'

'Thank you, Commander. May I have your permission to dispense with this loathsome form?'

'Has the lock that the Time Lord damaged with his sonic device been repaired yet?' asked Balaak, turning to a Zygon scientist working at a nearby console.

There was a quiver in the white Zygon's fluting voice. 'Not yet, Commander. It was not considered a priority task.'

Balaak gave a hiss of annoyance and turned back to Veidra. 'I want the lock repaired without delay. No detail, however small, must be overlooked. Do it now, Veidra, and retain your human form until the task is completed.'

'Yes, Commander,' Veidra said and walked out of the control room.

'Well, at least I know Litefoot's still alive,' the Doctor said, aware that the Zygons would otherwise have been unable to use his body print. 'I trust Sam is, too?'

'Certainly, Doctor,' said Balaak. 'Would you like to see her?'

'The real her or the poor imitation, do you mean?'

'Your gibes are pointless, Doctor,' Balaak said. 'They are a waste of your limited breath.'

'Oh, I don't know,' the Doctor sighed. 'I mean, if you can't laugh, what can you do?'

This time Balaak ignored him. Instead the Zygon warlord turned and beckoned to the scientist who had spoken a few moments before. The scientist came forward, evidently nervous. In contrast to Balaak, its features were delicate, almost feline.

'Tuval will accompany you to your time craft,' Balaak said to the Doctor. 'You will explain to Tuval how it operates, and then the two of you will pilot the craft back here. While you are gone, we will be monitoring Tuval's synchron response constantly. If you attempt to injure Tuval, the synchron response will fluctuate and your friends will be fed to our Skarasen. If you deceive but do not physically harm Tuval, Tuval will transmit a telepathic message on a frequency that again will cause the synchron response to fluctuate. I hope you will be wise, therefore, Doctor, and not try to take advantage of your partial liberty.'

'Oh, I will,' said the Doctor humbly, and raised his eyebrows. 'Telepathic abilities, eh? When did you make that little evolutionary jump?'

'It is a skill like any other. My scientists perfected the technique after many years of dedicated research. There is nothing, Doctor, that we Zygons cannot achieve in time. Even here, stranded on this primitive planet, we continue to progress.'

'Your ambition does you credit,' said the Doctor. 'I suppose you control your Skarasen telepathically now too?'

'Of course,' said Balaak.

The Doctor whistled. 'Well, I must say you're a bit more advanced than the last mob of Zygons I ran into – or rather, am going to run into in a century or so. Mind you, they were all warriors like yourself, Balaak. No brains, no imagination, no means to procreate…'

'Your attempts to goad me are pathetic, Doctor. I find your company, not to mention your physical appearance, repugnant. It is time for you to go. Tuval.'

The Zygon scientist gave a nod of acknowledgement and immediately a reddish aura appeared around its body. The aura thickened, became a swirling, incandescent cocoon of pure, localised energy that was difficult to focus upon. Within the cocoon, the Doctor, squinting, saw Tuval's delicate features shimmer and start to change. Within moments the process was complete. The reddish aura faded. Standing in front of the Doctor now, looking up at him, face expressionless, was a perfect facsimile of Sam.

Surprising himself, Albert Rudge blurted suddenly, 'There was something mighty peculiar about the manner of our gentleman tonight.'

Ever since he and Jack had begun pursuit of their quarry, Albert had wanted to express the misgivings he had had all evening, his notion that their employer knew exactly what they were up to. Because he had been afraid of Jack's response, however, the words had lodged firmly in his throat each time he had tried to speak. Albert knew all too well that once Jack had hit upon a scheme that gave him an excellent opportunity to line his pockets, he did not take kindly to any utterance from his colleagues that might be construed as doubt or anxiety or dissent. For this reason Albert felt a sense not of relief but apprehension at the fact that he had finally managed to express what was on his mind.

Sitting in front of him, his voice muffled by drizzle and fog, Jack growled, 'What the deuce are you babbling about now?'

Instantly Albert felt what little resolve he had evaporating. Gamely, however, he said, 'You must have taken notice of him, Jack. He was not himself this evening.'

'Who was he then?' Jack muttered dangerously.

'He was… he was the same man and yet not the same. There was a change about him. The way he looked at us, the way he moved and spoke. My fear is that he may have got wind of our plan.'

'Ha! And who has told him? You?'

'Not I! I've not breathed a word to no one.'

'Nor I. So it appears, as ever, that you're whistling in the dark, Albert, old chum.'

Though the words in themselves seemed friendly, Jack's manner was not. Albert was all too aware that should he push Jack too far, Jack would very likely knock him off the back of Ned Cockles's nag and then urge the animal to trample all over him for good measure. Nevertheless he felt compelled to add, 'All the same, Jack, I fancy caution should be the order of the day.'

Jack shook his head, rain spinning off the brim of his hat. 'Here

I am, trying to make you rich, and all you do to repay me is babble in my ear like a frightened old crone! Perhaps you believe this gentleman of ours has been secretly observing us at work, listening to our every exchange? Or perhaps he has a twin brother... No, wait, perhaps there's an entire army of 'em. Perhaps they are lying in wait even as we speak, making ready to leap on us from all sides, wielding knives to cut our throats and slice out our gizzards with! Would it please you to find this to be the case, Albert? Simply to be proven right?'

'Of course not,' Albert responded miserably. 'I was merely –'

'Hush' Jack growled.

At first Albert thought Jack had urged him to silence simply because he was tired of hearing his voice. Then he realised that the sound they had been following for some time, that of the slow clop of hooves and the rumble of their employer's cart over stony, uneven ground, had ceased.

Albert did not know whether to feel apprehensive or hopeful. He recalled Jack's words and suddenly pictured in his mind a dozen caped gentlemen, their faces covered, advancing upon them from all sides. He looked around nervously, but saw nothing except fog drifting across the hazy, sharp-angled surfaces of buildings. Their quarry had not led them far. They were currently pursuing him through the factory-lined streets, silent at this hour, that meandered down to the river. It was Albert's hope that their employer would meet a boat at the river's edge and set out upon it together with his cargo, thus bringing their night's adventure to an end.

'It seems we've lost him,' Albert said, trying to keep the glee from his voice. 'What should we do now?'

'Bah, you give up too easily, Albert,' Jack said. 'We go forward of course.'

'But if he's waiting for us up ahead?'

'Then we shall see his cart through the fog before we get too close.'

'And if he confronts us? Demands that we should explain ourselves?'

'Then we shall do so. If it's a battle of wits he wants, Albert, I know who I shall favour.'

Jack urged the nag forward, but they had advanced no more than two dozen yards when he was tugging on the reins to halt it again. Through the murk up ahead, both Jack and Albert could see the faint outline of their employer's transport, the horse waiting patiently before a set of tall factory gates, one of which stood open. Albert began to shiver and hoped that Jack would not notice. Suddenly, a dark figure in a cape and top hat appeared through the gate, leapt nimbly up on to the driver's seat of the cart, and steered the horse through the gate and into the factory grounds.

Moments later the huge wrought-iron gate swung shut with a low clang whose echo was quickly swallowed by the fog. 'Come on, Albert,' Jack said, dismounting from the horse so swiftly that he was in danger of dragging Albert off with him. He tied the horse to the factory railings and set off at a shambling run, Albert struggling to keep up.

'Where are we going?' Albert wheezed between gasps for breath.

'Down to the river. There'll likely be a way of entering the factory grounds from there.'

There was, and soon the two men were creeping between the fog-enshrouded outbuildings behind the factory, searching for their employer's horse and cart. After ten minutes, however, during which they traversed the entire area and peered into every outbuilding and factory window they could reach, they still had not found it.

'We've lost him,' Albert said, trying to sound both disappointed and to prevent his teeth from chattering. 'We might as well go back.'

'Go back when we're so close to exposing our man's secret? Your reasoning dazzles me, Albert.'

'But our quarry is nowhere to be found, Jack. Perhaps if we were to return in daylight…'

'In daylight these grounds would be full of workers. We'd never get near the place. Besides, our man and his cargo would be long gone by then. No, he's close by. We both know it.'

'Then where is he? Perhaps he knew of our presence, after all, and he's deceived us, led us on a wild-goose chase.'

'He must be in the factory,' Jack said. 'He and his cargo.'

'But the factory is locked up tight as the Old Lady herself, Jack. Let's face it, we're beaten.'

'Never,' Jack said. 'There's always a way. Follow me.'

He led the way round the back of the factory, and stopping beside a likely window, looked around until he spotted a chunk of wood. He picked it up, hefted it in his hand, then drew it back to strike the glass.

'Jack, don't,' Albert squeaked. 'We'll be overheard and caught. We'll swing for sure.'

'There's no one to hear us, besides the man we want to speak to,' Jack said.

He brought his arm forward and the glass exploded with a shattering crash. Quickly he used the wood to batter out the jagged shards that still clung to the frame. That done, he threw the wood aside and looked at Albert, savage triumph and determination on his face. 'Come on,' he said, then reached out with both hands, grasped each side of the window frame and hauled himself into the factory.

'Sixteen hours?' exclaimed the Doctor. 'That must be the longest snooze I've had for centuries, give or take the odd coma. Why didn't somebody wake me?'

'Acquiring your time craft is not vital to our plan. Therefore it was not considered a priority task,' said Tuval.

'How insulting,' murmured the Doctor, nonplussed. 'Here we are.'

They came to a halt on the towpath in front of the TARDIS. As the Doctor rooted through his pockets for the key, Tuval, still in the form of Sam, gazed up at the tall blue box without expression.

'Well?' said the Doctor. 'Aren't you going to say it?'

'What am I required to say?'

'Well, most people say "Is this it?" or "Isn't it rather small?" or even "A police box?"'

Tuval gazed at the Doctor as if he had told a joke whose punchline was beyond him. 'Why would I say this when I know from your mind print that your craft is dimensionally transcendental and has an operating chameleon circuit?'

'Why indeed?' mused the Doctor, and then rather grouchily added, 'But for your information, my chameleon circuit isn't operating. It's jammed.'

He produced the key with a flourish and inserted it into the lock. As the door swung open, he said, 'Sorry about the mess. If I'd known you were going to drop in I'd have pushed a hoover around.'

He led the way inside, calling, 'Shut the door behind you, would you? We don't want stray Skarasen wandering in with muddy feet, dripping water everywhere and knocking things over.' He strode across the floor, jumped up on to the raised dais and patted the console affectionately. 'Hello, old girl.' Turning back to Tuval, he said, 'Feel free to have a look around. I'll put the kettle on and make us both some tea. Darjeeling all right? I think I've got some simnel cake somewhere.'

As the Doctor made tea, he kept an eye on Tuval, and despite the circumstances, could not suppress a smile. The Zygon scientist was looking around the TARDIS with wonder and excitement on its borrowed face. The Doctor had quickly discovered after being released from the Zygon ship that Tuval, though taciturn and somewhat humourless, was far less aggressive and arrogant than the several Zygon warriors he had spoken to. When the tea was ready, he carried it across to the console on a tray, where Tuval was peering raptly at the time rotor.

'What do you think?' the Doctor asked.

Tuval looked at him, blinking as though roused from sleep. 'Intriguing technology.' The Zygon referred to what appeared to be nothing more than a rock inset with hundreds of tiny glittering crystals that it held in the palm of its hand. The crystals were changing colour constantly in apparently random patterns. 'Many of these materials appear inorganic, and yet my readings indicate an unknown organic component present in each separate structure, which therefore seems to indicate an organic uniformity, not entirely unlike our own technology.'

'Really?' said the Doctor, as if this was news to him.

'Furthermore, I am picking up energy emissions which are… structured but nonrepetitive. Incredibly complex.'

'Like thought patterns, do you mean?' asked the Doctor innocently, and nodded. 'Yes, the old girl has always been a deep thinker.'

'Your craft is alive?' said Tuval, astonished.

'In a sense,' said the Doctor. 'It's an inevitable consequence when technology gets pushed beyond a certain barrier. After all, Tuval, what are you and I but organic machines?' Picking up a cup from the tray, he offered it to the Zygon scientist. 'Drink up before it gets cold.'

Tuval eyed the cup suspiciously. 'What is this?'

'Tea,' said the Doctor. 'It's a liquid refreshment, native to this planet. Surely you've come across it before? How long have you been here?'

'By the time scale of this planet, almost three centuries. But this is the first time I have been outside our craft.'

'What? Three hundred years without a works outing? You ought to have a word with your shop steward.'

Tuval frowned. 'I'm afraid I do not understand your Time Lord humour.'

'Yes, a lot of people have the same problem,' said the Doctor with a sigh, and put Tuval's cup down on the console. 'I'll just leave it here, shall I? You drink it if you feel like it. There's cake on the plate if you want some. Bit dry, though, I'm afraid.'

'I do not understand why you are being pleasant to me, Doctor.'

The Doctor shrugged. 'Well, it's just the way I am.' He took a sip of his tea. 'Tell me, Tuval, what's your story? What are your people doing on this planet?'

Tuval looked thoughtful for a moment, as if unsure whether to answer the Doctor's question. Then the Zygon said, 'Five centuries ago, our home planet, Zygor, was destroyed in a stellar explosion instigated by our enemies, the Xaranti. Since then we have become a nomadic race, searching the galaxies for new planets to colonise. Three centuries ago, a fleet of our craft were engaged on such a mission when we were ambushed by a Xaranti attack force. Most of our fleet was destroyed, but our craft, and perhaps others, was merely damaged and managed to crash-land on Earth. Since then we scientists have been working on ways of augmenting Zygon physiology and technology. Within the past two decades we have managed to create an effective breeding programme for our Skarasen. It has been a long, hard struggle with many failures, but now we are finally in a position to push forward our plan to eradicate humankind and then to alter the planet's ecology, turning it into a new Zygor.'

The Doctor looked glum. 'I suppose by giving you my TARDIS I'll at least be saving the Earth from that fate, then.'

'What do you mean, Doctor?'

'Well, the TARDIS is plenty big enough for all your people. Once you have it, you'll be able to go away and leave Earth alone, find somewhere more appropriate to live, somewhere uninhabited where the ecology is already close to what you need.' He frowned. 'Why are you shaking your head like that, Tuval?'

'Forgive me, Doctor, but your words betray a lack of understanding of Zygon mentality. Once a Zygon warlord has decreed that its subordinates must follow a certain path, it is subsequently considered a sign of weakness to veer from that path, whatever the changing circumstances. Procuring your time craft will not, therefore, halt Balaak's original plan. Balaak has promised our people that Earth will become the new Zygor, and therefore it will; there is no doubting the matter.'

'So Balaak would be prepared to commit genocide just to save face?' said the Doctor.

Tuval shrugged. 'It is the Zygon way, Doctor.'

'It's barbaric,' said the Doctor. 'Typical of the military mind. But what about you, Tuval? You're a scientist. Surely you can't condone such an action?'

Tuval looked uncomfortable. 'I have no choice, Doctor. Balaak is our commander. Our commander's word is law.'

'I'm not asking you what your obligations are, I'm asking for your opinion. Do you think Balaak's action is justified?'

For a long moment Tuval did not answer. Then the scientist said, 'I must confess, it is a regrettable state of affairs.'

'Spoken like a true Victorian,' muttered the Doctor. He finished his tea with a gulp. 'Is there any way that together you and I could make Balaak see sense?'

Now Tuval looked alarmed. 'I would not even wish to try, Doctor. To question my commander's decision, particularly when persuaded to do so by an alien, would be the worst crime I, as a Zygon, could commit. I would be summarily executed.'

'Ah well, we can't have that, can we?' said the Doctor, and sighed. 'I suppose if Balaak won't listen to us, then there's nothing more we can do. I might as well show you how this works.' He began to move around the TARDIS console, flicking switches, making minute adjustments. He pointed to a row of coloured lights and what looked like a computer keyboard, though the keys were imprinted not with letters but esoteric symbols. 'This is interesting. I've been working on it just recently, tying up a few loose connections. I call it the state-of-grace circuitry, mainly because I can't remember what the technical term for it is. It's linked in to the TARDIS's telepathic circuits and when it's fully working, it negates all hostile and aggressive actions within the TARDIS itself. But – and this is the clever part – I've not only finally got round to repairing it, but I've actually added a few modifications of my own. I've built in what I call a stasis circuit, so that if the TARDIS is ever invaded, the aggressors can be rendered harmless – like so!'

The Doctor suddenly sprang forward and stabbed at a key in the top right-hand corner of the panel. Instantly the console room was filled with a screeching sound that was like a cross between an alarm and a tortured animal. Tuval tried to raise its hands to its ears, but found that it couldn't move. The Zygon scientist was unharmed but utterly helpless.

'Sorry, Tuval,' the Doctor shouted above the din, 'but I'm afraid I can't simply stand by and allow your people to wipe out an entire species. If Balaak won't listen to reason, then I'm afraid I'm going to have to do something about it.'

He jumped down from the console dais and hurried across to what appeared to be a dusty display area for many and varied kinds of timepieces, which was situated next to the library. He hurried through this humming, ticking, pulsing jungle, and disappeared through a small wooden door that blended so perfectly into the wall that Tuval would not have known it was there had he not seen the Doctor open it. Some minutes later, the Doctor reappeared, carrying a carpet bag. He put the bag down, hurried across to the console, and scurried from one panel to another, his fingers rippling over the instrumentation.

Finally he stepped back and smiled at Tuval. 'Contingency plan,' he said. He gestured vaguely around him. 'Sorry about the noise. I'll be back as soon as I can. I know you have to take your lactic fluid at regular intervals, but you're trapped in a time bubble, which I've set to loop back to the beginning every ten minutes, so your bodily needs and functions won't be affected. It also means that as far as you're concerned I'll be explaining this bit to you with sickening regularity, but as your mind will be wiped clean each time, hopefully you won't get too bored, and after all, it'll be a bit of company for you, won't it? What else? Oh yes, your synchron response won't be affected, and I'm afraid any telepathic messages you try to send won't get through, so I wouldn't bother. And... well, that's about it really. Cheerio.'

'Not a soul to be seen,' said Albert. 'We may as well face it, Jack: our bird has flown.'

After entering the factory, Albert and Jack had scoured the factory floor and searched the offices above, to no avail. Now they were back on the factory floor, Jack striding up the aisles between the dark hulks of machinery, Albert trailing him like an obedient dog.

'We're not beaten yet,' Jack growled. 'Our quarry must be here somewhere, lying low.' He stopped suddenly and rounded on Albert. Albert quailed, certain that his companion's frustration and rage was finally about to be turned on him. Rather than getting busy with his fists, however, Jack said almost thoughtfully, 'If it was you, Albert, where would you conceal two dozen cadavers?'

'I'm sure I don't know,' Albert said, and then added unhelpfully, 'Somewhere they wouldn't be so easily discovered. Somewhere cold and dark. A secret place.'

Jack nodded, though seemed lost in his own thoughts. 'A building such as this would have to have a cellar, wouldn't it?'

'I fancy so,' said Albert doubtfully, 'but how would our man get a horse and cart down there? No, Jack, it's my belief that he's given us the slip.'

'That's what you'd like to believe, you mean? Perhaps I ought to slice out your liver, Albert, just to see how yellow it is.'

'I was merely being practical, Jack,' Albert protested feebly.

'Practical, hah! You were attempting to preserve your miserable skin, as always. Well, it won't do, Albert. It won't do at all!'

Albert felt his companion's spittle fleck his face as he raised his voice. He held up his hands in an attempt to calm him. 'You misunderstand me, Jack,' he jabbered. 'I'm with you all the way; wherever you go, I follow. I was merely trying to prevent us heading off on a wild goose chase and thus causing our man's trail to grow ever colder.'

Jack nodded ponderously. 'Certainly you were. Just so long as we understand each other, Albert.'

'Oh, I'm sure that we do,' Albert said.

'Good,' Jack muttered, fixing his companion with a fierce glare. After a moment he looked away, releasing Albert as a man might release a worm from a hook. 'Now, this cellar, if it exists, must have two entrances, must it not? One situated outside, and big enough to provide access for a horse and cart, and one inside, to provide easy access for the workers.'

'That's very clever reasoning, Jack,' Albert said encouragingly. 'I'm sure you're right.'

'I'm sure of it too,' Jack said drily. 'In which case, let us not waste another moment. You look over there, Albert, and I will look over here. If you find a likely-looking entrance, whistle, and keep whistling until I find you.'

In fact, it was Jack himself who came across the barred and padlocked door several minutes later. He gave a shrill whistle, and by the time Albert had joined him, had already succeeded in removing the lock with the jemmy that he carried around with him at all times. As Jack pushed the door open, Albert shivered at the chill breeze that blew up and over them from the depths below. Although it was dark in the cellar, it was not entirely so. From somewhere below came the faint, flickering glimmer of candlelight.

'The trail grows warm once again,' Jack hissed. He hefted the jemmy and grinned savagely. 'Follow me, Albert, and not a word. I want our gentleman friend to enjoy his surprise.'

Though a big man, Jack could move with nimble, silent steps when he wished to. He did so now, creeping down the stone stairway, Albert, as ever, trailing miserably at his heels. The candlelight grew brighter as they descended, though only a little. As they reached the bottom of the steps, both men could see that the light shone from a small arched alcove leading off from the main room.

Jack grinned at Albert again, evidently enjoying himself, and holding the jemmy at shoulder height, crept towards the alcove. Looking round, Albert noted that there seemed to be no other way in to the cellar apart from a large grille in the corner of the room that presumably led down to the sewer beneath the factory. Perhaps there would be nobody down here then, after all. Perhaps they would find a mysteriously flickering candle and nothing else.

His vain hope was short-lived, however. Jack reached the alcove before him, and as he did so, Albert saw his grin widen, saw him raise the jemmy a little higher above his head.

A moment later he was standing at his friend's shoulder, looking down at a well-dressed, grey-haired man who was crouching down, attending to something on the floor, his back to them. So far the man was unaware of their presence. But then Jack stepped forward and struck the seeping stone wall savagely with the jemmy. Even before the loud clang had begun to echo in the confined space, the man had spun round and jumped to his feet.

'So! Unveiled at last!' Jack snarled.

The man who had been revealed to them was around sixty. He had rather refined features and a neatly clipped grey moustache. Albert felt a measure of relief. If this was their employer, then he was not as fearsome as Albert had been expecting. His eyes were cold, certainly, but their effect appeared diminished when the entirety of his face was uncovered. For the first time since Jack had proposed it, Albert began to see the sense in his friend's plan.

The man stood there in a semi-crouch, his teeth bared, a look of intense hostility on his face. Jack laughed. 'Have you nothing to say for yourself, sir?'

By way of reply, the man raised his hands, palms out, towards them. Albert thought that he was about to throw himself on their mercy, but then, to his horror, he saw strange, bloodless wounds open in the man's palms, and the next instant vicious thorns were springing like tiger's claws from the apertures.

Albert saw the expression on Jack's face change immediately from supreme confidence to wide-eyed disbelief. Showing remarkable agility for one so old, the man suddenly sprang forward, hissing like a snake. Jack, veteran of many a street brawl, reacted instantly, stepping aside and swinging the jemmy at the man's grey head. The man staggered as the jemmy caught him a glancing blow, but rather than halting his attack, Jack merely succeeded in deflecting it.

Albert tried to dodge out of the way as the man lunged at him, but the alcove contained so little space to manoeuvre that he could do no more than step back smartly into the stone wall, banging his head. Next second the man was on him, his thorned palms tearing at Albert's face. Albert screamed as he felt his skin part like paper, then screamed again in a far shriller voice as he felt the wounds begin to sting and burn horrendously. The burning sensation seemed to rip into his body, and for a few agonising seconds his veins were full of fire. Then he felt the fire closing around his heart. There was a sudden crushing pain, then blackness…

Jack, for his part, saw the thorns in the old man's palms shred Albert's cheeks. The next instant green stuff, bubbling and hissing, was mingling with Albert's blood. Albert was screaming with fear and agony, but almost immediately his screams tailed off, his eyes rolled up into his head, and he hit the floor like a sack of coal.

Jack had no time to react to his companion's death. The instinct of self-preservation, always strong in him, had hold of him now. Before the old man could turn his attention away from Albert, Jack waded forward and struck him twice more across the crown of his head with the jemmy. Then, almost calmly, he extracted a long-bladed knife from his jacket, reached around the man's body, and with expert precision plunged the knife in to his heart.

The man gave a high, warbling scream in a voice that did not sound even remotely human. Jack shoved him violently away. The man stumbled, his legs giving way beneath him, and crashed head first into the opposite wall. To Jack's horrified astonishment, a swirling red vapour suddenly seemed to pour from the man's body, streaming from his mouth and nostrils and eyes. The vapour surrounded the man's body, shimmering with a strange light that hurt Jack's eyes to look at it.

Eventually the vapour with its strange light dispersed, but what was revealed now was an even more terrible sight. In place of the man who had killed Albert, and whom Jack had killed in turn, was a creature that Jack could not have envisaged in his worst nightmares. It was the colour of a blood orange, covered in suckers and with a vast, domed head. It looked to Jack like an evil, diseased, man-sized parody of a baby.

Worse still, it was not yet dead. It was twitching and writhing, and from its throat came a shrill whistling sound. Jack started to back out of the alcove, not wishing to take his eyes from the creature for a moment, fearing that if he did it would leap up, pluck the knife from its chest, and come howling after him.

He did turn away, however, when, stepping out of the alcove, he heard a scrabbling sound behind him. To his utter horror he saw a huge silvery animal, larger than any man, sliding up out of the grate in the corner of the room. Jack was not a man to whom fear was a close companion, but it transfixed him now. He felt as rooted to the spot as a bird under the spell of a cat as the creature hauled itself up out of the hole in the floor and lumbered towards him.

Opening its vast jaws, the creature gave a shrieking bellow that Jack felt sure would burst his eardrums. Its head waved from side to side, its eyes rolled, and then with another terrifying bellow it lunged at Jack.

He braced himself for the impact of that massive body striking his own, and hoped his death would be mercifully swift. But to his amazement, the creature bypassed him, heading instead for the alcove.

For several seconds Jack simply stood there, unable to believe his good fortune. He could only think that the creature had ignored him because it had smelled the blood issuing from the wounds in poor Albert's body. 'Thank you, Albert,' he croaked, and at last found that he could move his limbs again. Behind him he heard the creature snarling like a dog as it began to tear and worry at his companion's cooling flesh. Leaving the monster to its grisly supper, Jack fled.

At the same instant that the Zygon wearing Litefoot's body breathed its last, Litefoot himself convulsed and woke up.

The first thing he became aware of was that he felt sick and light-headed. Immediately, however, this was superseded by the horrifying realisation that he was blind. He raised his hands to his face and felt what seemed to be ropes trailing over his arms. Had he been tied up and blindfolded? He couldn't remember. Then he touched the thing that was covering his eyes, and encountered a cold, jelly-like mass, and as his hands jerked in shock from his face the memories came flooding back.

Revulsion seized him, accompanied by a rising sense of panic. At once he recalled the Doctor's voice; it resounded in his head, urging him to remain calm. Deep breaths, George, he ordered himself, and after a few moments his racing heart quietened, resuming its normal rhythm. Once again, tentatively, he touched the cowl that covered his head and the upper part of his face. He half expected it to react – to squirm or pulse or tighten its grip – but it appeared to be inert.

He found the edge of the cowl with his fingers and experimentally tried to peel it away. To his surprise he managed to lift it from his skin with no discomfort whatever. As it came away, it made a slight sucking noise, like a rubber mask that his own sweat had caused to adhere to his face. Within seconds he had tugged the cowl from his head and pushed it distastefully away from him. It dangled beside him, like a dead jellyfish suspended on a fleshy rope.

The tentacular bonds that had earlier entwined his body and held him rigid while the cowl lowered itself over his head, were now hanging limp, some twitching feebly, as if confused. Litefoot pushed them aside with ease and stepped out of the alcove.

Apart from the usual burbles and rumbles from within the walls, this area of the ship was silent. Groggily, Litefoot moved from one alcove to the next, endeavouring to ascertain whether any of his fellow captives had awoken as he had.

The answer was no, though Litefoot noted with an odd blend of hope and alarm that the Doctor's alcove was empty. Sam, however, was still held tight by her bonds, the pulsing cowl clamped tight to her head and the upper part of her face like an acorn's cap. Her mouth was open as if in a silent scream. Litefoot gave an experimental tug at the tentacles coiled around her, but they were immovable.

For a few moments he hovered there, wondering what to do next. Liberty was all very well, but where could he go? He no longer even had his revolver; somewhere along the way it had been taken from him. In the end he decided that his only option was to find either the Doctor or a way out. If he fell into the clutches of those hideous Zygon creatures again, then so be it. He tried not to think that there were worse things they could do than escort him back to what he thought of as the cell area.

He set off, moving on tiptoe even though there was no real reason for it. The cell area narrowed to a crystalline door. As he approached it, it slid up and away from him. Litefoot reflected smugly that the Zygons' security arrangements were somewhat inadequate, but then he supposed they believed that they were so superior to the inhabitants of Earth that they could not be threatened. 'Well, we'll see about that,' he muttered defiantly. 'Get on the wrong side of George Litefoot and you'll soon find yourself with rather more than you bargained for.'

For a while he wandered aimlessly, with no real idea where he was going. The Zygon ship seemed a mishmash of irregularly shaped chambers, control rooms and observation areas. Litefoot was not sure whether these were the same rooms he and his companions had passed through while being escorted to the cell area earlier. If they were, he did not recognise them, but then such was the nature of this place that he thought he could very likely wander for days with no inkling of whether or not he was retreading the same ground.

As he blundered along, he found himself thinking about the nature of the astonishing beings whose clutches he and his friends had fallen in to. Did they have such things as crew quarters? he mused. And if so, were they full of personal effects? Did they read books, create works of art, take photographs of family and friends? Did they require love and affection? Did they laugh with joy and grieve for their dead? Did they feel pain? Were they physically attracted to one another despite being genderless?

His reverie was interrupted by the sound of movement from somewhere up ahead. He was in a corridor like a gigantic pipe whose sides were the texture of gnarled and twisted tree bark encrusted with limpet-like crystals. Though the crystals gave off a faint ochre luminescence, the way ahead was little more than a mass of brownish shadow. Litefoot halted and listened. The sounds were coming towards him. Hastily he retraced his steps, retreating back along the corridor and through a door into one of the Zygons' control rooms.

Here he concealed himself behind the largest control panel he could find, a strange construction from which sprouted a mass of trumpet-like growths. His back and knees creaked with age as he pulled himself into a ball. Moments later the door to the room slid open and two Zygon scientists entered. They busied themselves tweaking and adjusting various controls around the room, talking in their high, fluting voices about 'diastellic readings' and 'trilanic responses'. Finally, each reeled off a long list of numbers which the other verified, and then they moved on, heading in the direction of the cell area.

Litefoot rose from his hiding place and crossed to the door that led into the pipe-like corridor, wincing at the pain in his knees. He passed through the door and moved along the corridor as quickly as he could, able to do no more than hope that somewhere along the way he would strike lucky in his quest for freedom. He had no doubt that if the Zygons entered the cell area and discovered him gone, they would instantly raise the alarm.

The corridor branched several times, and each time, acting on instinct, Litefoot took the fork to the right. This part of the ship was dark and under-manned, and more than once Litefoot had to assure himself that he was not lost, that all he had to do to find his way back was to turn and continually follow the left-hand path.

Eventually he found himself in a roughly spherical chamber that immediately made him realise what it was that this section of the Zygon ship had been reminding him of. His journey latterly, he thought, had been like travelling through a gigantic rabbit warren, and now here he was in some form of central chamber or junction point, where there were no crystalline doors, but merely holes which were the entrances to what appeared to be secondary tunnels, leading off in all directions.

Some of the tunnels looked dark and narrow, singularly uninviting, but there were several in the low roof above his head that reminded him of the chute by which he and his friends had entered the ship from the factory. There was even one that was ridged like a giant windpipe, and which therefore looked as though he might be able to make an attempt to climb it.

He hesitated a moment, and then decided to try it. He could go on, but what did he expect to find? A door marked EXIT which would lead him straight out on to a London street where a landau would be waiting to take him home? No, if he desired his freedom then he had to grasp any opportunity that might present itself, and thus far this was the only one that had.

He stood beneath the shaft, reached up and took hold of the lowest of the bone-like ridges. They were more pronounced than he could have hoped for, almost like the rungs of a ladder. He took several deep breaths, and then, using all his strength, attempted to haul himself up into the shaft. At first he thought he was not going to make it, that the strength in his arms would not be equal to that required to pull himself up. He felt his arms beginning to tremble, his fingers slipping. He forced himself to recall the awful sensation of the cowl coming down over his head, sliding across his eyes. This encouraged him to grit his teeth and redouble his efforts. He would not fail here, he promised himself: he would escape from this place or die in the attempt.

Slowly he managed to bend his elbows until his head and then his shoulders had risen above them. That done, he shifted his weight to jam himself against the side of the shaft and brought his right knee up. Now he was secure enough to be able to reach up for the next rung with one hand and then the other. In this way he dragged himself painstakingly upwards until at last his flailing right foot managed to find purchase on the shaft's lowest rung.

He paused a moment to regain his breath. His head swam, his

stomach roiled with nausea, and his body felt hot and damp beneath his clothes. With grim humour he recalled how he had voiced his doubt about his heart's ability to take the strain should his life become as eventful as it briefly had five years ago. Well, George, he told himself, if you *are* going to die, at least this will be an interesting place in which to do so. His rest over, he began to climb the shaft, taking it steadily, pausing every now and again to rest his aching legs. Soon the bottom of the shaft was so far below him that it was no longer in sight.

He had been climbing for what he estimated to be the best part of half an hour when an odd ripple ran through the shaft. Litefoot paused, looking above and below him in an attempt to ascertain what might have caused the movement. Seeing nothing, he carried on, dismissing the matter as nothing more than another vagary of the Zygons' peculiar vessel. Several minutes later, however, the shaft rippled again, more markedly this time, and no sooner had that passed than it actually began to convulse, to bend and flex violently like the inside of a concertina.

The movements, continual and prolonged, almost dislodged Litefoot from his perch. He clung on, desperately hoping that the frightful disturbances would soon pass. He couldn't help but wonder, however, whether the shaft was convulsing because of his presence. If it was, then he was in dire trouble indeed.

All at once he heard a rushing sound beneath him and glanced down. Next moment an incredibly powerful blast of stinking air raced up the shaft – so powerful, in fact, that it tore Litefoot from his perch and propelled him upwards at an astonishing speed. A single thought leapt into his mind – I'm being sneezed out! – before suddenly, shockingly, he found himself immersed in black, freezing-cold water. His entire body clenched; for a few seconds his heart seemed to freeze, and he honestly believed he was about to die.

Then his heart gave a kick and began to thud hard in his chest. His limbs seemed to unlock, his extremities tingling inside even as the cold water numbed them. He forced himself to open his eyes wide and look upwards, vainly searching for the surface. He saw nothing but blackness, but began to swim anyway, kicking his legs, shovelling water aside with his hands as though it was earth he was burrowing through.

It was no use. The climb up the shaft had exhausted him, his sodden clothes ballooned about him, weighing him down, and his body quickly used up what little oxygen had been stored in it prior to entering the water. As he began to panic through lack of air, his movements first became frantic and then turned languid, his limbs becoming leaden and unresponsive. A great dark pressure grew inside him, crushing his brain and his lungs; black shapes swarmed in his vision and seemed to cut him off from his thoughts. Just before unconsciousness engulfed him, he saw a bright glittering light shining somewhere ahead of him, spinning like a whirlpool. Thinking dreamily that the light was the single most beautiful sight he had ever seen, he imagined himself stretching out his arms towards it.

CHAPTER 7
A PLACE OF EVIL

In the main control room of the Zygon ship, a Zygon warrior suddenly hissed, 'Commander, Veidra's synchron response has ceased.'

'What?' screeched Balaak, twisting its upper body towards its subordinate. The warrior flinched but repeated the information. Balaak's black, deep-set eyes seemed to flare orange as it stumped across to the console manned by the warrior and examined the readings. Instantly the Zygon warlord made a sound like a spitting cat. 'Veidra must have been eliminated. Zorva, I want you and Schivaal to go up on to the surface and assess the situation. Bring Veidra's remains back here. And if the perpetrators of this outrage are still in the vicinity, destroy them.'

'Immediately, Commander,' said Zorva, and stalked from the room together with another Zygon warrior.

'Chumaak, what is the status of the human captive whose body print Veidra was using?' asked Balaak.

A Zygon scientist twisted a number of controls on a nearby console and examined a veined, bubble-like screen. Its eyes widened and its delicate features quivered. Timorously it said, 'Veidra's elimination has induced a Trauma One response in the assimilation system's protoplasmic core, Commander. All systems are non-functional, including the Response Monitor. It therefore seems reasonable to assume that the human subject is now conscious and at liberty.'

Eyes blazing, Balaak let loose a gurgling roar that reverberated around the console room. 'Alert all stations. I want the human creature recaptured at once.'

'Yes, Commander.' Chumaak scampered across to what appeared to be a gnarled conglomeration of tubers on spiny stems that were growing from the wall and began to knot them together in a complex pattern. Then the Zygon scientist pressed a swelling on the wall beside the tubers and instantly an animal-like warbling filled the control room.

'Mowgra, what is Tuval's current status?' Balaak asked.

A Zygon warrior crossed to the console recently vacated by Zorva and made some adjustments to the controls. 'Tuval's synchron response is unchanged, Commander.'

Balaak inclined its great domed head slightly and gave a soft hiss. 'That is something at least. Monitor Tuval's progress, Mowgra, and report to me if there is any fluctuation in the synchron response.'

'Yes, Commander.'

Somewhere out there, thought the Doctor, standing on the towpath and looking out at the points of light shattering and reforming on the otherwise unseen, tar-black Thames. Fog curled around his ankles, while drizzle darkened the shoulders of his coat and formed a halo of fine droplets on his thick, wavy hair.

He pulled back his sleeve and checked the device strapped to his wrist. It resembled a digital compass with its own light source. A needle hovered on a dial ringed with strange symbols. The central section contained several rows of ever-changing numerical readings.

He tapped the device as though it was a watch whose batteries were running down, then nodded in satisfaction. Humming a Draconian lament, he placed the carpet bag he was carrying on the wet cobbles and opened it. He extracted a bulging waterproof hip pack attached to a belt, a diver's face-mask, a pair of flippers, a small, slim oxygen cylinder and mouthpiece, and finally a worn and dusty-looking wet suit, which he laid on the ground and which immediately began to turn shiny black with the rain.

Quickly he stripped down to a pair of thermal long johns, expertly folding each item of clothing as he removed it and placing it in the carpet bag, then donned the wet suit and flippers. He clipped the belt to his waist, buckled on the oxygen cylinder and covered his eyes and nose with the face-mask, adjusting it until it was comfortable.

At last he took a deep breath. Everything seemed fine.

After concealing the carpet bag as best he could beneath a nearby bench, he patted the hip pack and checked the device on his wrist once again. Not wishing to alarm anybody, or worse, be the cause of a rescue attempt, he glanced both ways along the towpath. Seeing no one, he murmured, 'Ready or not, here I come,' then flapped over to the nearest set of steps that led down to the river. He descended awkwardly until he reached the level of the water, then turned and allowed himself to flop backward into the Thames. There was a splash and a brief churning as the black water closed over him. Within seconds, however, the surface of the river was still and silent once more.

For those present in the Whitechapel gin palace known locally as the Doldrums, 13 January 1894 was a day to remember. At approximately 2 a.m. the door burst open and in staggered big Jack Howe, looking as no one had ever seen him before. His eyes were bulging, sweat was running down his face and he was shaking like a child. He stumbled to the bar and ordered gin in a weak, jabbering voice that was far removed from the arrogant growl that he usually employed. Once the glass was in his hand, he threw the gin down his throat and demanded another. This happened thrice more, after which Jack pushed the glass away from him and sank on to a bar stool, his head in his trembling hands.

The Doldrums was generally a rowdy, violent place, but for a full half-minute after Jack's entrance there was silence as those present looked at each other and at the big man himself, and tried to reckon up in their own minds what unutterably dreadful event could possibly have transpired to reduce Jack Howe to such a state. Finally Henry Peterson, one of Jack's drinking cronies, a florid-faced man with a nose so crooked it appeared to be almost at a right angle to the rest of his features, sidled up and tentatively inquired, 'What ails you, Jack?'

Slowly Jack raised his head from the mask of his hands. Peterson took a hasty step back, looking like a boy who has jabbed a dead dog with a stick only to find that it isn't dead, after all. However, there was no anger on Jack's face, merely a bleary, fearful incomprehension. In a barely audible voice, he muttered, 'I've witnessed some terrible things tonight, Henry, terrible things indeed. Things the like of which no living man should ever have to see. I've seen Albert killed by a creature spawned from hell itself. And I've seen a dragon too, the length of four men, with teeth as long as my hand.' He held out his hand to demonstrate his point, then stared at it, fear swirling in his eyes, as if his memories were threatening to engulf him once more.

A murmur ran round the room, part superstitious dread, part disbelief. Then a youth hovering at Henry Peterson's shoulder, perhaps emboldened by Jack's sorry state, piped up, 'I've seen such creatures oft-times myself. They reside at the bottom of my glass.'

There was a smattering of nervous laughter, a release of tension more than anything, but Jack was not amused. With a sudden roar, he barged Henry Peterson out of the way and launched himself at the youth. Before the youth knew what was happening, Jack had grabbed him around the throat with one huge hand and slammed him up so hard against the bar that his back bent like a bow. With his free hand Jack snatched up a half-full glass and smashed it into the startled youth's face.

Blood poured from the youth's lacerated mouth and from Jack's cut fingers, but the big man seemed oblivious to his own wounds. He forced the gurgling youth's mouth open with one massive, grimy hand and started shoving chunks of broken glass into it with the other.

'Don't you mock me!' he roared. 'Don't you ever mock me! I'll have your tongue out, you bloody maggot!'

The youth's eyes rolled and blood poured down his chin and spattered on the bar. He began to squeal as best he could as Jack selected a large and viciously sharp chunk of glass from the debris, and holding it in his blood-slippery fingers started hacking away inside the youth's mouth.

No one moved to intervene in the one-sided contest, partly because they were too afraid of Jack Howe to do so, and partly because they were enjoying the show. Indeed, a number of Jack's cronies clapped and cheered as Jack suddenly straightened up, holding aloft a sizeable portion of the youth's tongue. After milking the applause for a moment, Jack tossed the bloody gobbet of flesh aside and turned away from the youth, who slid to the floor, barely conscious, blood spilling from his slashed mouth.

'Gin,' Jack ordered, not even bothering to clean the blood from his hands. When the drink arrived, he knocked it back as before, then immediately ordered another.

His cronies gathered around him, eager to bask in his dangerous aura. 'What about these creatures you saw then, Jack?' someone shouted.

'What about 'em?' Jack growled.

'Where did you see 'em?' someone else asked.

'In the basement of Seers's factory, down by the river. Poor old Albert and I had a bit of business there, if you get my meaning.'

Though Jack was not exactly his old self, his encounter with the youth, who was still lying unattended in a widening pool of his own blood, had restored his spirits a little.

'It seems to me that something ought to be done about 'em,' Henry Peterson said.

There was a drunken ripple of assent.

Jack looked around at his cronies and after a moment he muttered, 'That factory's a place of evil. I say we burn it to the ground.'

This time the ripple raised itself to a roar. Glasses were clashed together. Jack grinned, tilted back his head and threw another gin down his throat.

All in all, it had been a quiet night on the manor. The light but incessant rain had persuaded those with homes to stay indoors. As PC Harry Bowman undertook his nightly patrol along the river bank he reflected that there was an added chill to the air this evening. Surely it would not be too much longer before the first snows of this so-far mild winter would begin to fall, casting a cold white blanket over the land, which would smother the lives of young and old alike.

Bowman knew only too well that December through to February were the truly savage months. Any infant or oldster still breathing by the time the first buds of spring appeared was considered hardy indeed. Many a time Harry and his colleagues had found entire groups of street urchins, having attempted to huddle together like puppies for warmth, frozen to death. The more privileged classes believed that this was merely nature's way of culling the surplus population, but they were not the ones who had the task of prising apart the rigid bodies of dead children.

It was just after 2 a.m. when Harry spied the body. At first he thought it was just a heap of old sacking washed up on the shingle below the towpath. He lowered his lantern over the edge for a closer look, but the fog was thick as soup. He was about to move on when the fog parted, only momentarily but enough for Harry to make out a white hand.

'My oath,' he muttered, and stumbled down the nearest set of slippery stone steps to the narrow bank. He hurried across to the body, which was lying on its face, half in and half out of the water. Floaters were not uncommon around these parts, but this fellow looked well dressed, which immediately suggested the possibility of foul play. Placing his lantern on the shingle, Harry grasped the body's sodden shoulder and turned it over.

Immediately he jerked back in shock. Good Lord, but he knew this fellow! It was Professor George Litefoot, eminent physician and police pathologist. The man was popular and well respected among rich and poor alike, and Harry wondered what could possibly have happened for him to have ended his days like this. It surely couldn't be suicide? No, more likely he'd been attacked and robbed while on an errand of mercy, and his body, dead or unconscious, dumped in the Thames.

Poor old duffer, Harry thought, looking at the man's grey hair plastered across his white face and his wide-open mouth dribbling river water. No one deserves to die like this.

Then Litefoot's body spasmed and he turned on to his side, retching. Next instant what looked like gallons of brownish water were spurting from his mouth.

Harry gaped at him for a moment, then did what he could to help. Litefoot's eyelids were flickering now, though he barely seemed conscious. When Litefoot had done vomiting, Harry dragged his body fully out of the water, and then, despite the rain, peeled off his wind-cheater and draped it over him. 'Professor,' he said urgently, 'I don't know if you can hear me, but you're safe now. I'm going to get you to a hospital. You just hold on there, sir.'

With one arm draped protectively around his charge, Harry pulled out his whistle, placed it in his mouth, and blew as hard as he could.

The Doctor pushed down through the murky water with powerful strokes. He constantly checked the device on his wrist, altering his course in accordance with the readings. The purpose of the device was to track the source of the Zygons' energy emissions and therefore lead him directly to their base. Despite his excellent sense of direction, the Doctor would have been hopelessly lost without it. The water was so filthy with raw sewage and rubbish and industrial waste that he could see no further than an arm's length ahead of him.

He had been swimming for long enough to make his arms and legs ache when he saw what appeared to be a huge dark shape looming up through the murk below. He paused for a moment, trying to keep as still as possible. The readings on his wrist monitor told him that the Zygon ship must now be very close, but that only made it all the more likely that this could be a patrolling Skarasen. He waited for several minutes, but the shape remained still. Finally, cautiously, he began to swim down towards it. He had to get very close before he could verify that it was indeed the Zygon base.

It was an awesome sight. Nestling on the river bed, it looked more like a living creature than a spacecraft. Vast and barnacled and fibrous, it resembled a cross between a lobster and a spider, though it was also strangely root-like, giving the jumbled impression that it was animal, vegetable, and mineral all rolled into one. Tubes, like sinewy-looking umbilical cords, stretched up from its carapace. The Doctor knew that these must be the Zygons' means of access to and from the surface, and that one of them was also the means by which he and his friends had entered the craft from the factory basement.

As the Doctor got closer, he saw that the Zygon ship had long, jointed legs which were tucked partly underneath its body, and that it was pulsing slightly, puffing up then deflating, as though breathing. Hoping that there were no exterior sensors to alert the crew to his presence, the Doctor kicked down towards the ship.

The thirty-strong group arrived swiftly and silently despite their drunkenness. They flooded like phantoms through the gates of Seers's factory, each of them carrying a stave bound with cloth and soaked in paraffin. Jack Howe was at their head, strutting on gin and adrenaline. As the last of the mob entered the cobbled courtyard, he turned to face them, raising his stave high in the air.

His face was dark and taut with a righteous anger, his eyes pooled with shadows cast by the brim of his billycock hat. From the pocket of his thick but ragged overcoat he produced a grimy box of matches which he held out towards Henry Peterson.

'Strike one of these for me, will you, Henry?' he growled.

Nervous but evidently considering it a privilege, Peterson hurried forward and took the box from Jack. Tucking his own stave under his arm, he fumbled the box open, extracted a match and lit it.

Fire flared, haloed by fog. Jack stepped forward and thrust the end of his stave into the flame.

A moment later he stepped back, brandishing his blazing torch.

'Come forward, one by one,' he ordered, vapour wreathing from his mouth. 'Once your torch is alight, find a window and throw it through. Break every pane of glass in the place.'

There was another rumble of assent. Henry Peterson stepped forward and Jack lit his stave with his own.

Soon the night was awash with flickering, bobbing teardrops of flame. It transformed the grey drizzle into a shower of glittering jewels.

The men ringed the factory, each selecting a window as Jack had ordered. Then, as though at some unspoken command, staves arced through the air. Glass shattered. Inside the dark building, flames leapt and danced as though in gleeful celebration of the chance to devour.

Jack stumped forward, selected his own window, and hurled his stave as hard as he could. It spun end over end before smashing through into the factory. Glass fell in shining splinters.

'Burn, you bastards,' he muttered. 'Burn all the way back to hell.'

'Commander,' Zorva hissed, sibilant voice echoing around the control room, 'a group of human creatures are attacking the factory.'

Balaak swivelled to glare at the Zygon warrior. This day was not turning out at all well. Though the warbling siren had ceased, the escaped human had still not been recaptured despite an extensive search of the ship. Also, Tuval and the Doctor were taking an inordinately long time to return, though Balaak knew that the Time Lords were a notoriously devious species; perhaps the complexities of his time craft were more involved than they had initially anticipated.

'Do they have weapons?' the Zygon warlord asked.

'No, Commander. Merely burning sticks. Their objective appears to be destruction rather than entry.'

Balaak was silent for a few moments, considering the options. If the humans were behaving in such a manner, then it seemed reasonable to assume that the Zygon presence on their miserable planet was no longer the secret it had once been. Balaak knew that the Zygons could deal with the humans easily, but that would only encourage more to come, and yet more after that. It could prove an irritating hindrance to their plans.

'Shall I send a Skarasen to destroy them, Commander?' Zorva asked.

'No,' said Balaak. 'It is too soon to engage the humans in open conflict. Besides, if they are intent on destroying the factory, then that is useless to us now. Relocate.'

'Yes, Commander,' hissed Zorva.

Like a pearl-diver, the Doctor moved slowly over the barnacled surface of the Zygon ship. He knew that the ship was a manufactured, nonsentient life form, and that its outer surface was pitted with 'breathing-holes', not entirely dissimilar in appearance to those possessed by whales. After several minutes of searching, he managed to find a breathing-hole that was large enough for his purpose. He knew that eventually the hole would open, and when it did he intended to be sucked in with the water from which the ship extracted oxygen to survive. As best he could, he settled down to wait.

He had been waiting for several minutes when the ship gave a sudden lurch. Bucked as though from a frisky horse, the Doctor scrabbled for a handhold. He was still trying to secure one when the ship's broad back tilted steeply. Even as the Doctor rolled down it, as though down an almost vertical cliff face, he realised what must be happening. The ship must be unfurling its long, spider-like legs from beneath it and rising unsteadily to its feet. The question was, why? It surely couldn't simply be to dislodge him. For some reason it must be altering its location, abandoning the web of influence it had woven around Seers's factory. The

Doctor rolled right to the edge of the gnarled back, unable to halt his momentum, and next moment was sinking blindly into a great swirling cloud of muddy water.

For several seconds it was like falling through nothingness, no points of reference above, below, or to either side of him. Then, with enough of an impact to dislodge his mouthpiece, he struck bottom. He lay there on his back for a moment, unable to breathe, mud curling around him like thick, enveloping smoke. As it cleared, he got a vague impression of the Zygon ship, its underbelly high above him and still rising, propelled by the straightening of its long, jointed legs. Even as the Doctor shook his head to clear his vision and groped for the mouthpiece which was floating in the murk somewhere in front of his face, he became aware of the ship beginning to move slowly forward along the river bed like a gigantic spider. He was so woozy that he didn't realise he was lying right in the ship's path, until suddenly, to his horror, he saw one of the craft's massive legs spearing down through the murky water towards him, threatening to skewer him as effectively as a javelin might skewer a beetle.

CHAPTER 8
THE BROTH OF OBLIVION

Gathering his wits, the Doctor hurled himself out of the way, rolling over and over in the soft mud, his oxygen cylinder jolting beneath him, digging into his back. The leg came crashing down into the place where his body had been just a second before. As it sank deep into the river bed, the Doctor scrambled to his feet and launched himself through the churning water towards it. Though the legs of the Zygon craft seemed spindly in comparison with the mass that they were supporting, the girth of the one nearest the Doctor was still akin to that of a good-sized oak tree. As the ship continued its remorseless advance along the river bed, the Doctor saw the leg tilt from one side to the other, and knew that any second now it would take its next step, pulling itself free from the mud and rising into the air. He gritted his teeth and pushed himself as hard as he could, his hands reaching for the leg with the same desperate eagerness as an Olympic swimmer reaching for the wall at the end of a race. Even as his fingers touched the granite-rough appendage, bristling with spiny hairs, he felt and saw the leg begin to slide upwards, dragging itself from the mud in readiness for its next step.

He grabbed hold and clung on, pressing his body up close against the leg, wrapping his limbs around it as best he could. As the leg rose up through the water with dizzying speed, he felt like someone trying to remain in his seat during a perilous funfair ride. Next moment the leg was plunging downwards again, and the Doctor closed his eyes as bubbles fizzed across the surface of his face-mask. When the leg came into contact with the soft river bed once more, it was still with enough of an impact to jolt the Doctor's head, causing the face-mask to clunk painfully against the leg's craggy surface.

He saw the dislodged mouthpiece floating on its length of tubing in front of his face and, grabbing it, clamped it between his teeth. He gulped oxygen to revive himself, knowing that he had only a few seconds before the leg started rising into the air again. Then, like an aquatic monkey, he pulled himself hand over hand as far up the tree-like limb as he could get, clinging on like a limpet as the leg again swooped him up and through the water.

This process was repeated at least a dozen times before the Doctor finally reached the top of the leg. During the next brief hiatus, he swam-scrambled over the bulbous joint securing the leg to the main body of the ship, and climbed on to the barnacled carapace that he knew was as impervious and adaptable to the pressures and problems found in the deepest regions of space as it was to those in the water.

Spread-eagled across the vessel's back, jolted by its movement, he began to search as before for a suitable breathing-hole. He used the craft's spines and nodules as hand-holds both to drag himself along and to secure himself when the ride became too bumpy.

Eventually he found what he was looking for. The breathing-hole resembled a puckered mouth in the centre of a wrinkled depression. As before, the Doctor settled down to wait, though this time he had to brace the muscles in his arms tightly to prevent himself slithering about.

Just as he was beginning to think that he wouldn't be able to hold on for much longer, the breathing-hole began to show signs of activity. First, the wrinkled depression began to flex and shiver like cold flesh. Then the mouth of the hole began to open, at first twisted and quivering, as though in a moue of pain, and then stretching wider, as if to yawn and cry out.

The Doctor saw the water that the ship was drawing into itself before he felt it. It appeared as a vortex, a shimmering whirlpool, above the hole. At first it was small, no larger than an ice-cream cone, but as the hole stretched wider, so the vortex increased in size and power. Now the Doctor could feel its pull, and he welcomed it. As the breathing-hole became the entrance to a cavern, and the vortex above it stretched to the size of a man, he rose slowly into a semi-standing position, then stepped forward.

Instantly the vortex had him, dragging him into itself. The Doctor felt himself spun and buffeted by an irresistible force. Though it went against his instincts, he tried not to resist, tried to relax and let it take him. It was impossible, however, not to close his eyes and cry out in pain when he felt himself being sucked down. The water was being drawn into the ship under such pressure that it felt as though his body was being pounded with chunks of concrete. As water smashed against his face and body, ripping off his face-mask and dislodging his mouthpiece once again, and the ship sucked him into blackness, he felt consciousness slipping away. His last coherent thought, before he was clubbed into submission, was to wonder whether this might have been a mistake.

The first thing the Doctor became aware of when he woke up was the sensation of water sloshing against his face. He opened one eye and saw that he was lying in a gourd-shaped chamber, the walls and floor of which were riddled with mouth-like openings. The whole place was dripping like a sea cave at low tide. Water was pooled in the depressions and hollows between the apertures. Groggily the Doctor climbed to his feet, his body stiff and bruised. 'Next time I'll avoid the tradesmen's entrance,' he murmured as he checked his wet suit for signs of damage.

There were none, which meant that, though battered, he was relatively dry. However, at some stage during the buffeting, his oxygen cylinder, as well as his face-mask, had been torn away and was now nowhere to be seen. The Doctor looked around, trying to get his bearings, and saw that the only exit, apart from the gaping opening above his head, was a cylindrical tunnel away to his left, which looked large enough for him to walk along in a stooped position. He sloshed his way over to it, the ground giving a little beneath his flippered feet. The texture of the walls and floor and ceiling was more fleshy than fibrous here, the ever-present nodules and ganglions and tentacle-like appendages resembling soft organs rather than knots of root.

It was hard going along the tunnel, even when he removed his flippers, rather like walking on a half-inflated bouncy castle. The walls glistened like slug flesh and were so clotted with shapeless growths from which feebly waving tentacles dangled that it was akin to wading through a sewer pipe infested with small octopuses. The tentacles slid across the Doctor's face and shoulders, trying to tug him back, but he pressed on doggedly. Eventually the tentacular growths became less and the tunnel widened out. It didn't exactly come to an end, but all at once the Doctor was walking straight-backed through a large open area rather than stooped through a narrow tunnel.

He came to a junction where tunnels led off in four different directions. He paused for a moment, assessing them, checking them for light and signs of usage, listening for sounds in the walls. 'Eeny, meeny, miny, mo,' he began, pointing with the flippers which he now carried in his hand. Then his voice trailed off and he looked once again at the left-hand tunnel. He wanted to get to the nerve centre of the ship and his instincts told him to take that route. 'Eeny,' he said firmly, and strode into the tunnel. What was it Ace had once said to him? That he must have a homing pigeon in his head. Not that he was always right, of course. Life would be boring if he was *always* right. He was right only ninety-nine per cent of the time... well, ninety-nine and a half per cent, maybe.

He wandered through the ship for twenty minutes or so, following his instincts whenever he came to a junction. He knew he was heading in the right direction: the veins in the walls were thickening into major arteries, the rooms were becoming larger and more packed with Zygon technology, and there were increasing numbers of Zygons wandering around too.

For a while the Doctor played a cat-and-mouse game with them, dodging into alcoves or narrow tunnels or hiding behind instrument banks whenever they appeared. Fortunately there were rarely more than three of them together at any one time and he was able to avoid them fairly easily.

Eventually, stepping through one of the many crystalline doors on the ship, and hoping that he wouldn't be met by a Zygon heading the other way, the Doctor found what he was looking for. The door led him out on to a creaking walkway that appeared to be composed of a great knot of cable-like roots. Below him was a vast cavern, on the floor of which lay a number of Skarasen, their limbs twitching and their eyes rolling sleepily as though anaesthetised. The Skarasen were each connected via their bellies to a profusion of suckered tentacles which descended direct from an enormous ovular receptacle, like a gigantic wasps' nest, attached to the wall just below the ceiling, above and in front of the Doctor. The tentacles were pulsing, and making a peculiarly greedy gulping noise as they extracted what the Doctor knew was lactic fluid from the

Skarasen's milk sacs. From the bottom of the ovular tank, more pipe-like tentacles, hanging in loops, carried the lactic fluid away through the walls, presumably to an area where it would be treated and made fit for Zygon consumption.

'The milking shed,' the Doctor murmured, noticing that at the far end of the walkway a number of gnarled protuberances jutting from the wall formed a set of steps leading down to the floor of the cavern. He made his way along and down and less than a minute later alighted on the cavern floor. Glancing up to make sure that he was not being observed, he made his way over to the nearest Skarasen. It was lying on its side, its great flanks heaving as it breathed in and out. One of its eyes rolled to observe the Doctor, but that was its only reaction.

'Hello, girl,' said the Doctor soothingly, and placed his hand on the creature's back. Its scales were cold and hard as metal. Like many of the creatures that this community of Zygons employed, this Skarasen was barely an infant, measuring no more than forty feet from nose to tail. The Doctor reached across and gave one of the tentacles clamped to the Skarasen's belly an experimental tug.

Finding it to be tightly secured at both ends, he nodded in satisfaction. He dropped the flippers to the floor and climbed up on to the dozing Skarasen. It didn't react as he took hold of the tentacle he had tugged a few moments before and began to shin up it. His body ached from his earlier exertions, but he forced himself on, hand over hand, leg over leg. The ovular receptacle was perhaps fifty feet above floor level, and by the time he reached it, he was coated in sweat beneath his wet suit, every muscle in his body crying out in pain.

He paused for a moment, breathing deeply, his aching arms and legs wrapped around the pulsing tentacle. Bracing himself, he let go of the tentacle with one hand and unzipped the bulging hip pack attached to the belt at his waist. He extracted a large, old-fashioned syringe and a slim transparent case full of needles. Awkwardly he removed a needle from the case and screwed it into the syringe. He clamped the syringe between his teeth, put the case back into the hip pack, and took out a vial full of colourless fluid. He drew the fluid into the syringe, then rammed the needle into the hive-like receptacle and depressed the plunger.

When all the fluid was gone, he pulled out the syringe and dropped it back into the hip pack. 'Sweet dreams,' he murmured, patting the hive as a man might pat a pet dog. He shinned back down the tentacle and less than two minutes later was again standing beside the dozing Skarasen.

He was about to make his way over to the steps when the crystalline door above him slid open and two Zygon scientists entered the milking chamber. Instantly the Doctor dived behind the snoozing Skarasen, flattening himself against the floor. He lay for a moment, listening for the sound of raised voices that would inform him that he had been spotted. However, hearing nothing except the greedy gulp of the lactic-fluid pumps, he crawled along the length of the Skarasen's body until he had reached its head, then peeked out from behind it.

The two Zygon scientists were making their way unhurriedly down the steps. It seemed inevitable that in a matter of moments they would be heading towards his hiding place. All the Doctor could do was lie there and hope for the best. 'Excuse me,' he whispered and pressed himself so tightly against the underside of the Skarasen's jaw that he could smell its breath, an odd combination of rancid meat and engine oil, and feel the nudge of a strong, steady pulse in its throat.

The Zygon scientists walked towards him, talking in their high, fluting voices. Suddenly they stopped and the Doctor heard one of them say, 'What is this?' He closed his eyes briefly. He had forgotten about the discarded flippers. Stupid, stupid, stupid. He heard the scrape of the flippers as one of the Zygons picked them up.

'They appear to be footwear of some kind,' one of them trilled.

'I agree,' said the other. 'Perhaps they belonged to the escaped human. They are certainly not of Zygon manufacture. I will raise the alarm immediately.'

'There's no need for that,' the Doctor said, abruptly jumping up and walking towards them. 'I'm sure we can talk this whole thing through like sensible aliens.'

The two Zygons looked almost comically surprised, and more than a little nervous. Knowing that the best way to retain an advantage was to keep talking, the Doctor babbled, 'I've just been taking a look at that Skarasen of yours, and I think it's got a touch of croup. Perhaps it might be best if you got a vet in to look at it. I mean, you can never be too careful about these things, can you?'

He was within hand-shaking distance of the Zygons now. One of them suddenly piped, 'You are not the escaped human.'

'No,' said the Doctor soothingly, 'I'm the Doctor. Tuval and I have been to fetch my TARDIS. We've just got back. Tuval's over there.'

He flipped a casual thumb towards the darkest corner of the cavern. As the two Zygons glanced in the direction he had indicated, the Doctor curled his hands into fists and thrust out his arms, punching the two Zygons full in the face simultaneously.

One of the Zygons crumpled to the floor without a sound, startlingly crimson blood spurting from one of its nostrils. The other reeled back, keening, bringing up its delicate white hands to protect itself.

'I'm truly sorry about this,' the Doctor said, jumping forward and drawing back his fist. He pulled the Zygon's hands away from its face, and before it could gather its wits enough to unsheathe the thorns in its palms, punched it again. This time the Zygon's legs gave way and it collapsed unconscious to the floor.

Knowing that he had had no alternative did not prevent the Doctor from being ashamed of his actions. He dragged the bodies quickly out of sight, examined them to ensure there was no permanent damage, then scooped up the flippers and made his way back across the cavern and up the steps on to the walkway. Moments later he was slipping barefoot through the burbling corridors of the Zygon ship, heading for what he hoped was the cell area. After taking two wrong turnings and retracing his steps, and having to conceal himself from several more patrolling Zygons, he found it.

He smiled when he saw that Litefoot's alcove was empty, recalling how the two Zygon scientists had mentioned an escaped human. Although it scuppered his plans to rescue Litefoot, he could only applaud his old friend's initiative. He wondered briefly where Litefoot was now and hoped that by being free the professor didn't land himself in more trouble than he would otherwise have been in.

He turned his attention to Sam, who was still lashed into her cubicle, the cowl covering her head and the upper part of her face. He supposed that her being here unharmed must mean that Tuval was still held by the time bubble in the TARDIS, and that the Zygon scientist's synchron response was still strong. The Doctor was pleased with himself for knocking up this extra embellishment to the TARDIS's defence systems; he hadn't known for certain how effective it would be. Discarding the flippers, he examined the nodular controls beside Sam's alcove and carefully manipulated them. Instantly a couple of the tentacles tethering Sam's body began to lash as though under attack. The Doctor made a hasty adjustment and their frantic activity subsided.

The Zygon controls in this area of the ship were subtle and sensitive, but it didn't take him long to work them out. '*Voilà*,' he murmured as the cowl slid from Sam's face with a faint sucking sound and ascended into the ceiling. At the same time the tentacles uncurled themselves from around her body and hung limp as ropes. Also immediately Sam began to stir, her lips parting, eyes flickering open.

'What time is it?' she asked, her voice faint, rusty.

'Time to go,' replied the Doctor. 'How are you feeling?'

Her eyes opened wide and she looked at him. 'Like something disgusting has been trying to suck out my brain.'

'Excellent,' said the Doctor. 'You're not delusional then. Come on.'

He helped her out of the alcove. Sam glanced behind her at the now dormant cowl curled up near the ceiling, and shuddered. 'That was a very uncool piece of headgear,' she said weakly. 'Not my style at all.'

'Oh, I don't know. I've got some rather fetching photographs. I thought we could blow them up and have them printed as T-shirts.'

Sam laughed a little forcedly. 'Maybe I could send one to my parents with a postcard. "Hi, Mum and Dad: having a great time. Here's me wearing an alien mind-sucking device. Wish you were here"...'

They made their way out of the cell area, the Doctor leading the way. They spent the next ten minutes as the Doctor had spent most of the past half-hour – sneaking around, avoiding Zygons.

'So what are we doing?' asked Sam eventually. 'Looking for the canteen?'

'Either that or a way out. Or Litefoot,' the Doctor added.

'Oh yeah, the professor. Where is he?'

'Escaped.'

'Escaped?' Her tone was a little indignant, as if she believed that should have been her prerogative. 'How did he manage that?'

'Your guess is as good as mine. I haven't been around.'

'So what *have* you been doing while I've been having my little snooze? Scuba-diving from the looks of it.'

'That and other things,' said the Doctor, smiling. 'Annoying people mostly.'

'It's reassuring to know that nothing changes,' said Sam.

They came to a small chamber with a hole in the ceiling.

'Aha,' said the Doctor. 'The emergency exit.' He unzipped his hip pack and produced a small transparent cube, which he handed to Sam. 'Here, put this on.'

Sam looked at it, unimpressed. 'What am I supposed to do with it? Wear it as a brooch?'

He smiled and produced another cube, which he held by the very tip of one of its corners between the thumb and forefinger of his right hand. He made a sudden flicking motion with his wrist as though cracking a whip, and instantly the cube unravelled, expanding its mass to a seemingly impossible degree as it did so.

Within seconds, dangling from the Doctor's hand was what appeared to be a large sheet of transparent jelly-like material.

'What is it?' asked Sam, somewhat awed by the way the material seemed to shimmer and become iridescent, almost as if it was alive.

'It's a daxamoil suit,' said the Doctor. 'I bought this one and the one that you're holding from a Verulonian dealer on Peluvia.

Once you put it on, it moulds itself instantly to your shape. It's self-sealing, flexible, waterproof and fireproof, and it automatically keeps the body of its wearer at the optimum temperature required for their particular species.'

'Sounds great,' said Sam. 'You should have got a job lot. We could have flogged them down Camden Market. Er... why do we have to put them on?'

'Because we're going outside,' said the Doctor.

'Outside meaning?'

'Well, we may get lucky, and this chute may lead straight up on to dry land. But if it doesn't we'll find ourselves spat out into the Thames, in which case we'll have to swim for it.'

'I was afraid you were going to say that.' She sighed. 'OK, so if that thing moulds itself to your body and then seals itself, how do we breathe?'

'Ah,' said the Doctor, 'now that's the clever bit. To quote the chap who sold me the suit, "Whenceforth ever your respiratory doings is, daxamoil will expungify the requisital elementals from its own self and henceforth make a donatory prize to your respiratory systematic. Comprendino?"'

'Just about,' said Sam. 'So what's the catch?'

'There isn't one. Not in our case anyway. Now, if you were to wear the suit for three or four hours, then there would be a problem, because the more chemical elements that the suit donates to the wearer to allow him or her to breathe, the more brittle and opaque it becomes. In the end, the suit would simply deteriorate, flake by flake, like dry skin.'

Sam nodded slowly. 'OK, so what do I do?'

'Just shake the suit out as I did, and then drape it around yourself like a blanket. The daxamoil will do the rest.'

Sam did as instructed, trying not to appear hesitant. She expected the daxamoil to feel cold and slippery as she draped it around her shoulders, but in fact it was pleasantly warm and smooth as silk. She braced herself as the strange substance flowed over her, not unlike an all-enveloping version of the Zygon cowl that had covered her head and face. Taking her cue from the Doctor, who appeared perfectly calm, she tried not to panic as the stuff adhered to her face, pressing against her eyeballs and lips and rushing up her nostrils. Fortunately, the sensation was not as unpleasant as she had been expecting; indeed, it was hardly unpleasant at all, merely peculiar. Within seconds she was entirely encased in a jelly-like epidermis so thin and light that she could tell she was wearing it only by the plasticky gleam of her skin and clothes. When the Doctor spoke to her, she heard his voice quite clearly.

'Of course, I did bring this second suit for George, but as he's nowhere to be found I suppose I might as well make use of it.'

'Might as well,' agreed Sam. 'Do you think the professor managed to get out?'

The Doctor looked doubtful. 'He might have. He's a game old bird. Perhaps I ought to stay and look for him.'

'It'd be like looking for a needle in a haystack,' said Sam. 'I feel as bad as you do about leaving him, but we've got no choice. He might not even be here, and we'd only end up getting captured again.'

'Yes, you're right,' sighed the Doctor. He meshed his fingers together in a stirrup for her to step into, and, abruptly cheerful, said, 'I hope you're feeling energetic. Guess what we're going to do now.'

'Climb?' she said.

'Climb,' he confirmed.

It felt as though someone had been jumping up and down on his sternum wearing hob-nailed boots. The instant consciousness returned to Litefoot, he sincerely wished it would go away again. His head was a jumble of confused images: dark, enclosed spaces, nightmarish creatures, black water from which he could not escape. At this last memory a feeling of panic gripped him and he lurched upright, gasping.

Instantly pain blazed in his chest and throat, and transformed his lungs into two bags of blazing hot coals. So agonising was the sensation that he could not even cry out. He sank back on to the unfamiliar bed and stared up at the unfamiliar ceiling, willing the pain to ebb away. Eventually it did, though an echo of it resounded each time he drew a breath. Moving only his head, he looked around to ascertain where he was.

Hospital, evidently, and a private room at that. He knew he was high up because the large window to the left of his iron-framed bed afforded him a view of nothing more than an early dawn sky, streaked with blueberry-coloured clouds.

He tried to piece his broken memories together. Yes, of course, he had been with the Doctor and Miss Samantha. As though the memory of the Doctor was the key that unlocked his mind, it suddenly all came flooding back to him.

The Zygons! Of course! My word, how could he have forgotten that? He had been expelled from their lair, hadn't he, effectively sneezed out into deep, dark water that had stolen his consciousness?

Frankly, now that he came to think of it, it was astounding that he had woken up at all. He must have been closer to the surface and the bank than he had realised. Someone must have spotted him and fished him out. If so, then he possessed the luck of the devil, though perhaps it might be prudent not to celebrate quite so soon. The river was so filthy that he might yet fall prey to all manner of lethal complaints. His body could be acting as an incubator for cholera or typhus even now.

What of the Doctor and Miss Samantha? he wondered. Were they still in peril, held captive by the Zygons? He wondered how long he had been unconscious. It could be hours or days.

'Nurse,' he called, the word sawing at his throat like a rusty hacksaw blade and emerging as a croak. Nevertheless, a nurse appeared within seconds, a mere slip of a girl, evidently nervous to be caring for so prominent a patient.

'Yes, sir?' she said.

'Could you tell me how long I've been here, my dear?'

'Yes, sir. Several hours, sir. Four at least.'

'Hours, not days? You're quite sure?' said Litefoot.

'Yes, sir.'

'Excellent. Then there's still hope. Fetch me my clothes, would you, my dear?'

'Your clothes, sir?' said the girl uncertainly.

'Yes, and quick about it if you please. I have some rather pressing business to attend to.'

'B-begging your pardon, sir,' stammered the nurse, 'but Dr Hollis gave express instructions that you were not to exert yourself; indeed, that you were to get plenty of rest.'

'Pooh,' said Litefoot dismissively. 'You forget, my dear, that I too am a physician, and I pronounce myself perfectly capable of resuming my daily duties.'

The nurse looked unhappy. 'That's as may be, sir, but a problem still remains.'

'And that is?'

'Your clothes, sir. We tried washing and drying them, but they were quite unsalvageable. I'm afraid we have had to throw them away.'

'Good Lord, that's not a problem,' said Litefoot. 'Send to my house for some more. My housekeeper, Mrs Hudson, will sort something out. I, of course, will reimburse any expenses incurred by the hospital. Now please make haste, my dear. I'm in a terrible hurry.'

Thoroughly cowed, the young nurse could only nod. 'Yes, sir. At once, sir.' Then she turned tail and all but fled from the room.

The Doctor and Sam *did* get lucky, the chute emerging in a culvert close to the river. At the top of the chute a crystalline panel slid back and then part of the floor of the culvert itself, allowing them to climb out, exhausted but triumphant.

Sam bent double, hands on knees. 'I'm knackered,' she gasped.

'Too much easy living, that's your trouble,' panted the Doctor. 'Come on.' He began to stroll away.

They made their way on to the towpath and headed for the TARDIS, the Doctor retrieving his carpet bag from beneath the bench when they passed it a few minutes later. The night was a flimsy veil which daylight was gradually shredding. The fog was dissipating too, allowing Sam her first view of the concrete-grey Thames. She saw boats bobbing on the water, far enough away for her smallest fingernail to blot them out, and the suggestion of buildings on the far side, a few of which were aglow with light.

The TARDIS appeared ahead of them, solid and dependable as ever. The Doctor unlocked the door and they went inside. Sam faltered on the threshold, her eyes widening.

'Bloody hell! That's me!'

Tuval, in Sam's body, was still standing by the TARDIS console. Without a word the Doctor strode across the room, hopped up on to the dais, where he dropped the carpet bag, and began to operate the controls with his usual dexterity, looking not unlike a down-at-heel superhero in his shimmering wet suit.

Getting over her shock, Sam moved forward, though her eyes remained glued on the immobile yet three-dimensional image of herself by the console.

'What's going on, Doctor?' she shouted, trying to make herself heard above the dreadful screeching sound that was filling the room. 'And what's that awful –'

The screeching abruptly stopped.

'– noise?'

The Doctor hopped down from the console as Tuval, released from the time bubble, staggered and almost fell. He took hold of the Zygon's arm and steered it towards the chair where Sam had dumped her Walkman a couple of days earlier. He looked at Sam and nodded at the Walkman. She hurried forward and scooped it out of the way a split second before Tuval dropped in to the chair with a thump. The Zygon blinked and looked around dazedly.

'Are you all right?' the Doctor asked.

'I am fine,' said Tuval. 'The defences of your ship are very effective. Thank you for showing them to me.'

'My pleasure,' smiled the Doctor.

Suddenly Tuval registered the Doctor's attire, and the Zygon's borrowed features creased in puzzlement. 'You have changed, Doctor.'

The Doctor looked momentarily alarmed. 'Not again, surely?' Then he relaxed. 'Oh, you mean the clothes. Yes,' he said vaguely. 'Tell me, Tuval, what do you remember?'

'I remember being unable to move, and you telling me that you were going to stop Balaak from carrying out our plan. The next moment I felt faint and you took me by the arm and led me to this chair. Tell me, Doctor, how do you intend to stop Balaak?'

'I already have,' said the Doctor. When Tuval looked puzzled, he said, 'I activated the stasis circuit and set up a localised time loop within it. To you, only moments have passed, but I've actually been away for several hours.'

Tuval looked at him in disbelief. 'Impossible.'

'I'm afraid not,' said the Doctor gently. 'If my clothes don't convince you, then here's someone that will.' He held out his hand. 'Sam.'

Sam, still not entirely sure what was going on, came forward warily, rounding the chair so that Tuval could see her. The Zygon stared at the human whose body print it was wearing, and then its shoulders seemed to slump in defeat.

'What have you done to my people?'

'Nothing,' said the Doctor. 'Or at least, nothing that you need worry about. You might say I'm working towards a mutually beneficial solution to this situation for all concerned.'

'Doctor,' interrupted Sam, 'who is this gorgeous person?' And then before the Doctor could reply, she blurted, 'Oh, don't tell me. It's a Zygon, isn't it, wearing my body? Bloody cheek! Is my nose really that big?'

'Only in certain lights,' said the Doctor, smiling. 'This is Tuval. Tuval, your twin here is called Sam.'

'Hi,' said Sam. 'I won't shake hands if you don't mind.' To the Doctor she hissed, 'Is she – I mean, it – dangerous?'

'Why don't you ask Tuval,' said the Doctor, and then raising his voice, 'You're not dangerous, are you, Tuval?'

The Zygon looked surprised by the question. 'I do not intend to harm you, if that is what you mean. I am a scientist, not a warrior.'

'There, you see,' said the Doctor. 'Besides, the state-of-grace circuits won't allow any aggressive action to be committed within the confines of the TARDIS. Well... not unless they break down again,' he added.

The Zygon scientist produced a vial of milky fluid from inside its jacket (which of course was identical to the jacket that Sam was wearing) and began sucking on it greedily.

'Hey,' said Sam, 'what are you doing?'

The Doctor put a hand on her arm. 'It's all right, Sam, it's lactic fluid. Zygons need regular infusions.' He crossed to the carpet bag, opened it and extracted a small spray canister. 'I think it's time we got these suits off, don't you?'

He squirted a fine spray from the canister over himself, like a man applying far too much deodorant, and immediately the daxamoil suit began to turn brittle and milky in appearance. Digging in his fingers, the Doctor was now able to tear the suit easily. He ripped it away from himself and dropped it on the floor, where it continued to deteriorate, then crossed to Sam and sprayed her too. As Tuval drained the vial of lactic fluid and sank back with a sigh, Sam stepped from the ruin of her suit like a snake shedding its skin.

Sated and much revived, the Zygon scientist inquired, 'You said something about a mutually beneficial solution, Doctor?'

'Yes, I did,' said the Doctor, unzipping his wet suit and discarding it with no inhibitions whatsoever. Seemingly oblivious to Sam, who was blushing wildly but trying to appear cool, he hopped back up on to the dais wearing only his long johns and began to get dressed while simultaneously resetting the TARDIS co-ordinates.

'I didn't much like Balaak's plan to commit genocide,' he said, buttoning up his trousers and tucking in his shirt. 'Too messy by half. So I popped back to your ship and laced your milk supply with one hundred millilitres of highly concentrated anaesthetic. Four hours from now every single Zygon on the ship will be sleeping like a baby.'

'Oh, I get it,' said Sam, still with a flush in her cheeks. 'We're going to hop forward in the TARDIS and...'

'And?' prompted the Doctor, shrugging on his frock coat.

She frowned. 'Tie them all up and tickle their feet until they promise to go away?'

The Doctor smiled. 'That was my first plan, but I spotted a couple of tiny flaws in it. So what I thought we'd do instead was materialise inside the Zygon ship, release all the captive humans, and then link the damaged Zygon drive systems into the TARDIS.'

'Which means you could then take their ship far away from Earth before any of them wake up,' said Sam triumphantly.

'Exactly! I'd pilot the ship to an uninhabited planet as closely allied to the Zygons' own ecosystem as possible where they can start a new life without having to annihilate anyone. What do you think, Tuval?'

Both the Doctor and Sam turned to Tuval, who was still sitting in the chair. The Zygon scientist looked thoughtful for a moment and then nodded. 'It seems the perfect solution, Doctor. My only concern is that our two technologies will be incompatible.'

The Doctor wafted a hand dismissively. 'Oh, don't worry about that. I'll cobble something up. I'm quite good at that kind of thing.'

The first thing Litefoot did after discharging himself from hospital was to hail a carriage and return home. Though he felt bruised and battered both inside and out, he was determined to help the Doctor and Miss Samantha. However he knew all too well how foolish it would be to rush headlong into danger without first procuring some means of defence. To avoid falling prey to his housekeeper's curiosity, he had informed the messenger who had been sent to fetch him a fresh set of clothes to explain that his previous attire had become so bespattered with unsavoury bodily fluids due to his gruesome work at the hospital that it had had to be incinerated. Upon arriving at Ranskill Gardens, he asked the cab driver to wait for him, then plodded wearily up the steps to his front door.

He was forced to knock because his keys, together with his pocket watch, pipe and other sundry items had been claimed by the unforgiving waters of the Thames. The instant she opened the door, Mrs Hudson recoiled as if slapped.

'Good heavens, sir, you looked whacked to the wide! You appear to have had quite a time of it.'

'Indeed I have, Mrs Hudson,' Litefoot murmured. 'Indeed I have.'

He entered the house, Mrs Hudson hovering concernedly by his shoulder.

'Can I rustle you up some hot broth, sir? Or some ham and eggs perhaps? Pardon me for saying so, but you do look as though you need a good square meal inside you.'

The offer was almost unbearably tempting, but Litefoot forced himself to shake his head. 'I don't have time, I'm afraid, Mrs Hudson. Duty beckons. I have a cab waiting outside as we speak.'

She tutted and shook her head. 'It's criminal, the way they treat you at that hospital, sir, if you don't mind me saying so, expecting you to work all hours God sends. Then of course there's all these policemen coming to the door, wanting you to do this and that. A body can only take so much, sir, before it gives up the ghost for good.'

'I'm sure you're right, Mrs Hudson,' Litefoot said hastily. 'Nevertheless, I really do have a rather pressing matter to attend to. So if you'll excuse me…'

'Yes, sir, of course, sir. Far be it from me to tell you how to go about your business.' Muttering tetchily, she bustled away down the hall.

Only when he heard the kitchen door slam behind her, did

Litefoot scuttle across to the door beneath the stairs that led to the cellar. He hurried through it, and reappeared moments later carrying a fearsome-looking weapon – a Chinese fowling piece, which his father had purchased in Peking many years before and handed down to him before their rift. It was a long-barrelled muzzle-loader, a cross between a rifle and a blunderbuss. Ironically, the last time it had been fired in anger had been during the Weng-Chiang business five years before. The other Doctor had used it to dispose of one of a number of giant rats that had been roaming the sewers of London.

Carrying the gun, Litefoot crept to the front door and opened it cautiously. However, he had to spin round, concealing the weapon behind him, as the kitchen door opened and Mrs Hudson reappeared.

'I was just wondering, sir, whether you would be in for supper,' she asked pointedly.

Litefoot's first instinct was to say he didn't know, but then he saw the look on her face. 'You can count on it, Mrs Hudson,' he said.

Once she had returned to the kitchen, he fled as swiftly as his ravaged body would allow to the carriage that was still waiting for him, and after giving instructions to the driver to take him to Seers's factory, climbed inside. He spent the journey loading the gun with powder and shot from a small canvas bag and desperately trying to dredge up a little energy from deep within his reserves. He closed his eyes and breathed shallowly; it still hurt when he breathed, but the pain in his lungs had faded to a dull ache. At some stage, the gun propped between his knees, its muzzle pointing up at the roof of the cab, he must have dozed off, for he was next aware of the cab driver calling, 'Here we are, guv.'

He roused himself, paid the driver and got out. The area was busy at this hour of the morning, factory workers arriving from all quarters in readiness to begin their toil. However, there was a markedly different atmosphere around the gates of Seers's factory than there was around the others. Workers were not filing through the big gates to begin work, but were milling around them in confused groups, the air full of chatter.

Litefoot approached a knot of male workers who were standing in a tight circle, smoking and talking. As they eyed him warily, Litefoot realised how incongruous he must look in top hat and overcoat, carrying a piece of hand artillery that was half as tall as himself.

Nevertheless, he tried to project an air of jovial authority as he strolled up. 'What's going on here?' he inquired.

The workers glanced at each other, and then one, electing himself spokesman, said, 'Factory's burnt to the ground, sir, during the night. See for yourself.'

Litefoot did so, people stepping aside to let him pass. He peered through the gates and saw that the man's words were true. The factory was a blackened, smoking ruin. A surprisingly large number of police officers were picking through the rubble like carrion crows. Litefoot strolled back to the group of workers he had spoken to, people again moving aside for him, regarding his appearance and his gun with expressions of puzzled respect.

'Would any of you happen to know what all these police officers are doing here?' he asked the men.

A number of them shuffled their feet and looked down at the ground. The same man who had spoken before said cautiously, 'Well, sir, we're none of us rightly sure, but there have been one or two stories...'

'What kinds of stories?' asked Litefoot.

'Well, sir, now I'm only repeating what I've heard, but it has been said that the owner's wife, Mrs Seers, has been found dead, horribly murdered, in her own home, and that Mr Seers and his daughter are nowhere to be found.'

'Indeed?' said Litefoot.

'Yes, sir. Now far be it from me to say whether or not these rumours are true, but that's what I've heard, sir.'

'Thank you,' said Litefoot. 'You've been most enlightening.'

'Not at all, sir. Glad to be of service.' The man hesitated for a moment and then said, 'I take it you're... er... not with the peelers then, sir?'

'Indeed, no,' said Litefoot. 'I'm a physician.'

'Off to do a spot of duck-hunting down by the river are you, sir?'

Litefoot chuckled. 'Who knows? Perhaps I might bag myself something a little larger, eh? Good day, gentlemen.' He doffed his hat.

The workers mumbled their goodbyes, tugging their forelocks or the brims of their caps. Litefoot took his leave, anxious to make himself scarce before a police officer could spot him and ask him why he had such a fearsome-looking weapon in his possession.

He made his way down to the river, his only plan now being to locate the strange blue box that the Doctor owned. The other Doctor had owned such a box, and as such it was Litefoot's only link with his mysterious friend and his equally mysterious but charming companion.

He didn't actually know what he was going to do when he arrived at his destination. Though the box was evidently important to the Doctor, he didn't appear to feel a need to remain in its vicinity. Litefoot had a vague notion that the box may provide him with some clue as to his friend's present whereabouts. If not, he supposed his only option was to wait until the Doctor appeared – but for how long?

Although the Doctor's cubicle in the Zygon craft had been empty, that did not necessarily mean he had made good his escape. The Zygons may have released him from his bonds and taken him away for some unspeakable purpose of their own. Litefoot tried to push these thoughts to the back of his mind as he strode along the towpath. He would not abandon hope until he was absolutely certain that all hope was gone.

The only occasion he had seen the Doctor's blue box had been on the evening – two, three days ago? – when he, the Doctor, Miss Samantha and the bogus Miss Emmeline had entered the factory via the sewer. Yet although the river and its environs looked somewhat different in the day light, he was still certain he knew precisely where the box was located. However, upon arriving there, there was no box to be seen. Perplexed, Litefoot looked up and down the length of the towpath and even walked a little further along, thinking he must have been mistaken.

Finally, he returned to the spot where he was certain the box had stood and examined the ground. Sure enough, there were slight indentations in the thick mud between the cobbles, substantiating his conviction. So the box had gone. And the Doctor? Had he gone too?

All at once, feeling terribly, terribly weary, Litefoot stumbled across to one of the iron benches that were placed at regular intervals along the towpath and sank down on to it.

'How long will the journey take, Doctor?' Tuval asked, watching the rods of light within the time rotor mesh and unmesh. The Zygon wore an expression of professional interest, which, thought Sam, either meant that 'she' (she couldn't stop thinking of Tuval as a she) was either impressed by the TARDIS and trying not to show it, or was unimpressed and didn't want to hurt the Doctor's feelings.

'How long is a piece of Taran grappling twine?' replied the Doctor cryptically. The TARDIS made a noise that sounded alarmingly like a cough, and the Doctor hit the console hard in a carefully chosen spot with the flat of his hand.

Immediately the familiar dematerialisation noise filled the room. Tuval looked alarmed.

'Don't worry, it means we're there,' Sam said.

'Magnificent,' the Doctor murmured, examining the readings once the straining of the TARDIS's ancient engines had faded. 'When it comes to the crunch, the old girl never lets me down.' He flicked a couple of switches. 'Now, a quick glance at the scanner.'

Instantly the readings on the scanner screen were replaced by a view of the Zygon control room. Both Sam and Tuval, side by side like Tweedledum and Tweedledee, stood and looked up at the screen.

'It's a bit murky,' said Sam. 'You can't really see what's what. Oh yeah, look, there's one of your lot, Tuval. And there's another. Just like you said, Doctor, they all seem to be having a bit of a kip.'

The Doctor came and stood behind them, a full head taller than them both, and peered up at the screen himself. He was silent for a long moment, hands in pockets, eyes narrowed, lips pursed.

Finally Sam twisted her head to look at him. 'Is something wrong, Doctor?'

'I'm not sure.' The Doctor sounded and looked troubled. Suddenly he jerked into life. 'You two wait here. I'm going to have a quick look round. If all's well, I'll give you a shout.'

He had leapt up on to the dais, operated the door control, and was halfway across the room before either of them could respond.

'Doctor –' Sam belatedly began to protest.

He held up a hand, and, his voice booming around the room, cried, 'One minute, that's all.' Then he plunged through the double doors and out of sight.

Once he was released from the protective confines of the TARDIS, the stench hit him immediately. Litefoot had once likened the smell inside the Zygon ship to the stomach contents of a day-old corpse, but this was far worse: this was like a corpse that had spoiled over several weeks.

Instantly, dread settled inside the Doctor's belly, heavy as an anvil. He looked slowly around, and as he did so his face filled with horror and disbelief. Every last Zygon that was sprawled on the floor or slumped across an instrument console was dead. And not only that, but their bodies were liquefying rapidly, turning mushy as slugs that had been doused in salt.

'What have I done?' he whispered, feeling as desolate as he could ever remember. He had washed his hands in the blood of his enemies many times in his past, had committed genocide on more than one occasion, and yet never could he remember having made such a monumental mistake before.

He could only stand and gape, and might have remained in that state for some considerable time, had he not sensed movement behind him. He turned to see Sam and Tuval emerging from the TARDIS. He could tell simply by the way they moved that Sam was in the lead.

He spun round, throwing his arms wide in the vain hope of concealing the terrible sight from them. 'Don't come out here!' he shouted.

'Why not?' asked Sam, and then she recoiled, screwing up her face. 'Christ, what a stink! I think I'm going to puke.'

Tuval was looking around, face blank and uncomprehending at first. Then, slowly, absolute horror dawned on the very human features that the Zygon was wearing.

'Tuval,' began the Doctor haltingly, 'I'm so sorry. Look, I didn't mean –'

'What have you done?' The words were jagged splinters of sound. 'You've murdered my people! You killed them all! You lied to me!'

'No.' The Doctor shook his head. 'No, this wasn't meant to happen.'

Sam had both hands pressed to her face. She looked as though she was trying to fight the urge to throw up. 'What's happened to them?' she moaned.

'Cellular breakdown,' said the Doctor in a hollow voice. 'They must have reacted to some chemical in the anaesthetic. I never dreamed…'

'You killed them,' Tuval whispered. 'You killed them.'

The stricken Zygon pressed its clenched fists to the side of its head and began to wail.

'I didn't mean to,' the Doctor said. His words were almost a plea. 'It was a terrible mistake. I had no idea that your people would react as they did.'

Forgetting her inhibitions, Sam put her arms around her weeping double. 'Can't you go back?' she asked. 'Put things right?'

He shook his head miserably. 'What's done is done. I can't change it.'

'But you're a Time Lord. All we have to do is get in the TARDIS and hop back a few hours.'

'*No!*' shouted the Doctor, displaying a rare flash of anger. 'We can't undo what's already happened, Sam. If we start to unravel the past, it will go on unravelling. We will do untold damage.'

'But you change things all the time,' she said. 'You're always interfering.'

'Only from the standpoint of the present. I can give little nudges here and there. Within the confines of the TARDIS I can even project future events and try to alter them before they happen. But I can't go back to undo what's already been done, Sam. Not ever. If I could we'd live in a perfect universe and then where would we be?'

Now it was her turn to be angry. She shook her head, scowling. 'Sometimes I don't understand you,' she said.

'No,' said the Doctor quietly, 'you don't.'

He turned from the carnage he had wreaked and took a step back towards the TARDIS. Suddenly there was a movement in the murky shadows behind him. Sam saw a hideous, bubbling shape rising from behind a nearby console. Before she could shout a warning, the Zygon warlord, Balaak, blisters erupting all over its body, gave a hissing roar and lurched across the room, arms outstretched. Sam caught a glimpse of the thorns projecting from its palms an instant before it clamped its hands to the sides of the Doctor's neck. The Doctor's face creased in agony and he collapsed, writhing, to the floor.

'You killed my people, Time Lord,' Balaak rasped, deep-set eyes burning with orange light. 'Now I kill you!'

CHAPTER 9
UNLEASHED

All at once Balaak staggered, and was prevented from falling only by the mushroom-like controls of a nearby console which the Zygon warlord managed to clutch hold of. Immediately Tuval pulled free of Sam's embrace and rushed to help Balaak, taking the dying leader's arm, offering support. Balaak was breathing stertorously, its flesh running with pus from the blisters bursting all over its body. The Doctor was lying on the floor in a question-mark shape, knees bent, back bowed, head tucked in, eyes closed.

Sam went to the Doctor and crouched beside him. His hands were pressed to the puncture wounds in his neck. She wondered what she should do. Suck out the poison before it got into his bloodstream? Unable to think of anything else, she took hold of his right wrist, intending to drag his hand away from the infected area.

His eyes opened. They were cloudy with pain, but not insensible with it. Through clenched teeth he muttered, 'Balaak dying... not enough poison... not fatal... Help me sit up.'

She did so, putting her arm around him and dragging him upright as best she could, allowing him to rest his lolling head against her shoulder.

'Balaak...' he croaked.

The Zygon warlord, still leaning against Tuval, raised its great, domed head with an effort.

'Didn't mean this to happen...' the Doctor gasped. 'Wanted peaceful solution... all this... terrible mistake... So sorry.'

There was no forgiveness in Balaak's eyes. The Zygon stared at the Doctor balefully.

'How did you kill us, Time Lord?' it gurgled.

'He trapped me in a time bubble in his TARDIS. Then he returned to our ship and introduced a concentrated anaesthetic into the lactic fluid supply, Commander,' explained Tuval. The Zygon scientist seemed about to say more, but then appeared to think better of it.

'Then that is why I, alone, am still alive,' rasped Balaak. 'In order to facilitate our plan I have foregone several of my nourishment periods.'

Suddenly Balaak doubled over, choking and gasping. Sam looked away as thick, brownish fluid spilled from the Zygon warlord's mouth and spattered on the floor.

'Commander!' cried Tuval in alarm as Balaak's legs began to give way. With Tuval's help and the support of a console, the Zygon warlord remained standing.

'Do something for me, Tuval,' Balaak hissed.

'Anything, Commander.'

Balaak's features were almost unrecognisable, engulfed in a mass of dribbling boils. 'Complete what I am unable to do. Kill the Doctor.'

There was a pause. Tuval looked at Sam and the Doctor, face unreadable. Sam stared back, alarmed but defiant.

'No,' she said suddenly, her voice spiralling to the high ceiling. 'I won't let you.'

She lowered the Doctor gently to the floor and stood in front of him, clenching her fists.

'Kill them both!' gurgled Balaak.

Tuval advanced, blank-faced. Sam raised her fists. 'Come any closer and you'll regret it.'

Suddenly Tuval ran at Sam. Sam lashed out, catching her opponent on the side of the head. Tuval staggered slightly, but kept on coming. Sam threw another punch, but this time her blow was parried. Then Tuval was thrusting its hands beneath her armpits and picking her up, its strength surprising her. The Zygon lifted her into the air as if she was a baby and hurled her savagely to one side. In her path was a console, which Sam, unable to halt her momentum, half expected to bounce off as if it was rubber. She hit it face first; it was like crashing into a tree. Stars exploded across her vision and she tasted blood in her mouth.

Then she blacked out.

The Doctor lay on his back and looked up as Tuval loomed over him. The Zygon's eyes in Sam's face were flickering with orange light. The pain of Balaak's poison was ebbing now as his own system dealt with it, but the warlord's attack had left him too weak to resist a further one.

He saw Tuval reach towards him, ironically resembling a healer about to perform a laying-on of hands. He saw the suckers open in Tuval's palms, the tips of the spines peek through, oozing poison. He looked up into Tuval's face, into Tuval's eyes, calm and unafraid.

Tuval gazed back at him. A long moment passed.

Then the spines retracted into Tuval's palms and the Zygon scientist half turned away.

'You are mistaken, Commander,' Tuval said. 'Your sting was strong enough to kill. The Time Lord is dead.'

The Doctor heard Balaak give a hiss of satisfaction. Tuval glanced back at him briefly. He gave the Zygon a tiny, grateful nod and closed his eyes, leaving a slit to peek through. He saw Tuval stand up and walk back over to Balaak.

'Help me… to the… main console,' Balaak rasped.

Tuval did as Balaak asked, the two of them shuffling through the putrid remains of their dead comrades. Once at the console,

Balaak all but fell against it with a gasp of pain, and weakly began manipulating the controls.

'Our plans... may be in ruins... but we can still take our revenge... on this loathsome planet.'

An ovular screen fizzed into life, showing a red-tinged view of the swamp area in which a number of Skarasen could be seen and heard snarling and splashing.

'What are you going to do, Commander?' asked Tuval.

'I will release... the Skarasen... into the city.'

'But they are not yet fully grown, Commander.'

'They will still be more than a match... for the humans,' Balaak gurgled gloatingly.

The Zygon warlord twisted a control, and a rushing sound crackled from the speakers, filling the room. On the screen the water level in the swamp area began noticeably to fall.

Beneath the Thames, the Zygon ship raised itself up on its spindly legs. A flap, like the mouth of a crab, opened in its base, and within seconds dozens of Skarasen were pouring out of it. Like a shoal of giant fish, they congregated for a moment, their bodies flashing silver. Then, as though reacting to some prearranged signal, they darted away, their powerful limbs propelling them in different directions.

Slumped over the main console, Balaak watched the Skarasen go, blistered face alive with savage glee. Then the Zygon warlord turned, and, with Tuval's help, limped over to a control unit set in its own alcove. This unit was shaped like a giant gnarled heart, held suspended by thick transparent tubes that ran out of the floor and up through the ceiling. Balaak's rasping breath reverberated around the control centre as it began to twist nodular growths that served as controls.

'What are you doing, Commander?' asked Tuval, alarmed.

'I am setting… the self-destructor unit.'

'But our ship…' Tuval protested weakly.

'Now that we have… the Doctor's time craft… it is of no further use to us… It pains me to abandon… our fallen comrades… but we must be ruthless, Tuval… It is imperative… that we leave none of our technology behind… for the humans to find.'

'Of course, Commander,' said Tuval, casting a glance at the Doctor. He was still lying motionless, his eyes closed. He looked as if he was truly dead, or at least unconscious.

The self-destructor unit began to burble quietly, and dark fluid appeared in the pipes jutting up through the floor and slowly began to rise towards the unit itself. 'It is done,' said Balaak weakly. The Zygon warlord turned with an effort and hobbled over to the TARDIS, Tuval in attendance. Pausing by the half-open TARDIS door, Balaak placed a pustulating, claw-like hand on the machine's battered blue exterior. 'Is it safe to enter?'

'Yes, Commander.'

Suddenly Balaak swayed as though about to collapse. 'Help me, Tuval.'

The words were not uttered plaintively, but as an order that Balaak fully expected to be obeyed. Sure enough, Tuval rushed forward to take the Zygon commander's liquefying right arm, and together the two of them shuffled into the TARDIS.

'How much did you learn… about the workings of the machine?' Balaak hissed, seemingly oblivious to the Gothic majesty of the console room.

'Only a little, Commander,' muttered Tuval doubtfully.

Balaak waved a dismissive claw. 'No matter. We are… Zygons. We will learn… quickly. Close… the doors, Tuval.'

After lowering Balaak carefully into the chair in the middle of the floor, Tuval crossed gingerly to the central dais, stepped up on to it, and examined the console with an air of authority that masked an ignorance bordering on panic. The Zygon scientist tried to recall how the Doctor had opened and closed the doors earlier. Finally spotting a likely-looking lever, Tuval took hold of it, and, offering a short prayer to the Zygon deity, Kaatu, pushed it down.

Instantly there was a hum of power and the doors closed. Tuval turned to Balaak, trying to hide the relief and satisfaction on the inordinately expressive human features that it wore.

'Now,' Balaak hissed, 'set the coordinates... for Zygor.'

One expression that Tuval could not conceal was surprise. 'But Commander, Zygor was destroyed many centuries ago.'

'Do not treat me like a fool, Tuval,' snarled Balaak. 'My body may be decaying... but my mind... for the moment... is still intact. You are forgetting that this... is a time craft... We are going to pilot the ship... into the past... to a time before Zygor was destroyed... by the Xaranti... I know it is too late for me... but I wish to die on my home planet... You, Tuval, must warn our people... about the Xaranti attack... and prevent Zygor from being destroyed.'

Tuval inclined its human head in obeisance. 'Of course, Commander.' The Zygon scientist hovered for a moment above the console, and then, hoping for the best, punched in what it believed to be were the spatial and temporal co-ordinates for Zygor. Glancing nervously at the monitor screen, Tuval was much reassured to see that the correct time and destination were indeed displayed there. Next, the Zygon reached for the lever that it was fairly sure would send the TARDIS into the time vortex. Flexing its human hand, it pulled down the lever.

Instantly a number of things happened. The most reassuring

was that the grinding, trumpeting din of the TARDIS's drive systems filled the room as, presumably, the craft dematerialised from the bridge of the Zygon ship. However, more alarmingly for Tuval, the console suddenly seemed to become 'live', threads of crackling blue light dancing across it and skittering up the outside of the time rotor like barbed wire made of electricity.

'Comman-' the Zygon scientist began, but then the light seemed to coalesce into an angry blue ball and rushed at Tuval. With a sizzling crack, it flung the Zygon backwards. Tuval felt a searing bolt of pain, and the next moment was flying through the air and crashing to the ground. A burning unconsciousness flooded in from all sides, dragging Tuval into the buzzing darkness at its centre. The last image that filled the scientist's mind was the Doctor's face, mouthing the words, 'Contingency plan'.

It was the sound of the TARDIS dematerialising that penetrated Sam's subconscious. As she spiralled up through the darkness, back towards the light, her other senses slammed into place like wooden blocks forced into holes that were slightly too small for them.

Her sense of smell was the one she could have done without. The stench of decay was so appalling that she recoiled, scrabbling upright into a sitting position. She gagged and clapped a hand to her mouth. Her stomach contents seemed to coil and twist like a bagful of snakes. Her eyes opened, at first into slits, and then wide when she realised what she was looking at. 'No,' she croaked, but it didn't stop the faint outline of the TARDIS from fading, dragging the trumpeting din of its engines along with it.

She scrambled to her feet, feeling panicked, confused, betrayed. Why had the Doctor gone off and left her here in this... this abattoir? Then she caught a flash of movement over to her right and whirled round. The Doctor was crouched over a thing that looked like a giant heart with fungus growing all over it, suspended in midair by thick tubes that sprouted up through the floor and down through the ceiling.

The heart thing was shaking, like a boiler about to explode. Steam was rising from its surface, and it was emitting a burbling, whistling noise that did not sound at all healthy. Nevertheless, although that, coupled with the Doctor's hunched stance and quick, darting movements, gave the clearest indication possible that the situation here was not good, Sam felt a rush of relief at the sight of his familiar figure. She went and stood beside him and watched him for a moment, secretly impressed by the assuredness with which he twisted and tweaked the alien controls. He didn't seem to be making much impression on the thing, but at least he looked as though he thought that what he was trying *might* work. She made a mental note to ask the Doctor for a crash course on alien technology sometime – that, of course, being dependent on whether or not they managed to get out of this particular spot of trouble.

She watched him for a bit longer, and then said, 'Is it my imagination or are we in trouble?'

He didn't pause in his task, but he did answer her. He spoke quickly, in little more than a mutter; she had to lean forward to hear him above the burbling shriek filling the bridge.

'This is the self-destructor unit, which Balaak activated before abandoning ship in my TARDIS. It works by feeding a volatile and highly toxic substance through the ship's veins. This effectively causes the ship to have a massive coronary, which sets off a series of chain reactions that eventually result in complete disintegration.'

'The words "Oh my God, we're all going to die" spring to mind,' said Sam, trying to sound more composed than she felt. 'Is there anything you can do?'

'Well, I can't reverse the process, but I think I can buy us a little time.'

'How?'

'In effect, by giving the ship an emergency heart bypass. In the short term, this will divert the toxin away from the most vital areas and keep the vessel operative. Aha!'

'What?'

'I think that's it. Listen.'

The Doctor raised his eyes to the ceiling and pointed above his head, as though the sound could be seen and tasted as well as heard. Sure enough, the burbling shriek, which had been rising to a crescendo, now seemed to have lost a little of its edge.

'You've done it,' said Sam.

'Only temporarily, but at least it gives us a fighting chance. Come on!'

'Where?' she asked, but he was already halfway across the control room. Forcing her still-wobbly legs into action, she hurried after him. For the next ten minutes, she followed his flying coat-tails along the burrow-like corridors of the Zygon ship. She felt like Alice desperately trying to keep the white rabbit in sight. However, despite her frustration, it was a relief to leave the appalling stench of decaying Zygons behind for a while. Eventually they came to a place she recognised.

'We need to wake them up,' the Doctor said, hurrying across the cell chamber to the row of alcoves against the wall.

'How?' asked Sam, diverting her eyes from the pulsing cowls covering each of the prisoners' faces and trying not to remember the sensation of one of them sliding across her own face like a giant slug.

The Doctor suddenly halted and turned to her. There was

apology in his eyes and voice. 'I know you want to help, Sam, but I honestly don't have the time to explain everything. Just this once I'm afraid you're going to have to leave it up to me.'

She nodded, tried to look mature. 'Sure, I understand. I can live with that. If there's nothing I can do –'

'No, actually, there *is* something. As these people wake up, they're going to be frightened, confused. I want you to talk to them, reassure them, try to calm them down if needs be. Emmeline and her father will need particularly careful handling. Although the Emmeline that appeared at Litefoot's house was a Zygon, I believe that much of the initial story we were told was true. This means that Emmeline thinks her father killed her mother, whereas Nathaniel Seers, poor chap, doesn't even know that his wife is dead.' He frowned. 'Come to think of it, your job is infinitely more difficult than mine. Perhaps it's unfair of me to –'

'I can handle it,' Sam said firmly.

The Doctor looked at her steadily for a moment. 'All right, if you're sure.' Then he turned to the first of the alcoves in which stood a pot-bellied man whose thick ginger side whiskers frothed from beneath the Zygon cowl.

The Doctor's fingers danced over the crystalline panel beside the cubicle, then he turned to the knot of trumpet-like growths jutting from the wall and began to twist and squeeze them. The tentacles around the fat man's body twitched and then retracted. A moment later the cowl rose from his head and ascended into the shadows near the ceiling.

Instantly the man shuddered and staggered, almost falling headlong out of the alcove. Sam and the Doctor rushed forward to help him, nearly going down themselves under his considerable weight. The man's eyes opened wide and his arms began to flail. 'Get away from me!' he yelled, his voice raw with panic. 'Get away from me, you fiends!'

The Doctor stepped smartly forward. Sam half expected him to slap the hysterical man across the face, but instead he reached out, caught hold of each of the man's flailing arms just above the elbow, and, showing remarkable strength for one so slight, clamped them to his sides.

The man stared at him, boggle-eyed, his face slack, almost stupid, with fear. A string of saliva drooled from his bottom lip before thinning and breaking and falling to the ground.

'Mr Stoker,' the Doctor said quietly, companionably. 'Mr Stoker, can you hear me?'

The man stared at him a moment longer, then blinked and nodded.

'Good. Now, Mr Stoker, you're among friends. Do you understand? Friends. You have nothing to fear from us. We're here to help you. But to do that we need *you* to help *us*. We need you to remain calm. If we're going to get out of here, we need everyone to remain calm. We all need to help each other. Do you understand that, Mr Stoker? You do want to get out of this place, don't you?'

The big man blinked, then whispered, 'Yes.'

'Good,' said the Doctor, beaming. He let go of Stoker's arms and held out a hand. 'I'm the Doctor and this is Sam.'

'Nice to meet you,' said Sam. She felt slightly grudging of the fact that the Doctor had taken away the task he'd held her responsible for before she had even had the chance to exercise that responsibility. However, she had to admit that part of her resentment came from the knowledge that she would have had neither the strength nor the authority to placate the man as the Doctor had done.

With Stoker quiescent, the Doctor moved on to the next alcove. There were a dozen people to awaken in all, eleven of whom were men.

Progress was slow but steady. All the Zygons' captives awoke disorientated and frightened, though none reacted as violently as Stoker had done. Employing the Doctor's methods as best she could, Sam soothed and cajoled and reassured, and though she couldn't help feeling like an inexperienced sheepdog in charge of a flock of rather nervous sheep, she was secretly pleased at how the men responded to her and were calmed by her.

The Doctor left Emmeline and Nathaniel Seers to the end. He awoke Emmeline first, greeting her with the charming smile and silken voice that Sam had observed him employ often in the past to get them out of awkward situations. She knew, not without a slight sense of superiority, that this kind of treatment would have caused most of her mates at Coal Hill to go weak at the knees. However, Emmeline had rather more to think about than the attentions of a dashing stranger.

'Mama,' she gasped, blinking at the Doctor. 'Where's Mama?'

She staggered forward. The Doctor held out his arms to catch her should she fall. 'I don't know,' he said gently. 'What's the last thing you remember?'

She looked bewildered, as if her mind was a complete blank, then horror crossed her face. 'My father,' she whispered. 'My father killed her. He had…' She held out her hands and looked at them as if they appalled her. A murmur of disquiet rippled around the group that the Doctor had awoken, most of whom were employees of Nathaniel Seers.

'No,' the Doctor said, raising his voice to be heard above the mounting hubbub. 'It wasn't your father who killed her. Your father is here, as much a prisoner as you are.' He indicated the cubicle beside Emmeline's. Emmeline turned, saw her father for the first time, gave a shriek and clutched at the Doctor.

'Listen to me, all of you,' said the Doctor, his tone demanding quiet. The group stopped their muttering and turned to look at him.

'What I'm going to tell you may be very hard for you to believe, but I assure you that it's true. All you have to do is look around you to confirm the truth of what I'm saying.'

Sam watched the faces of the group as the Doctor told them about the Zygons. About how they could transform themselves into those whose bodies they copied; about the giant machine creatures, the Skarasen, that served them; about their ship, like a massive living creature which had been secreted beneath the waters of the Thames, and which they were now all trapped within.

He flooded them with information, told them how he had inadvertently destroyed the Zygon race, and about how Balaak, their leader, had set the self-destructor unit before escaping.

'So you see,' he said, speaking as calmly and clearly as if he was delivering a lecture at some revered institute, 'it is imperative that we all work together to effect the quickest possible escape from this place. To do this I need you all to trust me. I need you to accept what I'm saying without question and to follow my instructions to the letter. Dissent will only lose us vitally precious seconds, even minutes. Now I know that this is an extraordinary and traumatic situation for all of you, which ideally you could all do with some time to come to terms with, but I'm afraid we don't have that time. The simple choice is this: work together under my guidance or perish. Which is it to be?'

The men's faces were still etched with fear and confusion, but there was something else there now too: a collective expression of awe. They looked, thought Sam, how she imagined cave dwellers might look when encountering modern man for the first time.

After a short silence it was Emmeline who spoke.

'I am certain I speak for us all, Doctor, when I say that we will all do precisely as you tell us. I for one wish to take my leave of this terrible place as swiftly as possible.'

There was a rumble of assent. Heads nodded vigorously.

'Well then, that's half the battle won,' said the Doctor. He turned to the alcove behind him, containing Nathaniel Seers's unconscious form. As his fingers played deftly over the crystalline panel, he leaned towards Emmeline and murmured, 'I think it best if you keep the news of your mother's death from your father for the time being. If we're going to get out of here, we all need to keep our wits about us as much as we can. Can I rely on you to give your father the emotional support he needs while at the same time impressing upon him the need for urgency?'

'Of course, Doctor,' said Emmeline firmly.

The Doctor twisted the trumpet-like controls and the cowl detached itself from Seers' head. Immediately the factory owner's mouth gaped and he released a low moan, then he slowly opened his eyes.

'Father?' Emmeline said hesitantly. 'Father, it's me – Emmeline.'

He looked at her with no recognition whatsoever for a moment. Then he blinked and his mouth struggled for articulation before he whispered, 'Emmeline?'

'Yes, Father. Oh yes, it's me!' She stepped forward, arms outstretched. Tears sparkled in her eyes.

He swayed, then stepped from the cubicle, unsteady as a toddler. As she flung her arms around him, he reciprocated, slowly raising his arms to enfold her in an embrace.

They stood there for long seconds, clutching each other, not saying anything. Finally the Doctor cleared his throat and Seers looked up.

'Good day, sir,' he said wonderingly. 'Whom do I have the

pleasure of…' Then his voice tailed off as he took in his surroundings. 'Where am I?'

'In danger,' said the Doctor, 'and I'm afraid there's no time to lose. Would you all follow me, please?'

'Danger?' mused Seers, but the Doctor had already turned and walked away. The rest of the men obediently trailed after him. Sam hung back to help Emmeline with her father.

'Is he all right?' she asked. The blank bemusement on Nathaniel Seers's face reminded her of her dad's gran, who'd suffered from Alzheimer's and had died at the age of eighty-eight when Sam was thirteen.

'I'm sure he'll be perfectly fine in a moment,' Emmeline said determinedly, holding her father's left arm and leading him along.

'I'm Sam,' said Sam. 'I've sort of met you before. That is, I've met your Zygon double. She seemed all right until she changed.'

Emmeline paled. 'Do you mean these hellish creatures created a facsimile of me? I dread to contemplate what fiendish acts it committed in my name.'

'Nothing too bad,' said Sam. 'Don't worry. They made a double of me too. She's quite nice as Zygons go, actually. It's really weird, though, meeting yourself.'

Between the two of them they managed to keep the tail-end of the Doctor's entourage in sight, and so guided Emmeline's father back towards the main control room. During the journey, Nathaniel Seers became gradually more aware of his surroundings, until finally, his voice stronger than before, he asked, 'What precisely is this place?'

'It's an alien spaceship,' said Sam airily, 'but it's probably best not to think about it.'

'A spaceship?' Seers looked momentarily bemused again, then his face cleared. 'I recall… creatures. Hideous creatures.'

'Zygons,' confirmed Sam. 'Don't worry, they're all dead. If you don't believe me, just breathe in.'

Sure enough, the stench of decay was getting stronger the closer they got to the main control room. Some of the men were evidently agitated by it. Before entering the room, the Doctor turned and held up his hands.

'Behind me is the centre of operations,' he said. 'My aim is to try to guide the ship on to dry land. Unfortunately, the drive systems are ailing even as we speak, but with a bit of luck we might just be able to do it before the ship blows up.

'Now, inside this room are many dead Zygons, all of which are in a rather unpleasant physical state. Try not to let the sight of them upset you. Once inside the room, I'm going to set each of you a task. Most of these tasks will be simple, but absolutely vital to the well-being of us all, and your utmost concentration will therefore be required. Do you all understand what I'm telling you?'

The men nodded. Even Sam, at the back of the group with Emmeline and her father, couldn't help but respond. The Doctor spent so much of his time being vague, unassuming, accommodating, and sometimes downright infuriating, that it became all too easy to forget how mesmerisingly impressive he could be when he put his mind to it. So much of the time his genius seemed intuitive, but how much of an act was that? Could a man really muddle absent-mindedly through the most appallingly dangerous situations and come up smelling of roses almost every time?

'Right then, ladies and gentlemen,' he said, and grinned as though he was genuinely enjoying himself, 'let's go to work.'

He turned and strode towards the crystalline door as if he intended to smash his way through it. However, the door slid up into the ceiling, releasing the stench of decaying Zygons which rolled over them like fog. The Doctor, seemingly unaffected, marched right into it. As if reacting to his presence, the burbling shriek of the self-destructor unit began to rise in pitch once more.

'There's not much time!' the Doctor shouted. 'Come along, gentlemen.'

He spent the next few minutes organising his troops, positioning them at consoles around the main control room and shouting out instructions: 'Apply pressure here'; 'Hold this steady'; 'Tell me if these readings fluctuate.' Then he scampered between those consoles that weren't manned, tugging and twisting and squeezing the Zygon controls, his hands at times moving so fast they were almost a blur.

From her post in front of an orange-tinged screen across which a seemingly random succession of symbols tumbled (she was to call out if a particular symbol, shaped like a denuded Christmas tree, began to proliferate), Sam kept an anxious eye on the Doctor. He reminded her of a plate-spinner at the circus who was trying to keep more plates going than he could comfortably handle. His hair hung down over his eyes and his lips moved feverishly as he muttered to himself. Finally, having tweaked and adjusted to his satisfaction, he crossed to the main console, absently stepping over a steaming Zygon skeleton which was lying in a gluey pool of liquefied flesh.

He cracked his knuckles loud enough to make Sam wince, then set to work. He manipulated controls until the image on the main screen altered to what Sam assumed was the ship's-eye view of what lay ahead of it, which at this moment was nothing but hundreds of thousands of gallons of murky water.

'Don't be alarmed if you feel a little turbulence,' the Doctor called. 'I've never piloted one of these things before, and I may be a little'– the ship gave a sudden lurch, causing them all to stagger – 'heavy-handed.'

He sprang forward to tweak and adjust, and almost immediately the ship steadied. 'That's it, old thing,' he said in the same coaxing voice he used when speaking to the TARDIS. 'You can do it.'

Debris-clogged water rushed in a frothing stream from the top to the bottom of the screen. 'Are we surfacing?' Sam asked.

'No,' said the Doctor, 'we're standing up.'

'You mean this thing has legs?'

'Ambulatory appendages, yes.'

Next moment Sam felt the floor of the ship rocking gently from side to side beneath her feet. She looked at the screen. Scraps of debris were now rushing towards it and then sliding away to the left or right.

'It's walking,' she said with an incredulous half-laugh. 'The bloody thing's walking.'

One or two of the Victorian gentlemen manning the consoles gaped at her, apparently more startled by her use of the vulgarism than by what had prompted her to utter it.

For approximately the next fifteen minutes, the ship continued its spider-like progress along the bed of the river. During this time the warbling scream of the self-destructor unit continued to rise steadily until it reached a point where Sam and the others were having to grit their teeth and intermittently jam their fingers in their ears.

'We can't be that far from the bank now,' Sam yelled at the Doctor.

He didn't respond.

'I said –' Sam began, but just then one of the men, whose blocky brown teeth gave him a rather simian appearance, excitedly blurted, 'Land ahoy! Land ahoy!'

The Doctor scurried across to the screen that the man had been doggedly watching. A grin appeared on his face. 'I do believe you're right, Mr Beech,' he said. 'Well done.'

The man looked absurdly proud of himself. The Doctor clapped him on the back, then hurried back to his post. 'Hang on, everybody!' he yelled above the ululating SD unit. 'Hard to starboard.' He twisted controls and the ship gave a pronounced, though not violent, tilt.

At that moment there was a sizzling, popping noise and acrid yellow smoke began to belch from a cluster of ganglia on the wall close to the door. The ganglia themselves began to thrash and writhe like an octopus in pain. Almost instantaneously the screen that Emmeline was concentratedly watching flickered and died.

The Doctor glanced round, then shouted, 'The toxin is getting through, disabling the subsidiary systems. We haven't much time.'

'Will we make it?' Sam yelled.

'We can only try.'

The control room was getting darker. Sam looked around, and saw that the veins in the walls were beginning to lose their glow. The liquid inside them was becoming turgid, lumpy, causing them to swell and in places burst, releasing a steaming ichor that made her think of mushy peas.

Suddenly there was a bang and one of the men jumped back from the console he was operating with a cry of alarm. Smoke was pouring from the console, which was beginning to blister and melt.

Like a chain reaction, there were several more explosions, and more of the consoles began to disintegrate. Screens died, as Emmeline's had, or simply burst like punctured eyeballs, revealing internal workings like a mass of fat worms writhing in colourless jelly.

The main console ruptured, the Doctor snatching his hand back as thick green fluid bubbled out of it. Then an interlacing of fine cracks appeared on the main screen and the picture faded to a hissing fog.

There was an almighty KKLAK! and the walls and ceiling split in several places at once. As the rifts widened, the ship lurched and they all stumbled, some of the men falling over. The floor was becoming gooey, as though covered with a carpet of mud. Green slime and what looked like lumps of decaying vegetation oozed from the widening rents in the walls and spattered down from the ceiling to the floor.

Everyone had left their posts now and was milling around in confusion, trying to avoid the falling debris. 'We'll have to swim for it!' the Doctor yelled. 'Follow me and try not to panic. We don't want to lose anyone.'

He ran for the door, the others bustling after him, Sam bringing up the rear. The Doctor led them on a nightmare journey through the convulsing, shuddering ship. The place was literally falling apart, turning to mush and ooze around them, the walls and floors and ceilings tearing like putrefying flesh.

There were places where great chasms had opened in the floor, others where they had to wade through showers of decaying matter that made Sam feel as if they were being pelted from above by rotting fruit. At last, bespattered and dripping but all relatively unscathed, they reached what Sam assumed to be their destination.

It was the Doctor who brought them to a halt, turning and holding up his hands. Immediately Sam looked around, searching for their likely escape route. They were in a large but unremarkable chamber, the walls running with rot. There were several gaping holes in the walls through which only blackness could be seen, but whether these had been fashioned or were simply another consequence of the ship's disintegration it was difficult to tell.

Sure enough, the Doctor led them over to one of the holes and pointed down into it. 'If my calculations are correct,' he yelled, 'this is a connecting chute down to the simulated Skarasen environment we saw earlier.'

'That swamp place?' shouted Sam.

He nodded. 'I'm fairly sure it will be flooded by now and there will be access directly into the Thames. We'll go down one by one. We'll be coming out directly under the ship, so I want everyone to take a deep breath, and once you find yourselves under water strike out to clear the ship and then head upwards for the surface. If you all remain calm, you should be able to do it. Once you've reached the surface, the shore shouldn't be far away. Now, who's first?'

The men hung back, fear in their eyes. It was Nathaniel Seers who stepped forward. He stripped off his sodden jacket and necktie. 'I will go first, Doctor,' he said.

'And then I,' said Emmeline. She was already peeling off her bulky outer layer of clothing. Even at this juncture, some of the men, Victorian to the core, were looking away, embarrassed.

Her show of mettle, however, did have the desired effect of shaming the rest of the men into stripping off their coats and jackets and lining up to await their turn. Before stepping into the chute, Nathaniel Seers proffered a hand to the Doctor.

'Good luck to you, sir, and God bless you for all you have done to help us.'

The Doctor grasped Seers's hand and shook it warmly. 'And good luck to you, Mr Seers. I'll see you soon.'

'Count on it,' said Seers, and launched himself feet first into the chute.

The blackness swallowed him almost immediately. Without hesitation, Emmeline occupied the gap left by her father. She looked at the Doctor and offered a tight smile. 'Thank you,' she whispered. Then she was gone.

One by one the men came forward, some looking determined, some apprehensive, some downright terrified. Eventually only Sam and the Doctor were left. She sat on the edge of the chute and nodded at his slime-encrusted frock coat.

'Hope that's not dry-clean only.'

He smiled. 'I've got others.'

'Gallifrey's answer to Imelda Marcos,' she said, rolling her eyes. 'Right then, see you later.'

She pushed herself forward and disappeared into the blackness. The Doctor gave her thirty seconds, then sat on the lip of the chute. With any luck, Nathaniel and Emmeline would have surfaced by now and be striking out for the shore. In the last few minutes it had been getting noticeably hotter in the ship as the drive systems approached critical mass. The Doctor estimated that he had only minutes before the systems were engulfed in one final devastating explosion. He pushed with his arms and next moment was rushing feet first into slippery darkness.

Even more quickly than he had been expecting, he found himself in water so icy that it almost punched the air from his lungs. He tried to look around, get his bearings, but saw only bubbles and blackness. Hoping he was heading in the right direction, he began to swim away from where he estimated the ship to be. Eventually he drifted upright and looked back. Sure enough, the ship was there behind him, a vast, dark, crab-like shape, convulsing uncontrollably, its outlines blurred by the water that was swirling and bubbling around it.

All at once the ship glowed a bright cherry-red and then flared white. The shock waves of the explosion billowed out towards him, and suddenly the Doctor found himself tossed about in a churning maelstrom of boiling water. He tried to curl himself into a ball and ride out the storm, but by the time the shock waves dissipated, he had completely lost his bearings and his tightening lungs were making him feel dizzy. He unfurled himself and clawed towards what he hoped was the surface. However, as the seconds seemed to stretch into minutes his limbs became unbearably heavy. Eventually, inevitably, unconsciousness began to steal over him. It seemed as black and sticky as the tar he felt he was crawling through.

CHAPTER 10
END OF THE WORLD

Twenty minutes after sinking on to the metal bench by the river's edge, Litefoot was still there. It was a chilly morning, but he was so weary that he felt disinclined to move. He looked out over the grey water and shuddered. It was hard to believe that he had so very nearly lost his life in there. When he thought about the experience now it seemed as vague as a half-remembered dream.

And what of the Doctor and Miss Samantha and those hideous Zygon creatures? Perhaps if he could convince himself that they too were merely part of some elaborate dream he could live the rest of his days in peace. If not, he would be forever tormented by his curiosity, wondering what had become of them. It had been bad enough the first time, when the previous Doctor and Miss Leela had vanished in front of his eyes, but at least there had been an end to that business. At least Magnus Greel and his cohorts had been defeated and destroyed.

He gave a deep sigh, which made his chest and lungs flare with pain. Perhaps it was time to retire, he thought. Or perhaps he ought simply to join Henry in Brighton and convalesce a little. As water lapped against the stone flood wall below, he shuddered again. The chill was beginning to seep into his bones.

Time to go, he told himself, and reached for his gun propped against the bench to his right. His hands had just closed around the cold metal of the barrel when a faint sound touched his ears.

He turned, his eyes widening. He had heard the sound only once before, some years ago, but it seemed as familiar to him as the chiming of his old grandfather clock. It was an ominous trumpeting sound, muted but growing steadily louder. Oddly it seemed directionless, as if it was not approaching from a distance, but already there, simply waiting for time to catch up with it.

A blue haze suddenly appeared where the Doctor's box had stood. Litefoot blinked, as if the haze was nothing but a speck of matter on his eyeball. However, when he opened his eyes again, not only was the haze still there, but its colour had deepened. And now a definite outline could be seen, transparent enough to see the stone wall of the towpath through it, but growing more solid all the time.

Even as Litefoot watched the Doctor's peculiar blue box appear out of thin air, his mind tried to deny the evidence of his own eyes. The swirling, grinding bellow of massive and ancient engines filled his head until he thought he would go mad with it. And then a moment arrived when the box was simply *there*, as solid and real as the objects that surrounded it. Litefoot gaped at it, his mind a stew of emotions. It was a peculiar thing to have one's wish fulfilled – wondrous and yet at the same time intensely alarming.

Much to his relief, the bellow of the engines faded quickly once the object had materialised. Slowly Litefoot rose to his feet, watching it warily all the while. The arrival of the box, momentous though the event had been to Litefoot, appeared to have gone unnoticed by the rest of the world. All around was silence, aside from the incessant lap of water against the wall below.

An age passed before the door opened. It did so slowly, almost ceremoniously. Beyond it, Litefoot could see nothing. It was not so much darkness as an emptiness, an absence, a void waiting to be filled. He picked up his gun and took a step towards the door on trembling legs.

'Doctor?' he called, his voice wavering. He cleared his throat and tried again. 'Doctor, are you there?'

A shape appeared in the doorway. 'Gad!' Litefoot gasped, and took a stumbling step back. It was not the Doctor who stood there, but a Zygon. If it had not been for the creature's lobster-coloured flesh and its great domed head, however, Litefoot might not have recognised it. The Zygon's body was horribly misshapen, reduced, liquefying like wax in a furnace. Boils were rising and bursting all over the creature's body, and even as Litefoot watched, gobbets of flesh were sliding from it, forming steaming pools around its feet.

Only its eyes seemed alive, blazing with furious fire. A maw opened in the mass of boils that served as the Zygon's face, and from it came a rattling, gurgling hiss.

'This... is not... Zygor,' the creature rasped. It swayed for a moment, and then seemed to notice Litefoot for the first time. It gave a blood-curdling screech and raised its hands, unsheathing the thorns in its palms. Then, with astonishing speed considering its condition, it rushed at him.

Instinctively, Litefoot raised the gun and pulled the trigger. The blast, at such close range, almost tore the creature apart. Bits of it flew everywhere, its left arm spinning through the air and landing with a splash in the water below. The creature's momentum carried it forward another two steps and then it pitched forward on to its face. It twitched for several seconds and then became still.

Now Litefoot expected people to come running. The echoes of the shotgun blast seemed to thrum and thrum in his ears. He looked down at his handiwork, sickened. The Zygon was crumbling to nothing even as he watched, its rate of decay accelerated even further by its death.

So mesmerised was he by the terrible sight that he didn't notice another figure had emerged from the blue box until it was no more than a few steps away. Sensing movement in his peripheral vision, he jerked the shotgun up, almost jabbing the figure in the chest. The girl looked at him, her face numb with shock and disbelief.

'Miss Samantha!' Litefoot gasped, hastily lowering the gun.

The girl stared at him for a moment, and then slowly shook her head. 'No,' she moaned. 'No... I am not Samantha.'

'My dear, you're upset. Why don't you –'

'I am Tuval,' the girl announced, pushing her shoulders back, holding her head up proudly. 'Last of the Zygons on this planet.'

Litefoot looked at her bemusedly for a moment, and then said, 'That's as may be, my dear, but I really think you should –'

'I wear a human body, but I *am* a Zygon. Look!'

The girl held up her hands and Litefoot saw the suckers open in her palms, the tips of the thorns emerge. Instantly he jerked the gun up again, staggering back a few paces.

'Just like Miss Emmeline,' he gasped. 'Then where's Miss Samantha? And where's the Doctor?'

'You are... Litefoot,' Tuval said. 'The Doctor's friend.'

'That's right. And if anything has happened to him, I promise you I'll avenge his death.'

The Zygon sighed and shook its head. 'The Doctor is a good man. He tried to arrange a peaceful solution for both our peoples. Sadly, it was not to be.'

Somewhat disarmed by the creature's apparent lack of aggression, Litefoot asked again, 'Where is he?'

Tuval swept an arm towards the river. 'Out there. Balaak set the self-destructor unit and abandoned him in our craft.'

'What precisely does that mean?'

'It means that our craft will soon disintegrate, if it hasn't already, and that the Doctor and his companion, together with all the other humans on board, will perish along with it.'

Litefoot was horrified. He looked out over the river. It looked grey and untroubled, the light shifting constantly as ripples danced gently over its surface. 'Is there nothing we can do?'

'Nothing.'

'What about the Doctor's blue box? Couldn't we use that?'

'No. There is a force field around the time controls which I suspect only the Doctor can disable.'

Litefoot looked anguished. 'There must be something... a boat perhaps? If you knew the exact whereabouts of this craft of yours...'

'There is no time. Once the self-destructor unit is set, the ship breaks down very quickly.'

'We have to try,' said Litefoot. 'We can't just leave them to their fate. Oh, damn those blasted Zygons!'

'I am a Zygon, Litefoot,' Tuval reminded him, and gestured at the gun. 'Are you going to destroy me with your weapon as you destroyed Balaak?'

Litefoot glanced at the gun almost shamefacedly. 'I acted in self-defence. Balaak, as you call him, attacked me.'

'And if I attack you,' said Tuval, 'for destroying my leader?'

'Then I suppose I would have to shoot you too, though it would give me no pleasure to do so.'

Tuval sighed. 'I will not attack you, Litefoot. There has been too much violence, too much death.'

Litefoot nodded sadly. 'There always is. What do you...'

His words tailed off as the surface of the Thames not twenty yards away suddenly began to boil and seethe. Litefoot and Tuval both turned as a monstrous reptilian head with rolling eyes and a jaw packed with savage teeth broke the surface. Water streamed from the creature's silver hide as it began to clamber up on to the towpath. It saw the two humanoid figures and gave an ear-splitting roar. Litefoot, stupefied by the proximity of the creature, suddenly felt a hand on his arm.

'Come Litefoot. We must seek refuge in the Doctor's time craft.'

Litefoot glanced at Tuval, and then at the TARDIS. 'A monster of that size would crush the box like matchwood.'

'It is not merely a box, it is a time machine, and it is stronger than it appears. Come on.'

With no other alternative, Litefoot allowed himself to be led. In his present condition, he had no hope of outrunning the creature, and neither could he even fire his gun at it. Despite what he had said to Tuval, it discharged once only before it had to be reloaded.

The creature had scrambled up on to the embankment now. It gave another bellow and charged at them. Litefoot, despite his burning lungs, ran as he had never run before, his hand clasped in Tuval's. They ran through the partly open doors of the box, and straight into a peculiar voidlike area beyond them. Litefoot experienced a moment of disorientation, and then he staggered to a halt, gazing around him in awe.

He found himself in what appeared to be a vast, shadowy cathedral, the ceiling of which was so high he could not even discern it. The cathedral was dominated not by an altar, however, but by a gigantic column filled with rods of light which was attached to a six-sided console. Part of the cathedral had been converted into a library, another part into a display for every conceivable type of chronometer. There was even a garden area with a bubbling stone fountain and a vast multidrawered cabinet covering one entire wall.

His senses assailed, Litefoot staggered to an overstuffed leather armchair set incongruously in the middle of the vast floor next to a small side table and slumped into it. Somewhere along the way, Tuval had let go of his hand and was now standing on the dais beside the console, tentatively reaching out towards a lever situated there. Litefoot saw the Zygon grit its teeth as it grasped the lever, as though it expected to be repelled. However, Tuval pulled the lever without mishap, an action that precipitated a boom and a puff of dust as the massive stone double doors through which they had entered the room swung closed.

Instantly there was an almighty crash and the room shuddered, spilling Litefoot from his armchair. Next moment the grinding roar of ancient engines filled Litefoot's head once again, and the rods of light within the central column began to rise and fall, meshing and separating. As the room settled, Litefoot noticed a screen beside the console flashing with the message: HOSTILE ACTION DISPLACEMENT SYSTEM OPERATIVE. The trumpeting of the engines faded and, aside from the splashing of the fountain and the intermittent bleeps and burbles coming from the console, the room became quiet once more.

Litefoot picked himself up, wincing. Tuval did likewise.

'Are you unharmed, Litefoot?' the Zygon asked.

'I think so,' Litefoot replied, 'relatively speaking.' He noticed his gun lying on the floor twenty feet away. He must have dropped it when he had entered this... this...

'Where precisely are we?' he inquired weakly.

'We are in the Doctor's time craft,' said Tuval. 'He calls it a TARDIS.'

'But we entered a small blue box.'

Tuval frowned as if Litefoot was being deliberately obtuse. 'Yes. This is its interior.'

'But that's preposterous!' spluttered Litefoot. 'The box was far too small to house a room of such... such magnitude.'

'Ah,' said Tuval, 'you are referring to the spatial inconsistency. It is accomplished by a Gallifreyan engineering technique known as dimensional transcendentalism.'

'I see,' said Litefoot feebly. 'Or rather, I don't. But never mind.'

The message on the screen had been replaced by a slow tracking shot of stone walls and grey water. 'Is that what's outside?' Litefoot asked.

Tuval nodded. 'It appears the time craft relocated to a point further along the bank when it came under attack from the Skarasen.'

'Jolly useful. That beast of yours will have gone back into the water now, I take it?'

'No,' said Tuval. 'Before vacating our craft, Balaak released the Skarasen and programmed them to invade the city, destroying all before them. We Zygons have a telepathic link with our Skarasen, but Balaak's programming is too strong. I cannot override it.'

Litefoot was appalled. 'Then it appears the killing has barely even begun. How many of these creatures are there?'

'By your numerical system, two hundred, perhaps more.'

'Two hundred,' spluttered Litefoot. 'And can they be stopped?'

Tuval's voice was apologetic. 'Not by any weapons that your race have yet devised.'

At first Jack thought that the shaking floor was not really shaking at all, that it was merely a consequence of his pounding head. He groaned and awoke in the stinking, rat-infested room that was his home, his body itching from the bugs that teemed in the bundle of straw-filled rags that he called his bed. He sat up slowly, and suddenly sensing movement beside him, whirled round, expecting to see a fat black rat baring its teeth at him. It would not have been the first time such a thing had occurred; he had once woken in the night with a cry of pain to find one of the hellish creatures gnawing at his toes through a hole in his boot.

However, it was not a rat that was sharing his bed but a woman – or rather, a poor excuse for one. Her hair was matted with clumps of dirt, boils sprouted in profusion on her cheeks, and the breath gushing from her toothless open mouth as she snored befouled the air with its stench.

Jack kicked her on the thigh, hard enough to raise a bruise, but the woman barely stirred. 'Hideous old drab,' he muttered, and struggling to his feet, stomped across to the window. There were no rats to be seen at present (though he could hear them scurrying in the walls), but there were cockroaches aplenty; Jack crunched as many of their shiny black bodies beneath his feet as possible as he crossed the wooden floor. His room was situated high in the building, and outside he could see a white sky bruised with the occasional dark cloud.

He was almost at the window when the light was blotted out by something vast and dark that rose up from beneath the sill.

Jack stepped back, unable to believe what he was looking at. It was an enormous rolling eye, surrounded by reptile skin whose individual scales were as big and shiny as silver shields. The eye seemed to regard him for a long moment; Jack saw blood vessels thick as rope pulsing in the whites. Then it swooped upward and was replaced by a huge mouth filled with row upon row of savage teeth. The mouth opened wide and a bellowing roar filled the room, almost splitting Jack's head and causing the floor to tremble beneath his feet.

He staggered backward, his only thought being that the creature, ten times larger than the one he had encountered in the factory, had come to seek revenge for his part in burning the factory to the ground last night. 'I'm sorry,' he bleated, 'I'm sorry.' Then he darted across to the bed and clamping his hand around the arm of the woman, who was still asleep and snoring despite the commotion, yanked her to her feet.

'Come on, you old slattern, get up,' he ordered, slapping her across her boil-encrusted face to rouse her.

The woman staggered, mumbled, her bleary, bloodshot eyes flickering open. Then she saw what was outside the window and suddenly she was wide awake.

She went rigid, letting loose an ear-shattering scream. 'Be quiet, for mercy's sake,' growled Jack, and swinging a lazy arm, punched her in the face, breaking her nose. As the woman began to gag and splutter, her nose streaming blood, Jack dragged her over to the window. 'Here, dragon,' he shouted, 'take her, not me.' He shoved the window open, then grabbed the woman's legs and lifted her up, intending to shove her head-first through the window into the creature's jaws.

Realising what he was trying to do, the woman retaliated, snarling and spitting and clawing at his face with filthy nails. Undeterred, Jack hit her again, snapping her head back. The woman went limp, all but unconscious, and Jack heaved her on to the windowsill. 'Here, dragon,' he called again, and gave the woman a shove. Her body fell fifty feet to the cobbled ground below. The monster pounced on it immediately.

Hoping its meal would distract it enough for him to make his escape, Jack turned and fled. He flew out of his room and down the stairs, trampling on a child who was sleeping on the landing. The monster was at the front of the building, and so Jack ran out of the back, into a yard and then down a filthy alleyway where the sewage was ankle-deep. There was a high wall to either side of him, and Jack began to laugh a little hysterically as he sloshed down the narrow passage between them.

'You'll never catch Jack Howe,' he panted, 'not in a hundred years. I'm too damned clever for the lot of you.'

The end of the alleyway was in sight now. Jack knew it led to a wider road, which offered him ample opportunities for escape. He was no more than twenty feet away from it, his head down as he ran, when a shadow fell across the opening. Jack plodded to a halt and looked up. The shadow edged forward into the alleyway, behind which Jack glimpsed a flash of silver.

'Merciful Lord, no,' he murmured as the flash resolved itself into another monster, this one smaller than the one at the front of the building. Jack knew, however, that although this creature was no more than twenty feet long from nose to tail, it was just as lethal.

The creature spied him and seemed to grin, showing him a mouthful of teeth like jagged knife blades. As it squeezed into the alleyway and came for him, its clawed feet scrabbling on the slippery cobbles, Jack turned once again and ran back towards the house. He was snivelling like a child now, terror causing his heart to crash in his chest, the sewage sucking at his boots, slowing him down. If he could only reach the cellar, he thought, and slam the door behind him, he might be safe.

Then his right foot slipped on the slick cobbles and suddenly he was falling.

The palms of his hands made a splat as they hit the stinking pool of sewage. Human waste shot up his nose and down his throat and into his eyes, blinding him. Choking, Jack tried to scramble to his feet, but before he could do so he felt a sharp tug on his ankle. Instinctively he put his hand down to his foot, but oddly there was no foot there. His groping fingers reached a little higher, and suddenly encountered what felt like a shattered stick where the lower half of his leg should have been.

He screamed then, realising what had happened, as hot, sticky fluid flowed over his hand. He dug his fingers into the sewage and tried to crawl away, but had managed to advance only a few feet when he felt something of immense strength dragging him back. Pain shot through him as what felt like gigantic meat hooks dug into his body.

Jack did not stop screaming for a long time.

Hands grabbed the Doctor and dragged him up through the water. Breaking the surface was like another explosion, light and sound assaulting his senses. The Doctor gulped air, then began to choke, water streaming from his nose and mouth. He could survive without air for far longer than any human being, but it really did feel as though he had been down there for hours.

He was hauled on to a stone banking and lowered gently to the ground. He lay for a moment, gasping, letting the water run off him and out of him. Already he could feel strength seeping back into his limbs. He pushed himself up on trembling arms and looked around. The first thing he saw was Sam's smiling face, her wet hair standing up in spikes. There were tears, or water, in her eyes. 'What kept you?' she asked.

The Doctor grinned. 'Had one or two things to do. You know how it is. Is everyone accounted for?'

Sam's lips pursed and she shook her head quickly. 'No. There are two missing and one who died after we pulled him out. I think he had a heart attack.'

The Doctor looked at the survivors. They were all shivering, hugging themselves, their eyes downcast and faces slack with the trauma of recent events. Their clothes were plastered to their bodies. Pools of water formed around their feet where they stood or sat. It was evident they had no more fight left in them. They were merely hanging around, waiting to be told what to do.

A little way away, a man lay on his back on the ground, his toes pointed upwards, his wet jacket laid over his face. The Doctor scrambled up and rushed over to him, pulled the jacket back. The man's face was purple, his eyes open and glazed.

'Emmeline and I gave him mouth-to-mouth and heart massage for ages, but he didn't respond,' said Sam. Her voice was calm, matter-of-fact, but suddenly she gave a deep, shuddering sob. The Doctor looked at her. Tears were rolling down her cheeks. She looked stricken, but tried to cover up the expression with the hand she clapped to her mouth.

'Sam,' he said, reaching towards her.

She stepped back and almost angrily said, 'I'm all right, just ignore me.'

'Sam, it's all right to let it out now and again.'

'No it isn't. You never do.'

She turned her back and walked away, further down the towpath. The Doctor sighed, then went after her. He stood three paces behind her and looked out over the river.

'Sam, I'm an alien,' he said gently. 'You don't want to use me as a role model. I'm different from you. I react differently.'

She made a spluttering sound that was halfway between weeping and laughing. 'Who said anything about role models? Arrogant sod.'

He smiled, and suddenly she swung round on him. Her nose and eyes were red, but her face was set. 'Don't you ever get upset?' she said. 'Don't you grieve when people die? Doesn't it ever all just get on top of you?'

'Oh yes,' he said quietly.

'Then why don't you bloody well show it?'

'I can't afford to,' he said. 'I keep it all in here.' He tapped himself on the chest.

'Well, that's no good for you, is it? You'll get an ulcer.'

'Probably.' He nodded towards the forlorn group clustered on the bank thirty yards away. 'Shall we go back? Rally the troops?'

'Yeah,' she sighed, and walked squelchingly back towards the group with him. 'Sorry for getting upset,' she said. 'I know it doesn't help.'

The Doctor put his arm around her and squeezed her briefly. 'Sam, believe me, you have absolutely nothing to be ashamed of.'

As they walked up to the group, Emmeline hurried towards them, her wet hair flapping about her face, her underwear sticking to her skin. With everything that had been happening, Sam had barely noticed before, but she now realised how clearly the outline of Emmeline's breasts could be seen through the wet material. She glanced at the Doctor, feeling a sudden confusion of emotions: possessiveness, jealousy, embarrassment, and even a measure of relief that the Doctor appeared to show no reaction whatsoever to the older girl's semi-nakedness.

Nevertheless, Sam positioned herself as surreptitiously as she could between the Doctor and Emmeline, as Emmeline said, 'Doctor, a number of us have just seen something break the surface of the water not forty yards away.'

'A body?' asked Sam.

'No. It could have been a submersible of some kind, though it looked more like a very large creature.'

'A Skarasen,' said the Doctor grimly, and turned to address the group. 'Excuse me everybody, could I say something?'

Faces turned towards him, expectant, eager, looking for direction. The Doctor had no words of succour to offer, however. He told them that they were not safe here, that even now Skarasen were emerging from the Thames and rampaging through the city. He told them that they should find somewhere safe and warm to hide and pray that the nightmare would soon be over.

'And what, may I ask, are you going to do, Doctor?' asked Nathaniel Seers, water still trickling from his impressive sideburns.

'I'm going to try and stop the Skarasen. Goodbye, everybody, and good luck.' He turned and began to walk away, Sam falling into step beside him.

Emmeline hurried after them. 'But Doctor, you can't simply abandon us!'

The Doctor sighed and turned back. 'I can't take you all with me either. If we travelled as a group we would be too slow and too conspicuous. Besides, Sam and I are going to have to put ourselves in considerable danger –'

'As usual,' said Sam.

'– and I simply can't expose you all to that. No, your best course of action is to follow my advice and find somewhere to hide. Believe me, you would have a far better chance of survival on your own than you would with me.'

'All the same,' said Emmeline firmly, 'I would like to come with you.'

'I too,' said her father, standing behind her.

The Doctor looked heavenwards, then said, 'All right, all right. But don't expect me to take responsibility for your safety.'

'Of course not,' said Emmeline indignantly.

'Good. Come on then.' He started to stride rapidly along the towpath before anyone else could decide that sticking with him was a better option than striking out on their own.

'Do you have a plan, Doctor?' panted Sam, jogging to keep up with him.

'Well, an inkling of one.'

'Like to share it with the group?'

'Not just yet if you don't mind. Time is of the essence.'

'Isn't it always?'

They came to a set of steps leading up to a sloping cobbled street lined with what appeared to be warehouses. The Doctor leapt up the steps two at a time.

'Could you not at least inform us of our present destination, sir?' gasped Seers.

'We're going back to the TARDIS,' said the Doctor, 'and before either of you ask,' he added, glancing at Emmeline, 'I really don't have time to explain what that is just now.'

'It's a big blue box,' Sam confided to Emmeline and her father. 'We live in it. Though the last time I saw it, it was being nicked by a couple of Zygons.' She turned to the Doctor and asked pointedly, 'How come you know where it is?'

'I preset the co-ordinates,' said the Doctor. 'Didn't I mention it?'

'No, you didn't.'

'Oh. Sorry.'

'So may I ask where this… TARDIS is?' said Emmeline.

'You already have,' said the Doctor, and pointed off to the left, arm thrust outwards like an indicating cyclist. 'It's on the towpath by the river, several miles in that direction.'

There was a brief, surprised silence, and then Nathaniel Seers said tentatively, 'Would it not be more prudent, therefore, sir, to follow the direct route along the river's edge?'

The Doctor stopped abruptly and turned round. He looked grumpy, which was unusual for him. 'No,' he said curtly, 'it would not. With no cover, we would be sitting targets for any Skarasen which happened to be swimming by. Our journey through the streets, although circuitous, will at least afford us greater cover, and give us a fighting chance of arriving at our destination in one piece. Now, are there any other questions you would like answering before we proceed, bearing in mind that the Skarasen are destroying this planet of yours even as we speak?'

There was an awkward silence and then Seers shook his head. 'No, sir. I apologise for my overbearing curiosity.'

The Doctor sighed and patted Seers on the shoulder. 'That's all right. I'll try to explain what I can later. It's just that now isn't the best time.'

'I understand, sir.'

They walked on, and had not gone very much further before they heard a faint but savage roar.

'Good Lord!' exclaimed Seers. 'That was the cry of one of these Skarasen creatures, I take it?'

'Well, it weren't no canary,' said Sam.

The Doctor led them into the heart of the East End, through back streets and alleyways, as if he had known the place all his life. The bellowing roars of Skarasen grew louder and more commonplace as they progressed, as did the shouts and screams of men, women and children fleeing before the rampaging cyborgs. The Doctor and his companions soon got used to the spectacle of people running through the streets in blind terror, of buildings reduced to rubble and twisted metal and broken glass, of lamp standards and post boxes crushed and mangled as if made of liquorice.

One thing they could not get used to, however, were the bodies strewn among the wreckage. Many were little more than half-devoured chunks of meat, no longer recognisable as human; others resembled bags of guts that had burst beneath the immense weight of Skarasen feet.

It was not until she saw the head of a child attached to nothing more than a bloody length of spinal column, however, that Sam felt her gorge rise.

'I hate to say this everybody, but I think I'm gonna puke,' she announced.

'Probably be a good thing,' murmured the Doctor, who had been urging them to keep close to the walls, his eyes darting everywhere. 'It would rid you of all those Zygon nutrients you've been ingesting for the past couple of days. I'm not sure they're entirely compatible with the human system.'

'Zygon nutrients?' said Sam, turning very pale. 'Excuse me a moment.' She slipped into a narrow alleyway and voided her stomach contents. Even as she was doing it, despite what she had seen, she felt ashamed of herself. Shouldn't Emmeline be the one doing this? Weren't Victorian women supposed to be sensitive and delicate, living cosy, cosseted lives, far removed from anything that might cause them the slightest distress?

When Sam re-emerged and mumbled an apology, Emmeline – who did admittedly look rather white-faced – offered her a sympathetic smile. The Doctor, however, merely grunted, his mind elsewhere.

Suddenly, from very close by, there came the crash of falling masonry and a shattering roar.

'Back!' the Doctor shouted, flapping his arms. 'Back! Back!'

Like a shoal of fish swimming before a shark, a group of perhaps two dozen people appeared around the corner, running for their lives. Behind them, claws scrabbling on the cobbles, threads of drool spilling from its massive jaws, was a Skarasen.

It filled the street, its head on a level with the roofs of the buildings. As it lumbered forward, the Doctor urged his friends into the very alleyway where Sam had been sick. They stood there, panting, their backs to the wall, as the crowd ran past. The shimmering hide of the Skarasen seemed to blot out the light for a very long time. Sam saw its claws gouge chunks from the road as it passed, saw it reduce a wall to a tumble of bricks with one flick of its tail.

All at once there was a hideous scream, which was immediately blotted out by the cyborg's triumphant roar. Sam looked at the Doctor and saw that he was gritting his teeth in anguish. Emmeline and her father were marble-skinned, their eyes wide and shocked. Emmeline, clad only in her damp chemise and knickerbockers and a pair of sodden boots, was shivering with either cold or fear, her hair a dark wet tangle around her face. Even the Doctor looked as grimy and exhausted as Sam herself felt; she couldn't help wondering how they could possibly hope to stop the carnage happening around them. Or was the Doctor's plan merely to get back to the TARDIS and leave London to its fate? Was that why he had been so reluctant for Emmeline and her father to accompany them? No, she couldn't believe that. She *wouldn't* believe it.

Eventually, its killing done and its meal over, the Skarasen blundered away, leaving devastation in its wake. The Doctor peeled himself from the wall and touched Sam's arm lightly.

'Come on.'

Those were the only words anyone spoke for some time. The Doctor led them through more wrecked streets, past more mangled bodies. Although the screams of the populous and the roars of the Skarasen provided a constant backdrop to their progress, for a while – via a combination of good luck and the Doctor's sound judgement – they managed to remain several streets distant from the bloodbath whose evidence lay all around them.

Their brief encounter with the Skarasen was almost twenty minutes past when Sam said, 'Doctor?'

'Hmm.'

'Do you mind if I ask you a question?'

'Must you?' he said, then glanced at her as she frowned. 'Go on then. Only don't turn it into an interrogation. We haven't the time.'

'I know that,' she said, the frown deepening to a scowl. 'Give me some credit.'

He held up a hand. 'Sorry, Sam. Go on.'

'What if the TARDIS isn't there? What if Tuval and Balaak have managed to override your preset thingamajig?'

'They won't have,' said the Doctor.

'What makes you so sure?'

'HADS.'

'You what?'

'I repaired the HADS – the Hostile Action Displacement System. It's been on the blink for ages.' He looked suddenly thoughtful. 'You know, I've been far more conscientious since I regenerated. I even keep my room tidy sometimes.'

'Congratulations,' said Sam drily. 'So you fixed the HADS. I assume this is relevant to our conversation?'

The Doctor halted them with a raised hand, listened for a moment, then beckoned them onwards. 'While I was repairing the HADS, I discovered that it was linked to an internal system that I managed to modify into a sort of bounceback circuit. I rigged it so that if anyone tried to take control of the TARDIS, she would defend herself by throwing up a force field around the console and returning automatically to a predesignated set of co-ordinates.'

'So you reckon that when Tuval tried to pilot it, it would've just jumped back to where you'd left it before?'

'Without a doubt,' said the Doctor and then pursed his lips. 'That's assuming that the elastic band hasn't snapped of course.'

'Elastic band!'

He grinned. 'I'm joking. It was one of those really thick ones. There's no way it would break.'

He led them into a deserted street where most of the buildings were still standing. Suddenly a raggedly dressed woman holding the hand of a girl of perhaps four or five appeared at the far end. Both woman and child were barefoot, both had stark, terrified expressions on their dirt-smeared faces, and both were running, the woman all but dragging the little girl in her wake. Seconds later, a huge dark shadow spilled across the road and buildings

256

behind them and a Skarasen appeared, its eyes rolling, its teeth stained red with gore. It snorted, steam spurting from its nostrils, and galloped towards the mother and child. It reminded Sam grotesquely of some monstrous puppy chasing a couple of scuttling insects.

All at once the little girl, her legs going faster than she could cope with, lost her footing and fell to the ground, her hand wrenching free from her mother's grasp. The woman's momentum carried her forward several steps before she realised what had happened and spun round. At the sight of the Skarasen bearing down on her daughter she screamed and froze, her hands flying to her mouth. The little girl lay on her stomach, crying but seemingly oblivious of the monster behind her, as if her greatest concern was not the prospect of being eaten alive but the pain of her grazed knees.

Before she even realised he had gone, Sam saw the Doctor running up the street. 'Hey!' he shouted, trying to attract the Skarasen's attention. 'Hey!'

Everything was happening so fast that he had almost reached the woman before it occurred to Sam that she ought to go after him. In contrast to the Doctor's legs, hers seemed to move in slow motion. The Doctor had bypassed the woman and reached the little girl now. He was fumbling in his pocket as he clumped to a halt. From Sam's position, fifty yards up the street, he appeared to be standing right between the Skarasen's two front paws.

'Hey, Fido!' she heard him shout. 'Catch!'

He whipped what looked like a canister from his pocket, twisted off the top and hurled it into the air. The Skarasen's head whipped round to catch the canister as it came level with its face. Its jaws came together and Sam heard a crunching, splintering sound. As the Doctor scooped up the child and ran for the shelter of a nearby building, there was a muffled boom and green smoke began to curl from between the Skarasen's jaws. The monster shook its head from side to side like a dog which had eaten a slug. Then it threw back its head and roared, enraged rather than harmed.

Despite the fact that her child had been rescued, the woman was still standing in the same spot, staring up at the Skarasen, hands clamped to her face, frozen in terror.

'Run!' the Doctor shouted from the shelter of the building within which he had taken refuge. 'Get away before it recovers.'

The woman did not move, did not even acknowledge him. Sam came to a halt still thirty yards away, unable to do anything but watch what was about to happen.

Muscles flexed in the Skarasen's neck and its head suddenly lunged forward and down, knocking the woman flat on her back with its snout. She lay there, looking up at the creature, not making a sound. It leaned down and sniffed at her, then nudged her with its snout once again.

It's playing with her, Sam thought, sickened, remembering how she had once seen a cat batting a squealing mouse with its paws, tossing it into the air. She had no desire to see the woman killed, but she couldn't simply turn away.

She was so mesmerised by what was happening that she didn't register the clattering behind her until the Doctor shouted her name. His voice jerked her from her trance and she spun round. She found herself standing in the path of four galloping and evidently panic-stricken black horses which were pulling a large, driverless carriage behind them. The carriage was bouncing on the rubble-strewn surface, its wheels leaving the road and then crashing back down. With the horses bearing down on her, Sam forced her legs into action, running and then diving to the side of the road. As the horses and the carriage thundered past, she caught a glimpse of the animals' crazed eyes, their shiny black bodies lathered in sweat.

The horses suddenly seemed to register what was in front of them and tried to change direction, their terrified whinnies sounding distressingly like human cries. However, the carriage, unused to such treatment, was unable to turn as abruptly as the horses wanted to. There was a screech of metal as the carriage teetered on two wheels, then an almighty crash as it toppled on to its side. The horses began to buck and thrash, their harnesses tethering them to the dead weight of the fallen carriage. The Skarasen looked up, attracted by the commotion. Its jaws were half open and stretched wide, which gave the bizarre impression that it was grinning.

It sniffed the air, then lumbered forward, stepping over the woman so that for a few moments she was thrown into the dark shadow of its body. Sam, who had picked herself up now, winced as the Skarasen's back feet thumped down, certain that the woman would be crushed like a bug. However, as the Skarasen advanced on the screaming horses, Sam saw the woman reappear behind it, still lying on the ground but undoubtedly alive.

The Skarasen reached the tethered horses and lunged forward, its jaws opening wide. Sam saw its huge claws smash into one horse and tear its body open like wet paper, felling it instantly. It clamped another of the horses in its jaws and lifted it high into the air, the leather harness that had prevented it from fleeing snapping like cotton. Sam turned away as the Skarasen began to shake the horse from side to side, but she couldn't blot out the sound of its awful screaming. It seemed to go on for a very long time.

The Skarasen ignored her as she ran past it on shaky legs. She ran up to the woman, who was still lying on her back, looking dazed. When Sam asked her if she was all right, the woman gazed at her as if she had no idea what language Sam was speaking in. She was willing enough to allow Sam to help her to her feet, however. Once she was upright, her eyes flickered and she murmured, 'Daisy... Where's my little Daisy?'

'She's safe,' Sam said. 'She's with the Doctor.'

'Doctor?' murmured the woman. 'She ain't hurt, is she?'

'No, she's... look, here they are.'

Sam pointed as the Doctor emerged from the shelter of the building, carrying the little girl in his arms. The girl seemed quite content to be with him. She was snuggled into his chest, sucking her thumb. The Doctor smiled and said, 'Here's a little girl who wants her mother.' He held her out and the woman took her gratefully. Despite his words, the girl barely seemed to have noticed that she had been passed from one person to another.

'Thank you, sir,' the woman said, a spark of real life returning to her eyes. 'Thank you most kindly.'

'Just take good care of her,' the Doctor said. 'Find somewhere to hide, and quickly. These creatures are everywhere.'

'Oh, I will, sir. Thank you, sir. Thank you.'

The woman hurried away, bowed down somewhat by the weight of her burden.

'Will they be all right?' Sam asked anxiously, watching them go.

The Doctor watched them too, his face troubled. 'Even I don't know everything,' he said softly.

Sam realised that the high-pitched screaming of the horse that the Skarasen had picked up had stopped behind them, though the others were still whinnying in panic. She turned to see the Skarasen lying on its stomach, holding the body of the now dead horse between its front paws and tearing at it with its teeth in much the same way as a lion will tear at a gazelle. The horse that the Skarasen had first attacked was lying dead beside the carriage, its body ripped open from its throat to its hindquarters.

The two remaining horses were still bucking and rearing in a desperate attempt to break free of their restraints, their eyes crazed and rolling, foam flying from their mouths.

Sam felt sick with helplessness. She wished there was something she could do. It was terrible to see the creatures suffering like this. Even a well-aimed bullet would have been kinder than walking away and leaving them to their fate. She looked beyond the Skarasen and the horses to where Emmeline and her father were still waiting, their eyes dark smudges in their pearl-white faces. She wondered whether Nathaniel had a revolver. Did Victorian gentlemen carry such things around with them? But no, even if he had had a weapon, the Zygons would have taken it or it would have got lost or ruined in the Thames.

Suddenly a thought came to her and she looked at the Doctor. 'That thing you chucked at the Skarasen, that firework thing.'

'What of it?'

'How come you were able to light it when you'd been in the water?'

'It wasn't a firework,' said the Doctor. 'It was a Pridian flare. Coated in dilumium. Completely waterproof.'

'You haven't got any more, have you? I thought maybe we could distract the Skarasen and rescue the horses.'

'Alas, no. I used all but one at the Festival of N'tapu on my last visit to Kakara. Nearly got executed for it, too. The locals thought I was trying to assassinate the High P'nbar.' He clapped Sam's upper arms lightly with both hands in a gesture of brisk affection. 'Why don't you go and rejoin Emmeline and Nathaniel? I'll be with you in a minute.'

'Why?' she asked suspiciously. 'What are you going to do?'

'I'm going to get the horses, as you so brilliantly suggested.'

She hated it when he was condescending, but this time she let it pass; there were more urgent matters to worry about.

'You can't,' she said.

'Why not?'

'Isn't it obvious? Go anywhere near that lot and you'll either end up as a Skarasen's dessert or get cut to ribbons by flying hooves.'

He glanced at the feeding Skarasen and rearing horses. 'Oh, I don't think so,' he said airily. 'The Skarasen's quite happy there. He won't bother me.'

'What about the horses?'

'I have a way with animals,' said the Doctor. 'See you in a minute.'

Before Sam could protest further he was heading towards the Skarasen at a brisk pace, his damp coat-tails flying behind him. Sam huffed angrily and almost went after him just to drag him back, but then thought better of it. He was exasperating sometimes, but she had to admit, however reluctantly, that his judgement was usually pretty sound. He never did something stupid just to make a point, though by the same token there were occasions when he seemed to think himself invincible.

What she didn't like really, she supposed, was the fact that he still saw a need to protect her at times, to keep her out of things, which seemed to suggest that he didn't think her as capable or as helpful as she liked to think she was. She wanted to be indispensable to him, wanted to be an equal half of a dynamic duo that would become feared and revered throughout the galaxy. She knew she'd made mistakes, shown weaknesses, but how could she put that right if he shielded her by rushing forward alone whenever they were in a perilous situation? For all that, she thought that now probably wasn't the right time to show her worth or argue the toss. She'd talk to him later, once all this was over, find out where she stood. That, of course, was if he didn't get gobbled up by a Skarasen or trampled to death by horses in the next couple of minutes.

She walked back to where Emmeline and her father were waiting, though kept her eyes on the Doctor the whole time, ready to rush in and provide what help she could if things got difficult for him. She saw the Doctor walk fearlessly up to the Skarasen, saw him stroll right past the end of its gore-coated snout, his body less than six feet from its massive, taloned claws. He stepped over the legs of the dead horse and came to a halt beside the two which were still rearing and whinnying, their bodies now coated in sweat so thick it was like foam. To Sam's horror, the Doctor suddenly slipped lithely beneath the body of one of the horses as it reared, ducking to evade its flailing hooves.

Now he was standing between the two frenzied animals. Sam expected him to be crushed between them, expected him to fall and be trampled into the ground. She saw him reach up and take hold of the reins of first one horse and then the other. Then she heard a strange, oddly haunting sound that it took her a moment to realise was the Doctor singing.

His voice was soft and lilting, but it seemed to fill the air. He was singing in a language she had never heard anyone speak on Earth, but for all that the words were soothing, hypnotic; incredibly she found herself wishing she could close her eyes, sink to the ground and go to sleep. The tune was familiar too, like a combination of all the carols and lullabies that had comforted her as a child. Immediately the horses stopped bucking and whinnying and pricked up their ears. Within seconds they were as docile as if they had been sedated.

Unhurriedly the Doctor untied them from the carriage to which they had been tethered. They waited calmly as he did so, and even allowed him to lead them past the Skarasen which was greedily and noisily devouring their stable-mate, bones and all.

'That was amazing,' said Sam when the Doctor came within earshot, the horses trotting at his heels like obedient pets.

Nathaniel and Emmeline Seers hurried forward. 'Quite astounding, sir!' Seers enthused. 'Quite astounding!'

'Whatever was that song you were singing, Doctor?' Emmeline asked. 'It was quite beautiful.'

'Venusian lullaby,' said the Doctor. 'The Royal Beast of Peladon was particularly fond of it.'

'Do you do requests?' asked Sam.

'Only by royal appointment.' He brought the horses to a standstill and offered the reins of one to Emmeline. 'Treat him gently, won't you? He's had a hard day.'

'You mean we're going to ride?' said Sam.

'Why not? One good turn deserves another.' Despite the lack of saddle or stirrups, the Doctor swung himself up on to the horse with practised ease, then reached out a hand for Sam to climb up behind him.

She did so, wrinkling her nose at the stink of sweat rising from the horse's hot flesh.

'Hi-yo, Silver,' she muttered.

'This is utterly intolerable,' Litefoot said. 'We must do *something*.'

Tuval, perched on the edge of the console dais, watched him pacing about. 'There is nothing we can do. We are safe in here.'

'Safe? Trapped is more to the point. How long do you suppose these creatures of yours will continue this infernal onslaught?'

'Until everything is destroyed,' Tuval replied phlegmatically. 'Until every man, woman and child is dead.'

'Barbarous,' breathed Litefoot. 'And once London has been razed? What then?'

'They will move further afield. They will continue to destroy all before them until this planet is nothing more than a wasteland.'

Litefoot shook his head as if such a notion was beyond his comprehension. 'But that would take years, centuries even.'

'The bodies of the Skarasen have been augmented by Zygon technology. They are equipped to live for millennia.'

'My God,' breathed Litefoot, and looked up at the scanner screen which was showing a now static view of the towpath and the Thames, a dark glimpse of buildings beyond. Could this really be it – the beginning of the end of the world? Were he and Tuval destined to live out the remainder of their days in this... this time craft of the Doctor's?

His gaze was wandering from the screen when a flicker of movement caught his eye. He looked again, and was both astonished and delighted to see a pair of black horses galloping along the towpath towards them, whose riders he recognised all too well.

'It's the Doctor!' he cried. 'And Miss Samantha! Quickly, Tuval, open the doors.'

Tuval glanced at the screen, then jumped on to the console dais and operated the door lever. There was a pause, then the doors ground slowly open. Next moment the Doctor breezed in, spinning the TARDIS key on its chain. Behind him, looking dirty, wet and exhausted, trailed Sam, a young lady in her underwear whom Litefoot recognised as Emmeline Seers, and an older man in his shirtsleeves whom the professor could only assume was the young lady's father, Nathaniel Seers.

'Professor!' cried the Doctor, pocketing the TARDIS key and reaching out to clasp Litefoot's right hand in both of his. 'How wonderful to see you again! We wondered where you'd got to, didn't we, Sam? Tell me, what do you think of my TARDIS?'

'Um... very impressive,' said Litefoot, taken aback by the Doctor's effusiveness.

'Yes it is, isn't it? *I* like it. And Tuval,' said the Doctor, releasing

Litefoot's hand and moving towards the Zygon still wearing Sam's body who was standing beside the console. His voice dropped an octave. 'How are you? I never got the chance to thank you for saving my life.'

Tuval stared at him blandly. 'I do not feel proud of disobeying the orders of my commander, Doctor, though neither do I believe in taking another's life simply for revenge.'

'And a good thing for me too,' said the Doctor. He looked around. 'I take it Balaak is dead?'

'Yes,' said Tuval simply.

'I'm sorry,' said the Doctor. 'For all that has happened, I'm truly sorry.'

'I too,' said Tuval. 'I am sorry that the Skarasen are laying waste to this world. I am also sorry that I was forced to injure you, Sam, the last time that we encountered each other. I trust that you sustained no permanent damage?'

'Nothing that a few weeks in traction won't cure,' said Sam, and then seeing Tuval's puzzled face: 'Nah, I'm joking, don't worry about it. It was a fair scrap.'

Nathaniel and Emmeline Seers were looking around them in awe, their mouths open. Nathaniel was swaying a little as if about to pass out.

'It's quite… quite impossible,' he said in a weak, tired voice.

'Yeah, it gets everyone like that at first,' said Sam. 'In the end, though, you just have to accept it. Either that or go stark staring bonkers.'

'Why don't you both sit down?' suggested the Doctor. 'There are plenty of seats knocking about. Sam, would you be kind enough to put the kettle on?'

She sighed. 'I suppose it *is* my turn. Is that what we're going to do now we're here? Have a tea party and wait for it all to blow over?'

'We'd be waiting a long time,' said the Doctor. 'No, I think a little direct action is called for.'

'What do you propose to do, Doctor?' asked Litefoot.

'It's more a case of what Tuval and I can do. Tuval, using my equipment, do you think we could replicate a Zygon summoning signal for the Skarasen?'

Tuval glanced at the console. 'It is possible, Doctor. Despite appearances, your technology is very advanced.'

'Thank you,' said the Doctor, straight-faced. He peeled off his damp coat and dropped it at the base of one of the leaning metal girders that supported the time rotor. 'Let's get to it, then.'

He began to flick switches and twist dials on the console. 'I'll just prepare the way. We don't want you burning your fingers, Tuval.'

'May I ask a question, Doctor?' asked Emmeline.

He nodded.

'What precisely will this... this summoning signal do?'

He looked up and grinned. 'It will draw the Skarasen to the TARDIS.'

'All of them?' said Litefoot, turning a little pale.

'Oh yes,' said the Doctor cheerfully.

Nathaniel Seers, slumped in a swivel chair made of some strange, pearly material, said, 'Forgive my insolence, sir, but wouldn't such a course of action be a little unwise?'

'Oh, probably,' said the Doctor, and then before anyone else could comment, he looked up and said, 'Ah, here's Sam with the tea. Excellent. Once you've drunk that you can all have a bath and put on some clean, dry clothes if you like. Sam will show you where everything is. This is going to take Tuval and me a bit of time to set up.'

He was not wrong. As he and Tuval set to work at the console, coaxing it to produce a variety of bleeps and burbles, Sam led

Emmeline and her father to the warehouse-sized TARDIS wardrobe and encouraged each of them to select a change of clothes for themselves. That done, she showed them where the TARDIS bathrooms were, provided each of them with soap and towels, then went off to have a shower in her own en-suite bathroom, telling them she'd see them back in the console room later.

She stood under the hot water for a long time, wreathed in steam, her eyes half closed. Though her body longed to sink in to her warm, soft bed and drift off to sleep, her mind wouldn't stop nagging at her, urging her to hurry up so that she didn't miss anything important.

Finally, reluctantly, she turned off the shower, dried herself and dressed in jeans, boots and a Greenpeace T-shirt. The Victorian clothes had been OK, but it was good to be wearing her own stuff again.

When she got back to the console room, she found the Doctor and Tuval still busy at the console, the Doctor explaining something to the Zygon, who was nodding gravely. Professor Litefoot, meanwhile, was rather inexplicably moving from one candelabrum to the next and blowing out all the candles.

The air was filled not only with blue smoke and the smell of candle wax, but also with an ear-splitting squealing sound which was emanating from the console and which changed in volume and pitch as the Doctor, aided by Tuval, made minor adjustments to the controls. Sam wandered over to Litefoot, and shouted into his ear, 'What are you doing, Professor?'

Litefoot whirled to face her. Sam raised a hand to apologise for startling him. The professor looked tired and drawn, but did a classic double-take at the sight of her clothes. Recovering his decorum quickly, he said, 'To be quite truthful, my dear, I'm not entirely sure. The Doctor set me this task when I offered my services. He said the candles were a fire hazard.'

'It's never bothered him before,' said Sam. 'I'll see what he's up to.'

She made her way over to the console, wincing as the squealing escalated to a burbling electronic shriek. The Doctor didn't seem to notice her until she was standing right beside him, but then, before she could say anything, he spun round and gripped her arms just above the elbows.

'Ah, Sam, the very person. Would you organise the removal of every item of furniture from the main floor area? You can stack it all in the library for now.'

'Why?' she asked.

'Because I don't want anything to get broken,' he replied. 'Would you mind doing it quickly? Tuval and I are nearly there.'

He turned away. She sighed, then muttered, 'Right,' and clumped back down off the dais to relay the Doctor's instructions to Litefoot. At that moment a door beside the enormous built-in filing cabinet opened and Emmeline and her father reappeared, looking much refreshed.

The four of them spent the next ten minutes transferring the chairs, side tables, lamps and candelabra to the library area as the Doctor had instructed. Throughout this time the hideous sound filling the console room altered by degrees until it became a deeper-pitched electronic burbling, at which point the Doctor stood back, hands half raised.

'I think that's it!' he shouted. 'What do you think, Tuval?'

The Zygon listened and nodded, then said something which Sam couldn't catch.

'Right everybody,' shouted the Doctor. 'If you would join me up here beside the console.'

Led by Sam, they did so.

'All right, Tuval,' shouted the Doctor. 'Open the doors.'

Tuval operated the lever and the doors swung slowly open.

'What exactly are you doing, Doctor?' asked Sam.

'I'm letting the Skarasen in,' he said.

Nathaniel Seers's eyes widened. 'Are you quite insane, sir? Those creatures will devour us all.'

The Doctor shook his head. 'A state of grace exists within the TARDIS. The Skarasen couldn't harm us even if they wanted to – which they won't anyway.'

'Aren't you forgetting one thing, Doctor?' asked Sam.

'I don't think so.'

'How will the really big ones get through the doors?'

The Doctor smiled. 'The TARDIS doors only look small because the chameleon circuit has fused. It's a matter of perception. Theoretically, the doors are as big or as small as I want them to be. To this end, I've managed to bypass the chameleon circuit and set up a localised mass inversion wave by tapping into the TARDIS's main drive systems.'

'What does that mean?'

'It means I've managed to break down the area around the doors into its raw state for a while. If I could do that for the whole TARDIS, I could probably get the chameleon circuit working again. The only problem is, it puts too much of a drain on the drive systems. The choice is either to have a TARDIS with no chameleon circuit or a chameleon circuit with no TARDIS.'

Sam nodded wisely. 'So what *is* its raw state?' she asked.

'Energy.'

'What kind of energy?'

'Just energy,' he said obscurely.

She sighed. 'Is it stable or unstable?'

'Oh, stable,' he said. 'Yes, quite definitely stable. Look, I'll show you.'

He operated a number of controls and a pearly haze began to form around the double doors that now stood wide open, revealing only blackness beyond. Sam blinked and tried to readjust her vision, but the doors refused to come into focus. The effect was not dissimilar to that of a painting left out in the rain, except for the fact that small sparks of energy were flickering around their edges like fireflies.

All at once Emmeline jabbed a finger at the TARDIS scanner screen and cried, 'Look!'

Sam turned her attention from the doors to the scanner. On the screen she saw a huge silvery shape dragging itself from the Thames and up on to the towpath, water streaming from its sides. Its savage head was weaving from side to side in a way that reminded Sam oddly of a toddler responding to a piece of music.

'Here they come,' cried the Doctor almost gleefully.

Though Sam watched the first Skarasen enter the TARDIS she wasn't entirely sure how it had done so. What appeared to happen was that the dark energy around the doors suddenly became agitated, dancing and sparking with light. Then there was a rush of silver, a kind of draining, sucking noise, and suddenly the Skarasen was there, its head stretching up on its sinewy neck towards the cobwebby darkness that Sam had always supposed must conceal a ceiling too high to be perceived.

Emmeline and her father clutched at each other as the creature looked around, then lumbered forward, its claws clattering on the floor. It opened its mouth and Sam braced herself, expecting its shattering roar to all but burst her eardrums in the relatively confined space. However, instead of roaring, the Skarasen uttered an extraordinary crooning sound that seemed to provide a peculiarly appropriate accompaniment to the electronic burble that had drawn it here.

'It's singing,' Sam said in wonder.

'The summoning signal acts as an aural sedative,' said the Doctor. 'It penetrates directly to the aggression centres in the Skarasen's brain and nullifies them.'

The energy haze around the door became agitated again and another, smaller, Skarasen appeared. It all but collided with the first Skarasen, but rather than retaliating, the larger creature simply ambled forward to give the newcomer room. This Skarasen too opened its mouth and crooned in response to the signal.

'They're quite sweet when they're not eating people, aren't they?' said Sam.

Over the course of the next half-hour more and more Skarasen appeared, until eventually they were entering the TARDIS at the rate of around two a minute. Though the console room was vast, it was not long before it was full of Skarasen, the creatures pressed together as closely as cattle in a truck.

'You'd better open the inner doors, Tuval,' the Doctor said. 'Let them wander around a bit. They won't come to any harm.'

'*They* won't, but what about the TARDIS?' said Sam. 'I don't want them going in my room, trampling all over my stuff.'

'Stuff can always be replaced, Sam,' said the Doctor. 'My motto is never become too attached to anything.'

'Does that include people?' she asked.

'Besides, you'll have closed your door so you've got nothing to worry about,' the Doctor said, ignoring the question.

She looked indignant. 'How do you know I'll have closed my door?'

'Human teenagers always do. Very secretive creatures.'

'Not unlike Time Lords then,' said Sam. 'Or at least, one particular Time Lord I could mention, who's standing not a million miles away.'

Tuval used a number of levers on the console to open the inner doors, and then set the mass inversion wave around them using a series of buttons like blue typewriter keys indicated by the Doctor. As soon as the dark haze began to appear around the doors, the Skarasen began to filter out into other parts of the TARDIS. For the next ninety minutes the creatures continued to file in through the main doors until at last the number of new arrivals started to dwindle. A few remaining stragglers appeared over the course of the next twenty minutes, but finally even they ceased coming.

'I think that's the lot,' said the Doctor at last, and abruptly thrust out a hand towards Litefoot. 'Time to go, Professor.'

Not for the first time Litefoot looked taken aback, though automatically met the Doctor's hand with his own. 'Oh,' he said, evidently disappointed. 'Is it?'

'Goodbye, Nathaniel. Goodbye, Emmeline,' said the Doctor abruptly, shaking each of their hands in turn. He held on to Emmeline's hand for a moment and said quietly, 'Look after your father, Emmeline, won't you?'

Emmeline's eyes clouded over briefly, then she gave a firm nod. 'Yes, Doctor, I will.'

'Forgive my pedantry, Doctor,' said Litefoot, 'but precisely how do you propose we get out of here?'

He gestured at the undulating silver sea of Skarasen blocking their way to the door. The Doctor grinned mischievously. 'Like this.'

He stepped down off the dais and then, without hesitation, clambered up the tail and on to the back of the nearest Skarasen. It didn't even so much as stir at his presence. The Doctor squatted on his haunches and offered a hand. 'Who's next?'

Nathaniel, Emmeline and the professor looked at each other for a moment, then Emmeline stepped forward and reached up towards him. The Doctor clasped her hand and hauled her effortlessly up on to the Skarasen's back. She swayed, her arms pinwheeling, but he steadied her. She bent and placed a hand on the creature's back.

'It's cold,' she said, 'and as smooth as glass.'

'Quite an experience, isn't it?' said the Doctor, and then called, 'Which of you two gentlemen is going to join us?'

Litefoot chuckled. 'In for a penny,' he said, and with the Doctor's help climbed awkwardly up beside him and Emmeline.

'Are you quite sure the creature won't mind the four of us clambering all over it?' asked Nathaniel Seers nervously.

'Quite sure,' said the Doctor.

'This has been a most singular day,' muttered Seers. 'A most singular day indeed.' Like the others before him, he stepped forward and reached out a hand.

'Which one of you's going to sing "I'm the king of the castle", then?' Sam asked once they were all standing in a row on the Skarasen's back.

'Ignore her,' said the Doctor. 'She's only jealous because she can't play. Follow me everybody.'

He turned, and using the backs of the tightly packed Skarasen as stepping stones, made his way to the TARDIS door.

The others followed gamely, Emmeline hitching up her long skirts, Litefoot stretching his arms out on either side of him like a tightrope walker. There was a narrow area of floor in front of the door which the Skarasen appeared to be avoiding, perhaps because of the disorientating effect of the mass inversion wave. The Doctor hopped from the back of the final Skarasen and landed on the floor, nimbly as a ballerina, bending his knees, then springing upright again on his toes.

Emmeline peered nervously down at him from a height of about twelve feet.

'You have two options,' said the Doctor. 'You can either climb down the tail or you can jump.' He stretched out his arms. 'If you jump I'll catch you.'

She jumped, and he did catch her. As she landed in his arms she let out a very unladylike whoop.

Litefoot and Seers elected to climb down the creature's tail, both of them slipping and sliding on its smooth skin. Finally all four of them stood in a group before the blurred doorway. Nathaniel Seers thrust out a hand.

'On behalf of us all, sir, I hope you will permit me to express our heart-felt gratitude for your quite astonishing efforts in what has been a most distressing and unusual matter. This country, and I dare say even the world, owes you a very great debt. Despite the foul nature of the events we have experienced, it has been a privilege to be acquainted with you, sir.'

'You too, Nathanial,' said the Doctor softly, almost shyly, taking his hand for the second time and shaking it.

'Goodbye, Doctor,' said Emmeline, presenting a hand which he took and kissed. 'I hope we shall meet again.'

'I'm sure we will,' murmured the Doctor. 'It's a small universe.'

Now Litefoot stepped forward to shake his hand. 'Goodbye, Doctor. I must say it's been both the best and the worst of times. However, I rather think that I've had my fill of adventuring now. I'm getting a little too old for it all.'

The Doctor flashed him a grin. 'Goodbye, Professor. Give my regards to Henry.'

'Oh, I shall. It's a great pity that you were unable to meet him.'

'Yes,' said the Doctor evasively and half turned away. He hated long goodbyes almost as much as he hated bus stations and burnt toast.

'It is quite safe, isn't it?' said Emmeline, gesturing at the energy wave suffusing the doorway.

'Quite safe,' said the Doctor. 'Just step through it. You'll feel a moment's disorientation, but you won't come to any harm.'

Perhaps wishing to make up for being the last to climb on to the Skarasen, Nathaniel went first, squaring his shoulders and stepping determinedly into the wave. It sucked him in and he disappeared. A moment later Sam shouted, 'He's outside. I can see him on the screen. He looks a bit groggy, but he's OK.'

Emmeline went next, blowing the Doctor and Litefoot a kiss before stepping through.

'I say,' commented Litefoot, but there was a twinkle in his eye. 'Well, goodbye again, Doctor. It's been most enlightening.' He stepped forward and in to the wave, and just before it sucked him in he raised a hand in farewell.

Instinctively the Doctor raised his own hand in return, but the professor was already gone.

EPILOGUE

Later that evening, Litefoot settled back in his favourite armchair, the old leather warmed and softened by the fire roaring in the grate. He cradled a glass of brandy and thought about the past few days.

For the second time in five years his life had been turned upside down, his perception of the world irrevocably altered. Yet despite all that he had witnessed and experienced, he felt surprisingly calm and controlled, as though his mind had expanded to accommodate the wealth of new and incredible information that had come flooding into it.

Did this make him dull witted or perhaps even mad, he wondered, the fact that he was so willing to believe and accept the impossible? No, on the contrary, madness surely occurred only when a mind persistently refused to accept the barrage of evidence being fed to it by way of its own senses. Such a mind, he mused, would be so unyielding, so rigid, it would certainly rupture, its boundaries straining until they burst, like the banks of a river after too much rain.

He glanced at the curtained window. There must be a multitude of poor, deranged souls wandering out there tonight, desperately trying to deny the evidence of their own eyes.

He had arrived home earlier that day utterly exhausted, his lungs aching from the walk. The only thing that had kept him going had been the thought of his warm bed and visions of Mrs Hudson's delicious beef broth, a pot of which she seemed to keep constantly on the boil. However, upon returning home, he had been informed by his housekeeper that there had been 'some form of commotion' in several of the poorer areas of London, and that his presence was required at the mortuary at his earliest convenience. Driven by duty, Litefoot had hailed a cab, which had carried him as far as it could until the streets became impassable, and then for the second time that day he had picked his weary way through once-familiar streets that now resembled a war zone, strewn with corpses, rubble and debris.

He had spent the remainder of that long day performing post-mortems on bodies that had been eviscerated, crushed, partly devoured, and sometimes all three. By the time a cab arrived that evening to take him home, the police having cleared a way through the streets, he was almost insensible with fatigue. Additionally, he had become so inured to the grisly nature of his work that he had had to be gently reminded by a police officer to wash off the gore that was coating his arms up to the elbows before donning his jacket and coat and staggering out into the night.

Now, though, he felt a little better. He had slept deeply in the cab, and then, upon arriving home, had devoured several bowlfuls of beef broth, half a loaf of bread, and a large pot of coffee. His aim now was to sip a brandy and clear his mind a little before heading up to bed. The last few days had been harrowing, no doubt about that, but exhilarating too. He wondered who the Doctor really was and where he had come from. Could he, like his colleague before him and their respective companions, have travelled back from the future to save the world? If so, despite the terrible events that had occurred today, the human race had many exciting times to look forward to.

Litefoot's eyelids were beginning to droop, these thoughts swirling hypnotically and somehow reassuringly in his head, when he heard a knock on his door.

He came awake and groaned. Surely the police were not here to request his services again tonight? He pushed himself up from his armchair with a great deal of effort, plodded through to the hallway and opened the door.

'Hello, Professor. I was passing so I thought I'd return this.'

The Doctor, looking fresh and alert, held out the Chinese fowling piece that Litefoot had used earlier that day to dispatch the Zygon leader, Balaak.

'Doctor,' said Litefoot, relieved. 'At this hour I must confess that you are one of the few people whom it is a genuine pleasure to see.'

'Thank you,' said the Doctor, sounding touched.

Litefoot took the gun. 'And thank you for this. In all the excitement I had quite forgotten about it. However, I'm sure I would have regretted its loss at some later date.'

He invited the Doctor in and led him through to the sitting room. Once the Doctor had accepted a chair by the fire and a cup of coffee, Litefoot asked, 'I trust you were able to dispose of your cargo satisfactorily?'

'My cargo?' said the Doctor, and then his face cleared. 'Oh, you mean the Skarasen? Yes, I dropped them off, together with Tuval, on an uninhabited planet ideal for their needs.' He gazed into the fire and said softly, 'That was all such a long time ago now. So much has happened since.'

'Indeed?' said Litefoot, surprised. 'Granted, several hours have passed, Doctor, since I last saw you –'

'There's one thing I didn't tell you about me, Professor,' interrupted the Doctor, his voice still soft but compelling. He looked up and suddenly he seemed older, more care-worn. 'I'm not of this world. I'm a traveller in time and space. I walk in eternity.'

There was a moment's silence and then Litefoot, his eyes shining, said wonderingly, 'I believe it. My Lord, I believe it.'

'I knew you would,' said the Doctor, and smiled suddenly, breaking the sombre mood. 'You know, time travel is a funny old stick. A few hours to one person can be several years to another. I visited Tuval recently. There's a thriving community on his world now. He has sixteen children and is a grandfather seventy times over.'

'Astonishing,' said Litefoot. 'And Miss Samantha? How is she?'

Suddenly the Doctor looked sombre again. 'Oh, fine,' he said evasively.

He tilted back his head, draining his coffee, and abruptly stood up. 'Ah well, I'd better be moving on. People to see, places to go. You know how it is.'

'Er... yes, of course,' said Litefoot, taken aback once again by the Doctor's unpredictable behaviour. He struggled to push himself up from his chair. 'Well, thank you for returning my gun, Doctor. I'm honoured that you came all this way merely to do so.'

'My mission was twofold, Professor,' said the Doctor as Litefoot trailed him to the door. 'I wanted to return your property, certainly, but I also wanted to buy a magazine which circumstances prevented me from obtaining the last time I was here.'

'Ah,' said Litefoot, 'and were you successful in your endeavours?'

'Oh yes,' said the Doctor, opening his coat to reveal the magazine folded neatly in the inside pocket. 'I have it here. I really must pop back some time and get dear Arthur to sign it.'

He reached the door and stretched out a hand. 'Well, goodbye, George. Perhaps our paths will cross again.'

'Oh, I do hope so, Doctor,' said Litefoot. 'You can always be certain of a warm welcome here – as can your colleague, the other Doctor. Will you be seeing him on your travels by any chance?'

The Doctor gave a little shudder. 'I sincerely hope not. Once was enough.' He opened the door, then turned and smiled. 'Mind you, in this universe anything is possible.'

Also available from BBC Books:

DOCTOR WHO
THE EIGHT DOCTORS
by Terrance Dicks

Booby-trapped by the Master, the Eighth Doctor finds himself suffering
from amnesia. He embarks on a dangerous quest to regain his lost memory
by meeting all his past selves...

ISBN 0 563 40563 5

VAMPIRE SCIENCE
by Jonathan Blum and Kate Orman

The Doctor and Sam come up against a vampire sect in present-day
San Francisco. Some of the vampires want to coexist with humans, but
some want to go out in a blaze of glory. Can the Doctor defuse the
situation without bloodshed?

ISBN 0 563 40566 X

GENOCIDE
by Paul Leonard

Arriving on Earth, the Doctor and Sam discover that humanity never
existed and that the peaceful Tractites rule the world. Trying to put things
right, the Doctor embarks on a hazardous quest to prehistoric Earth.

ISBN 0 563 40572 4

Other *Doctor Who* adventures featuring past incarnations of
the Doctor:

THE DEVIL GOBLINS FROM NEPTUNE
by Keith Topping and Martin Day
(Featuring the Third Doctor, Liz Shaw and UNIT)

Hideous creatures from the fringes of the solar system, the deadly Waro,
have established a bridgehead on Earth. But what are the Waro actually
after – and can there really be traitors in UNIT?

ISBN 0 563 40565 1

THE MURDER GAME

by Steve Lyons
(Featuring the Second Doctor, Ben and Polly)

Landing in a decrepit hotel in space, the time travellers are soon
embroiled in a deadly game of murder and intrigue – all the while
monitored by the occupants of a sinister alien craft…

ISBN 0 563 40565 1

THE ULTIMATE TREASURE

by Christopher Bulis
(Featuring the Fifth Doctor and Peri)

The fabled treasure of the infintely wealthy Rovan Cartovall is hidden
somewhere on the planet Gelsandor, and the Doctor is forced to join
the latest perilous search. But can even he find a safe path through the
deadly traps and tricks that lie ahead?

ISBN 0 563 40571 6

Doctor Who adventures out on BBC Video:

THE WAR MACHINES

An exciting adventure featuring the First Doctor pitting his wits against
super-computer WOTAN – with newly restored footage.
BBCV 6183

THE AWAKENING/FRONTIOS

A double bill of Fifth Doctor stories… a rural village hides a terrible
secret from the Civil War in _The Awakening_, while the distant world of
Frontios sees a fledgling colony of humans under attack from the
gravity-controlling Tractators…
BBCV 5803

THE HAPPINESS PATROL

The Seventh Doctor battles for the freedom of an oppressed colony
where misery is a sin…
BBCV 5803